A Palette for Murder

A LANA DAVIS MYSTERY

A PALETTE FOR MURDER

VANESSA A. RYAN

FIVE STAR
A part of Gale, Cengage Learning

GALE
CENGAGE Learning·

Farmington Hills, Mich • San Francisco • New York • Waterville, Maine
Meriden, Conn • Mason, Ohio • Chicago

LIBRARY OF CONGRESS CATALOGING-IN-PUBLICATION DATA

Ryan, Vanessa A.
    A palette for murder / Vanessa A. Ryan.
      pages cm. — (A Lana Davis mystery)
      ISBN 978-1-4328-3041-0 (hardcover) — ISBN 1-4328-3041-4
(hardcover) — ISBN 978-1-4328-3028-1 (ebook) ISBN 1-4328-
3028-7 (ebook)
      1. Insurance policies—Fiction. 2. Beneficiaries—Fiction. 3.
Murder—Investigation—Fiction. I. Title.
PS3618.Y347P35 2015
813'.6—dc23   2014042016

First Edition. First Printing: April 2015
Find us on Facebook– https://www.facebook.com/FiveStarCengage
Visit our website– http://www.gale.cengage.com/fivestar/
Contact Five Star™ Publishing at FiveStar@cengage.com

To Barbara

CHAPTER ONE

Miguel Garcia raised his fists and got in my face. I rolled my chair back. I didn't want to be in the line of fire if things escalated. Where was Security when you needed them?

"I'm the one who signed on her death certificate, Ms. Whatever," Miguel insisted.

The sign on my desk stated my name was Lana Davis, but I didn't want to push the issue.

"Antonio hasn't been around for years," Mario growled. I took care of her, and he thinks he gets everything. He's just a little guy . . . with a *big guy* complex. A nothing."

Maybe everything Miguel said was true. His cousin Antonio was a bragging little runt who'd never amount to anything. Miguel was a big guy, so he knew what that meant. But as a six-foot blond female, I knew what that meant, so I found myself sympathizing with Antonio's plight, especially when I considered the source of the complaint against him. Miguel had an ax to grind. He wasn't the one getting the money. Antonio was.

I glanced at the death certificate Miguel threw on my desk. "Mr. Garcia, thank you for bringing this to our attention, but it states on your great-aunt's policy, Antonio Chavez is her beneficiary. I'm sorry. We can't authorize any payment to you."

Somehow, I didn't picture Miguel as a loving caretaker. But that wasn't for me to speculate. His great-aunt had lived until eighty and died before her policy lapsed. Her file seemed to be in order and now one of her grandnephews, a certain Antonio

Chavez, was to inherit five-hundred-thousand dollars. As of yet, he hadn't come forward to claim it.

"I'm next in line," Miguel said. "If you don't find Antonio, you have to give it to me. It says so in her will."

Whether it did or not was above my pay grade. "We'll let you know, Mr. Garcia." My response did little to placate Miguel. But I didn't care. If I let all the Miguels of the world bully me . . . besides, the security guard had wandered by, and I felt safe.

It wasn't my job to find Antonio Chavez, or any beneficiaries of policies issued by First Century Life, where I worked. It was up to Antonio Chavez to find us to get his money. Most of the time we didn't know about the death of a policyholder, unless a beneficiary came forward. But with large policies, such as this one for Maria Escobar, Miguel Garcia's great-aunt, we got letters from lawyers or trustees handling the estates.

Although it was unusual for an heir, especially one not named on a policy, to come into our office, I would have forgotten about it, except someone claiming to be Antonio Chavez showed up a day after Miguel did. He fit Miguel's description of Antonio. He was a little guy with a big mustache and big muscles, despite his short stature. My boss Charley, a big, white-haired Swede with a ruddy complexion and an infectious laugh, told him to wait in my office. I didn't say much to the man. I knew Charley was checking out his story.

Twenty minutes later two uniformed police officers entered my office. "Mr. Chavez, is it? We need you to come with us," one of them said.

They escorted the man out. Charley told me later the man showed up with a phony driver's license.

A few weeks later Miguel Garcia filed a complaint against us with the state and with the Better Business Bureau. Of course, the complaints were bogus. We couldn't give him the money. But Charley felt the complaints affected our ratings with the public, so he hired a detective agency to find Antonio Chavez. After they charged mega bucks and turned up empty-handed, Charley was in a quandary. To make matters worse, Miguel posted nasty comments about First Century Life on Internet complaint sites.

The claims department, where Charley and I worked, was on the second floor of the First Century Life building in West L.A. And now the big boys on the penthouse level, ten floors up, were on Charley's case. But they wouldn't give him much of a budget to hire another detective agency. That's when Charley turned to me. "How would you like to go to Santa Fe?" he said.

"Yeah. Are we having a conference there?"

"No. But that's the last known address for Antonio Chavez. It's your claim. You're going to have to find him. So don't get us fired."

Great. "What do I know about finding anybody?"

Charley stared at me. "I know what you do on your lunch hour."

It was a common but unspoken practice that employees at First Century Life often used the company's accounts at official research sites to look up people for unofficial reasons. The company conducted their own background checks on all employees and on certain policyholders, and that's why they had these accounts. I had undergone such a background check before First Century Life hired me.

The searches themselves, with the exception of the credit checks, weren't illegal. People could do them online, if they paid. But using the company's accounts was cause for termination. Yet we did it anyway, considering it one of the perks of the job. I caught Charley doing a search once. He didn't realize I saw him. I knew better than to mention that now. And I knew Charley. He liked me, but when push came to shove, if didn't find Antonio, I'd be the one fired, not him.

That detective agency wasn't stupid. Most likely, they had combed that town looking for him. The one positive aspect of this bummer assignment, aside from playing tourist in Santa Fe, was earlier in the year, during one of my searches, I discovered an old boyfriend lived there. To use the cliché, he was the man who got away. What would happen when I came face-to-face with Alan Finley in Santa Fe? It might be fun to find out, especially when I didn't have to pay for the trip. Maybe he'd take me in if First Century fired me.

Landing in Albuquerque, where even the airport looked happy with its friendly, Southwestern architecture and bright orange colors, convinced me my life was about to change for the better, despite the whole Antonio Chavez thing looming over me. This, after all, was the land of enchantment, where anything was possible, if I believed my new-age friends. The serenity I felt when I gazed at white hills dotted with the dark green shrubs of the Southwest, further convinced me. I figured if this wasn't the moon or a planet other than Earth, it was close to it. What really got me was the silence. The weird silence. Silence like this cost a mint in L.A. And here it was free.

If New Mexico was like another planet, its people were earthy. Most of them had liquor on their breaths. The lack of greenery and the dry air must have made them thirsty. From the guy at the car rental in Albuquerque, to the bellhop at the Zimoro Hotel on the Plaza in Santa Fe where I was staying, everyone had imbibed, and it wasn't quite ten in the morning.

I knew the drill. My ex-husband was an alcoholic. Something he wouldn't admit to. In the three years since my divorce, I had not missed him one bit. I didn't drink anymore. It reminded me of the bad times with my ex-husband. Maybe someday I'd get over it. I used to enjoy a glass of wine with dinner.

The Zimoro Hotel's brochure didn't lie. The place was luxurious, if a bit touristy. My room was no exception. Its carved, wood-beamed ceilings, Navaho rugs on Saltillo-tiled floors and Southwestern-style furnishings and paintings gave me the feeling I had walked into the life of some glamorous movie star from the past. Although expensive, the room and the car rental cost less than hiring another detective agency. And it gave Charley an excuse to blame me if things didn't go right.

After I tipped the bellhop for carrying my bags to my room, I took the elevator downstairs to see the concierge, a petite, young Hispanic woman with large, bird-like dark eyes. Her name was Angelica Ortiz, according to the badge on her blue suit. She wore a gold, heart-shaped locket with a small diamond in the center around her neck.

"Angelica, I just checked in and I wondered if I could have a map of the area."

Angelica smiled, but her eyes looked somber. "Of course, ma'am. Where do you want to go?"

"I'm trying to find Route Eighty. I couldn't locate it on my GPS driving over here, and I couldn't find it on the map I got at the airport." I didn't smell liquor on her breath, but judging from the way she stared at the bellhop, who meandered by and who resembled her, he was the reason for her less than enthusiastic attitude. Not to belabor the point, but I knew what liquor could do.

Angelica retrieved a map from behind the counter and handed it to me. "This may help. Sorry you're having so much trouble." But Angelica didn't look sorry. In fact, I felt she regarded me with guarded hostility. Well, the woman had a drunk for a brother and most likely, despite that pricey gem around her neck, the hotel didn't pay great wages. She figured me for a rich, blue-eyed blonde from California who took more of her time than she wanted. Most of that was true, except for the rich part. My salary at First Century Life didn't pay enough to put me in that category.

"Thanks," I said. Still, I pressed on. "See, here's the address I'm trying to find."

Angelica frowned as she looked at a scrap of paper I showed her. She hesitated. "Uh, I think you just need to look on the map. It should be there."

I had seen frowns like that before. It usually meant people knew more than they let on. "I'm looking for Antonio Chavez. I think he lives there, or used to. Do you know him?"

Angelica stared at me and then shook her head. "It's a common name. I don't know what else to tell you."

"I'm with First Century Life. I'm trying to find him. He's inherited some money." I gave Angelica my business card.

"Sorry, I don't know him. I wish I could help you." With a nod and a polite smile, she dismissed me.

I studied the map Angelica gave me, but I couldn't find Route Eighty. I got the rental car out of the lot near the hotel and drove to a gas station. Someone there might know.

A white-haired man was filling his car at the pump when I drove up. "Excuse me," I called out. "I'm looking for Route Eighty. I can't find it on a map."

The man smiled. "Those routes are used for mailing addresses. The streets don't go by that. But I don't know where that one is. That's all I can tell you."

"Believe it or not, you gave me what I need. Thanks."

I parked and went online to check the address on Land Title's website. First Century had an account with them. I probably should have done that before I left L.A.

A cross-check search of Route Eighty revealed the real name of the street was Calle Fernando, and the property didn't belong to Antonio Chavez. A company called the Blackwell Corporation owned it. The company listed Route Eighty as its mailing address. Calle Fernando was off West Alameda, a long road leading to one of the more rural parts of the city. West Alameda was about nine miles from the Plaza.

On Alameda, I passed a cemetery. It reminded me that I was almost forty, divorced, childless and alone. And I was about to chase after some guy who probably didn't remember me. Unless I got lost in these hills and never came back.

A few miles later, when I turned on Selvin Road, the asphalt turned into dirt, the hills disappeared and the land became flat. Every house had several acres between them. Some were in the Santa Fe style, with flat wooden roofs, while others had pitched roofs and looked like farmhouses. All of them seemed to be made of red, brown or beige adobe. Turning on Calle Duma, the next dirt road on the map, the terrain got hilly and rugged— four-wheel-drive country in the winter snow or the rainy season.

Calle Duma dead-ended with a right turn at Calle Fernando. The houses were far back from the road, so I saw only their mailboxes with the route numbers printed on them.

I found the address. I parked and walked up a long dirt driveway. At the top of a hill, covered with junipers and native plants, was the house, a sprawling, one-story red adobe with a pitched roof and turquoise window sills. Turquoise was a big color in New Mexico.

"Hey! Get out of here."

Startled, I turned around and saw a man with gray hair. He wore an old pair of jeans and a dirty white sweatshirt. His red, swollen nose gave him away as a heavy drinker. He also held a rifle, though he didn't aim it at me.

"Hello. I'm Lana Davis. I'm looking for Antonio Chavez. I have this as his last address."

The man rested the butt of his rifle on the ground. "What do you want with Lefty?"

"Lefty? Why do you call him that?"

"Everyone does. Why do you need to find him?"

"I've got news for him. But he never answered the letters I sent." I wasn't about to tell this man about the inheritance. I didn't want him thinking I had it on me and shoot me for it.

"You don't look like you're related," the man said. "Who are you?"

"I represent people who *are* related to him. Does he still live here?"

"He did. But maybe he went back to the reservation. His woman is a Suique from Los Rios. I guess you know that."

I nodded, as if I did.

"Maybe he didn't go there," the man continued. "Maybe he just went away. He had a room here. He owes me rent. Maybe you can pay me."

"Well, sure. How much does he owe?"

"Six, but I'll take five—hundred. When you find him, I'll get the rest."

I didn't have that much on me and told him.

The man pointed his rifle at me. "You must want Lefty bad. What'd he do?"

I freaked. "Uh . . . nothing, really."

The man laughed. "You're okay." He lowered the rifle, pointing it away from me. Then he stuck his hand out. "Now give me the money."

"I don't have that kind of money. I told you."

He aimed the rifle in my face again. "Then give me what you have."

I shelled out two one-hundred dollar bills from my wallet. That seemed to satisfy him. I'd put this down as a miscellaneous expense on First Century's books.

"Since I paid you two hundred dollars, how about letting me see his room? Maybe I'll find something that shows us where he went."

"He didn't leave anything."

14

"You never know. I might find something you overlooked."

"You might. But you aren't." The man pointed his rifle at me again and marched me to the road.

I looked in the rearview mirror as I drove off. The man stood in the road, aiming his rifle at my tires. I gunned the motor and sped away, with shots ringing behind me. Fortunately, he was a bad shot. He didn't hit the tires, or even graze the car.

Maybe Angelica Ortiz knew Antonio as Lefty. Regardless, she knew something about that house on Calle Fernando. I just felt it. But when I got to the Zimoro, Angelica wasn't at the concierge desk. Instead, a young man stood behind the counter. He spoke to me with a Texas accent. "Can I help you, ma'am?" I could have sworn he had tears in his eyes.

"I'm looking for Angelica Ortiz. Do you know when she'll be back?"

He looked aghast. "I'm so sorry. Angelica . . . she . . ."

"What is it? I was here an hour ago. I talked to her."

"I'm sorry, ma'am. She was shot. The police are with her. There's an ambulance . . ."

"Oh! Is she . . . all right?"

"If you're a friend or family, go over there . . ." He pointed to an exit. Overcome with the situation, he didn't say anything more.

I rushed through the exit door and saw the ambulance in the street. The paramedics were loading Angelica into the van. She had her uniform on. It looked like she was still alive. I ran up to them, but a police officer stopped me. "You'll need to step back, ma'am," the man said. His face was a blur. I backed off.

At First Century Life, I talked about death, dismemberment, broken limbs, even stab wounds as if they were nothing, just words. But seeing Angelica's unconscious body, her face strangely gray in color, unnerved me. This was real pain. Real misery. I felt like crying, or screaming. I leaned against a wall to calm myself.

I remembered something. In a daze, I headed toward a police officer. I didn't know whether he was the same one who stopped me before. I just knew I needed to tell him this. "The woman wore a gold locket with a diamond in it. But it's not there now."

"You're sure about that?" the officer said.

"Yes. I am. I talked to her only a few hours ago. I'm staying at the hotel."

"Your name, ma'am?"

"Lana Davis. Room three-fifteen."

"Thank you. If you think of anything else, call me. Here's my card. Maybe you should go to your room now. We need to keep the area clear."

CHAPTER TWO

I didn't go to my room. I didn't want to be alone. I needed to be around people, noisy people. I went to the hotel restaurant. It opened to the Plaza. Its casual, elegant interior, furnished with wicker chairs, plants and adobe-red tablecloths, calmed my nerves.

A hostess in a long, black velvet dress studded with Indian turquoise stones steered me to a table near the Plaza. The woman acted oblivious to the ambulance outside. I didn't enlighten her. When the waitress came, I ordered a sandwich, a salad and dessert.

I thought about Angelica. But what could I do? Whoever shot her must have taken her locket. It was valuable, though maybe not enough to kill for—but that was relative. People got killed over less. I should have told that police officer about the old man who shot at me. Maybe Angelica had some connection with him or the house on Calle Fernando, because I didn't think I imagined her odd reaction when I asked her about the address.

Dream on. If only finding Antonio was as simple as asking Angelica about a guy named Lefty. Santa Fe had lots of people. Angelica's problems probably didn't have anything to do with my job.

After lunch, I felt better. But never again would I speak so flippantly about human suffering or loss of life. Still, I had a job to do here. Two, in fact, if I counted seeing Alan again.

I set out for Los Rios, an easy place to find on my GPS. Far from being a poor district, Los Rios looked upscale, with rambling adobe houses. I stopped at the Village Market. The girl at the cash register, a blonde with long hair, looked like a hippy chick from the nineteen-seventies. "I'm trying to find a guy named Lefty Chavez," I said. "He may have a wife or a girlfriend who's from the Suique tribe. Do you know him?"

"Sam," she called out, "know a guy named Lefty? He goes with a Suique."

Sam, an older, chunky guy with dark hair, came to the counter. "Hi, how can I help you?"

"I'm trying to find a guy named Lefty Chavez. His real name is Antonio Chavez. I heard he lives around here." I gave him my card. "He's an heir of an estate I represent."

"Sure, he used to come around here. He did a few odd jobs for me. But I haven't seen him in a while." Sam smiled. "I think he once worked at the pueblo casino, but they parted ways. He wasn't reliable, if you know what I mean."

"Do you know any other people he did odd jobs for?"

Sam raised his eyebrows while he searched his mind. "Well. Let me think. He might have worked for some art gallery in Santa Fe. You know, hanging drywall, fixing things. I don't know which one. I haven't seen him at the pueblo in a while. He was a good craftsman when he showed up. He had a finger missing on his left hand. That's why they call him Lefty. But he still did a good job."

"Did he have a car that you remember?"

"Hmm . . . I think he had an old Dodge pickup. But he didn't have it for the last job he did for me. I remember I had to get the supplies myself."

"So how did he get here?"

Sam shrugged. "Someone dropped him off."

"Could you give me his number?"

"He had a cell phone. I don't think it works anymore. I'll look it up for you, though."

No car, no address, no phone. And over two hundred galleries in the Santa Fe area, not counting places calling themselves galleries, but were just furniture or gift stores. I thanked Sam and got Lefty's number anyway.

I called Lefty's cell phone. The recording came on telling me this was a disconnect. Maybe he got another cell phone. Unlikely.

So where did people go when they dropped off the planet? The word *morgue* popped into my head. Yeah, I'd have to pursue that angle, but I sure hoped it came up a dead end, no pun intended. I couldn't stand the thought of Miguel Garcia getting anything, if he was the next in line.

I checked with the county—no missing person's report for Antonio. No arrest record, or impending trial either. Nobody at the morgue, funeral homes or the hospital had heard of him. So it looked like I still had a fighting chance of cutting Miguel out of his great-aunt's money.

I started on Canyon Road, the famous gallery row in Santa Fe, where some adobe buildings dated back to the early eighteen hundreds. With parking spaces nonexistent, I parked my car back at the Zimoro, several blocks over, and walked.

I meandered up the street, working my way in and out of the galleries. I didn't find anyone who knew Lefty, but every gallery invited me to come back after five when they had their Friday-night wine and cheese receptions. At the top of Canyon Road was El Casita, one of the best bars in the city and a great restaurant. I had gone there for dinner on my honeymoon. Frequented by artists, writers and tourists, the building had housed one restaurant or another since eighteen-thirty-five. It looked like something out of the Wild West with its woodsy, dark-paneled interior and sawdust-covered floor.

Lunch was over and dinner hadn't started, so the people eating and drinking on the patio were most likely the locals beginning their Friday happy hour early. I plunged over and, as it looked like open seating, I asked a group of people if I could share their table.

"Sure," said a guy in a black shirt. He wore a black cowboy hat. His friend, who wore a brown cowboy hat and a beige shirt, slid a chair out for me and then put his arm around a young woman with long, black hair seated next to him. "I'm Jeremy," he said. His accent was from Texas. Texans liked Santa Fe, it seemed. "This is my girlfriend Sandy," he said.

"I'm Tyler Veller," the guy in the black hat said. He had watery blue eyes and blond hair tied in a short ponytail. He wasn't bad looking either, in a rugged kind of way. But never mind. He looked like trouble.

"I'm Lana. Nice to meet all of you. Thanks for letting me share your table."

"What'll you have?" Tyler asked.

Lana smiled. "I'm just going to have some mineral water."

"Well, then allow me," Tyler said. "I sure am happy you decided to share our table."

I smiled again and thanked him. Men in New Mexico were sexier than they were in L.A. Or maybe I was just a sucker for a guy in a cowboy hat. "So what do you and your friends do in Santa Fe?" I asked.

"We're artists," Tyler said. "I'm a painter."

"We paint too," Sandy said. "I've got a show at the Esner Gallery down the street. The opening's tonight. You're welcome to come."

I showed her a postcard I had picked up from that gallery. It had a photograph of an abstract painting on it. "So you're Sandy Pelkon. This is a beautiful painting. Sure, I'll come." I hadn't met many artists in my life. I didn't know much about art, except for the one art history class I took in college.

"Are you new in town?" Tyler asked. "I haven't seen you around here before."

"I'm here on business. I'm from L.A. I'm an insurance administrator. I'm trying to find a guy named Antonio Chavez, sometimes known as Lefty. He has a wife or a girlfriend who's a Suique from Los Rios. But I didn't find him there. I heard he's a handyman. He worked at some gallery. He's got a missing finger on his left hand."

"What's he wanted for? Did he kill somebody?" Sandy asked.

"No. I need to find him about an inheritance."

"Well, you've come to the right place," Tyler said. "People here either have a trust fund or want to find someone who does." He took a sip of his beer. "Yeah, there's nothing like family money when times are lean. I wish I could get more of it."

"What about your paintings?" I said.

"I have a show now and then, but—"

"There's nothing like family money," Jeremy agreed. Sandy nodded.

"Except when you don't get any," Tyler added.

They all laughed. I had to admit their honesty was refreshing. I finished my drink and fidgeted in my chair. "Thanks for the drink, Tyler. I should get back to my quest. I'll see you all at the gallery later."

"Let me get your number," Tyler said. "I know lots of artists. Someone will probably know the guy you're trying to find."

I smiled. No way would I go out with him, but there might be some truth in what he said. "I'm at the Zimoro Hotel. Last name is Davis. What's your number?"

Sandy and Jeremy looked at each other.

Tyler laughed. "I don't have a phone. Never put one in."

"What about a cell phone?"

"No."

"Where do you live?"

"Near Elamos. I'm a caretaker for a lady who lives out of state. She's got a small house and twenty acres. I fixed up her barn and she lets me live in it. I keep the grounds planted. I've got the whole place to myself most of the time. She's hardly ever there."

"That sounds nice. People like to shoot guns here a lot, don't they?" I said. I gave them an abbreviated version of what happened on Calle Fernando, leaving out the part about the two hundred dollars. No need to tell them about the shakedown I experienced. I didn't want these three getting any ideas of subjecting me to another one. I didn't mention what happened to Angelica.

"Gotta be careful," Tyler said. "Could be a meth lab or something. You don't want to mess with them."

Jeremy and Sandy nodded.

"I hadn't thought of that," I said.

Santa Fe had a way of making urgent tasks seem less urgent. Instead of continuing my search for Antonio, I ended up having dinner with the three of them and paying for it, at my insistence. First Century could afford it. Afterward, I went to the hotel for a quick shower and a change of clothes. I met them at Sandy's reception. The gallery, several blocks down from El Casita, was packed. True to his word, Tyler introduced me to everyone he knew, which was about half the people there, though he let me do the talking.

"I know Lefty," a lanky, soft-spoken man said. He was about thirty, six-foot-three, with a muscular build and a face scorched by the sun.

"What can you tell me about him?" I asked.

"He's little guy."

I repeated Miguel Garcia's words. "Little guy with a big guy complex, huh?"

He stared at me for a second. "Yeah. I see you met him."

"No. Someone told me that."

"He's about five-four. Always acting like he's better than everybody. And he's not."

"Do you know where I can find him?"

"Listen, you don't want Lefty. I can do the job for your gallery better and faster."

He had looked at my hair in much the same way as Angelica had, sans her scowl. Expensive blond highlights marked me as rich enough to own a gallery. Maybe in Santa Fe. But in L.A., even poor women spent money on their hair.

"I don't own a gallery. I just need to talk to him."

"If you know where he is, why don't you just tell her?" Tyler demanded.

The guy shrugged and started to walk off. But he added, "I think he did some work for the Merryweather Galleries."

"Are they having a reception tonight?"

"Probably," Tyler said. "I'll take you there. We've spent enough time with Sandy's show."

I was leery of driving in a car with Tyler. He already had consumed two glasses of wine at the gallery, as well as a few beers at El Casita. I didn't need another drunk in my life, even if he seemed to hold his liquor. "Are you going to have a show soon?" I said. I wanted to distract him.

Tyler smiled. "I'm still working on it. I hope this gallery will give me a show."

"Well, maybe you shouldn't leave. You should let the gallery know you're here."

"Eh, you're probably right. I could talk to the director. I'll introduce you to him. He's the one standing next to Sandy."

Now I had my excuse. After Tyler said hello to the gallery director and introduced me, I congratulated Sandy again on her show. Then I said I was tired and was going to call it a night.

"I'll call you," Tyler whispered.

"Thanks for the drink," I whispered back.

I *was* tired. I had just flown in this morning, but I got back to my car and drove to the Merryweather Galleries.

The gallery was on Madison Street, near the Georgia O'Keefe Museum. It was this huge white, contemporary building with polished cement floors. The place was mobbed and somewhat overwhelming. As I mingled with the diverse crowd of artists in jeans and cowboy hats, conservative art collectors in gray suits and tourists in loud colors, I spotted a sleek blonde in an elegant white dress.

I waited until the woman stopped talking to a man in a mustard-colored jacket. "Excuse me, do you know where I can find the manager?"

The woman glanced briefly at my plain black dress, but my blond highlights made her pause. "I'm Carone Merryweather, the owner. How can I help you?" In the next breath she said, "Rodney, you have everything, don't you?"

The man in the mustard-colored jacket nodded before he walked away. He gave me a backward glance as he approached a group of people looking at a painting.

"I'm Lana Davis. I was told that you may have hired Antonio Chavez, also known as Lefty, to do some work in your gallery— putting up walls—things like that."

Carone's delicate forehead frowned. "You really have to talk to my staff. They deal with things like that. Now if you'll excuse me, I'm very busy."

"If you could just point out some of your staff to me. I'm a claims administrator for an insurance company—"

That seemed to catch her interest. "Really? And why are you interested in finding this person?"

"It's a personal matter for him. But it's good news."

"And who told you he might have worked here?"

"An artist I met at another gallery tonight. I don't know his name, but he also did drywall work for galleries. He was one of Antonio's competitors—for handyman work."

Carone took a deep breath. "I don't have time to talk and as you can see, I need my staff to converse with collectors and potential collectors. But come by tomorrow, about one. What did you say your name was?"

"Lana Davis."

Carone took my card and drifted back to the crowd.

Well, I found Antonio. One small issue solved. Two larger ones to go. Somehow I had to persuade Charley to let my all-expenses-paid vacation last longer, and I needed to have my all-important, face-to-face encounter with Alan—the most important reason for coming here.

I didn't know it then, but in the days that followed, tackling these would be the least of my problems.

CHAPTER THREE

I saw Carone at the front desk when I arrived at the Merry-weather Galleries. At first, she seemed surprised. "Oh, that's right. You were coming in today. We need to go into my office." She looked annoyed. "Where is everyone?"

Rodney, still in his mustard-colored jacket, came out of one of the rooms partitioned for exhibiting paintings and hurried toward Carone. "Carone, I'll cover the front desk, if you'd like."

"Thanks, Rodney," Carone said. She signaled to me. "Come this way, please."

I followed Carone through a large double door behind the reception desk into the administrative wing of the gallery. Several pairs of curious eyes stared at me as I strolled down the corridor after Carone. While the floors of the public areas in the gallery were cement, this wing had white carpeting. I hoped the bottoms of my shoes didn't leave marks.

We went into an office at the end of the hall. "Please sit down and close the door," Carone said. She took a seat behind a massive, white-lacquered desk. Carone stared at me for a moment. Then she got up and walked to the window, standing with her back to me.

I made a quick survey of Carone's office. Everything was bright, white and expensive. There were no books or magazines in view, and the stark light in the room almost hurt my eyes. On the far wall were some black-and-white drawings that might have been Picassos or Matisses. I remembered seeing images like those in my art history class.

Carone stared out the window for a long time. I didn't rush her. But whatever Carone knew about Lefty, I would know before this meeting was over because I wasn't going to leave until she told me.

In the meantime, I sized her up. She was about my age—in her late thirties—and about my dress size—a seven or eight, though I was taller. With our blond hair and blue eyes, we could almost have been sisters, but there the resemblance ended. Carone had an aristocratic air about her that spelled money, while I just had nice blond highlights.

Carone stopped staring and paced back and forth, as though wrestling with some decision she had to make. Her glamorous white suit, which had just the right silver pin on its lapel, matched the white carpet of her office. Even her elegant, black opal earrings—suitable for the power lunches she most likely attended—looked perfect against her pale, oval face, which, unlike mine, had never experienced a sunburn or grit from a sandy beach.

If Carone wanted her long silence to make me feel insignificant, she failed. I'd wait as long as I had to for Antonio's address. Just when I became impatient enough to demand information about Antonio's whereabouts, Carone said something in a voice so small I almost missed it. "Is anyone ever above corruption?"

Carone seemed to be talking more to herself than to me, but it was an odd thing to say after such a long silence. I said, "Well, sure—not everybody's corrupt."

Carone turned toward me and gave me a cold, appraising look. "You think so?" she said.

No, I didn't. I was as corrupt as the next one.

In a superior tone, Carone added, "How do you know? Anyway, that's why you're here. I hope you'll prove me wrong."

What was she getting at? What would she think of me if she knew about my quasi-legal lunchtime searches?

Carone sat down behind her desk and faced me. "You're a claims administrator?"

"That's right."

"I think I can use your services," Carone said. "Can we talk about this?"

"I'm here to find an heir, Antonio Chavez, for an estate in California. I don't know how I can help you unless you're the beneficiary of a policy from my company."

Carone waved her well-manicured hands at me. "What does that matter? I want you to work for me. You can be an employee, can't you? Aren't claims administrators just like detectives? I'll pay you well. And you can still find your missing heir at the same time."

A tempting offer. Double dipping. Every office worker's dream—not moonlighting, but getting paid for two jobs at the same time. Well, Charley *had* thrown me to the wolves. But I needed to think about this. "First, I have to find Antonio Chavez. You said you knew him. How can I get in touch with him?"

"Oh . . . I don't know where he is. He . . . may have worked for me. He was so unreliable. He didn't show up one day, and we had to find someone else. Stay here and work for me, and maybe you'll end up finding him."

My heart sank. "But you told me you knew where Antonio Chavez was."

"I said I knew him. That's all."

Oh, brother. Good thing I didn't tell Charley I found Antonio. "So why do you need a detective? I just handle claims. I'm not a detective."

"I've seen private investigators. They all look like police officers. You look like you could work in a gallery. Your hair, your

28

clothes—though that dress is old. You can wear some of mine. We're almost the same size, except for your height. They might be a little short on you. Maybe not. You have long legs, but your torso is short. I think they'll work. I'll have my housekeeper gather ones I'm ready to donate to charity."

Gee, thanks. Didn't realize I looked like a charity case. "I don't know much about art. I took one art history class in college . . ."

I couldn't believe I said that. The only excuse I could give her was, I didn't know much about art? What about my job? My life? And hey, I'm not your servant, lady. I didn't sign up for this. And you told me you knew where Antonio was.

"You look the part and I need someone now," she said.

"Humph."

Carone took that for a yes. "You may not know this, but Merryweather Galleries specializes in modern masters such as Miro, Picasso, Giacometti, as well as in young, emerging artists."

I shook my head. What was I getting into?

Carone ignored my negative gesture. She whispered, "We've been having a problem in the gallery. Someone is taking the work of the modern masters out of the gallery. It's almost as if they borrow them for a few days and then return them—unharmed."

"Why don't you call the police?"

"Shh. Don't say that so loud. I don't want any publicity," Carone said. "I also don't know who is doing this—I can't imagine it could be one of my staff, or our collectors, but I've got to find out. It's someone with an inside knowledge of the gallery."

"Why is that?" Not that I cared, because at that moment I felt like screaming at her.

"We have a very good security system, and the public doesn't have the freedom to walk around without being observed by my staff. However, some collectors have been in the stacks—the back rooms—usually at my invitation. They've been instrumental in getting us started in the resale market for modern masters, but I can't be too obvious about questioning them. That's why *you're* here."

Carone looked at a piece of paper on her desk and then clipped it to a manila folder. "I want you to find the Picasso for me," she whispered.

Despite my rising anger at being misled, I leaned forward in my chair. I wanted to hear more. "What Picasso?"

"As I said, I will pay you well."

"I appreciate the offer. But if a Picasso is missing, shouldn't you call the police? They're more prepared to deal with something like this."

"My whole business is at stake here. The Picasso is the only painting that hasn't come back. The other paintings that disappeared belonged to my family's collection. We display them in the gallery for educational purposes. But this Picasso belongs to one of my collectors."

"What do you mean, 'collectors'?"

"In your industry, you might refer to them as clients, or . . . policy owners. This collector brought the Picasso in for resale, and I can't let her know it's missing. It was the last painting Picasso ever finished. It's a portrait of an unknown woman. The collector bought it personally from Picasso the week before he died. Picasso wouldn't tell her who the woman was. It's almost priceless. It would ruin me if word got out it was missing. And I'd have to pay her for it."

"But if your whole business is at stake, it doesn't make sense to hire me. I don't know anything about finding missing paintings, let alone a Picasso."

Carone tilted her head. "Then you'll learn."

She stared at me with such anxiety I couldn't help feeling

sorry for her. Poor little rich girl. "It just seems that with your money, you would be better off finding—"

"I know what I'm better off doing," Carone said. "I admit it's unorthodox, but that's how I am. And I'm usually right. I have a feeling you'll rise to the occasion."

I let her wait a few minutes while I thought it over. Something about Carone's story seemed phony. And what would I do about my job? Sure, I wanted to prolong my stay—for a week or two, but this could take a lot longer. Though . . . maybe I'd see Alan and we'd fall madly in love and I'd never go back. Yeah. Stupid fantasy. Or should I take a leap of faith and say yes? I could work for this woman and find Antonio. Whichever came first would decide my fate, because since my divorce I hadn't been able to make a strong move in any direction. I existed, one day at a time.

"So when do I start?" I heard myself say.

The anxious look on Carone's face cleared up. She gave me a confident smile, as if she knew I wouldn't refuse. "Why don't you come in tomorrow? Say, about one, again. We'll start by telling everyone you're a new consultant hired to curate a new show of modern masters. We sometimes curate the resale paintings of our collectors into shows of my family's collection, so it won't look strange if you meet some of our collectors. Oh and here's my address." She wrote it on a slip of paper and gave it to me. "Come to my house at noon tomorrow, before you come here. My housekeeper will give you some things to wear. You can keep them, or donate them when you get your first check from me."

I nodded. "I still need to do the job I came here for. I have to find Antonio—Lefty—Chavez. So if you know anything—"

"I don't," she said. "You'll have time to find him, since I'll be the one doing the work on the show you're supposedly curating. I expect you to be discreet. If you tell anyone the real reason you're working at the gallery, I will deny it and terminate your employment."

"I'm not going to tell anyone. How much are you paying me?"

Carone pulled out some papers from her desk. "I drew up an employment contract," she said. "You need to sign it. It's two thousand a month. I can't pay you more than that because you're part time. I don't want my staff to become suspicious. We pay twice a month. You just need to be here three days a week—to keep up appearances and to watch who goes in or out—and at our receptions, if you haven't found the Picasso by then."

An extra two thousand for not doing much. Not bad. I could afford to buy a few trinkets during this trip. Carone never thought I'd refuse her offer, not when she'd appraised my little black dress last night at the gallery. I might fool poor people into thinking I was rich, but not rich ones.

"As you can see, there isn't anything about the Picasso in the contract," Carone said.

"I see. But—"

"But what?" Carone looked irritated.

"Well, what if—this gets—dangerous?"

"It's not that sort of crime . . . oh, now that I recall, when I hired Lefty, he helped put up partitions in the gallery and cleaned up after opening receptions—that's the night an exhibition opens. One night, after an opening, I caught him in the stacks. That's where we store the art we're not exhibiting. He wasn't supposed to be there. He'd been drinking. I told him the stacks were off limits. That was a few months ago. I don't know if he had anything to do with the thefts—he was an artist, of sorts. I think he made jewelry. I hired him to set up for our last exhibit, but he never showed up. So I don't know where he is."

"Why didn't you tell me that in the first place?"

"You caught me at a busy time. I didn't think of it," Carone said.

Sure you didn't. You tricked me. And I fell for it.

I never would have come back if I thought she didn't know where Antonio was. Then again, I wouldn't be getting the extra two thousand per month. "So how long did you employ Lefty?"

Carone sighed. "I don't know. He didn't work every day. Maybe about six months."

Six months. If Carone had told me that last night, I could have spent this morning searching the other galleries. "Maybe his disappearance is connected to the thefts."

"That's ridiculous," Carone said. "He was drunk. That's why he hid in the stacks."

"If I'm going to find this Picasso, you need to tell me everything. I have the feeling you're holding something back. How long has it been missing?"

"A month or two."

"And you haven't done anything about it?" I found this hard to believe.

Carone shook her head. "If I did, it would arouse suspicion. I can't let anyone know."

This woman lived in La-La Land if she thought I could save her. "Do you suspect someone?" I asked.

Carone tensed. Her hands shook. "No, I don't know who it is. The one thing I can tell you is when Lefty didn't show up last month, I hired someone else. Max Beely. He was an older man. I don't think this has anything to do with anything, but I don't want you to be surprised if somebody talks about it. After he worked here, hanging a show last week, he was killed. Shot. The police questioned me and my staff."

"Because he worked for you?"

Carone sighed. "No. He was killed in the alley behind the gallery. I don't think it had anything to do with us."

"I see."

"We managed to keep the fact that he worked here out of the news. We don't want our collectors to feel unsafe here."

"And you didn't tell the police about the thefts?"

"No, but Max couldn't have had anything to do with it. He knew nothing about art, or its value. I mean, really. He was a handyman."

I get it, lady. A lower class of humans. "Except, two people, working in the same capacity for you, are no longer here. One is dead and the other has disappeared, along with a Picasso. Does that seem like a coincidence? What if either or both of them saw something they shouldn't have? Or, that Antonio is the thief?"

"I doubt it. Both were drifters. They'd work a little here and there. Antonio had a drinking problem. He's probably sleeping it off somewhere."

"Maybe he killed Max."

"No. That wouldn't make sense. Anyway, this doesn't pertain to anything. His disappearance has nothing to do with the gallery. Nothing."

"But Max's death must have."

"No. There's a restaurant across the alley. It has a bar . . . it was a random killing. A tragedy."

I didn't know what to make of this. Crimes happened in the nicest places in Santa Fe. First, the hotel, and now at this upscale gallery. I supposed a handyman who drank too much and didn't come back to work wasn't unheard of. Maybe that was the story of Antonio as well.

"One more thing," I said. "How did you pay Lefty? Was he an employee? Did he have a pay stub?"

"I paid him in cash. I didn't want to, but he didn't have a bank account."

No paystubs. No death or marriage records that anyone could find. Nothing to go on but the house on Calle Fernando. And I couldn't gain entrance there unless I shot my way in or paid another four hundred bucks.

"So it's settled," Carone said. "You'll be in tomorrow. We're open every day. Here's a layout of the gallery. That may be helpful to you." Carone handed me a folder. "There's a list of all my staff with their work schedules."

I nodded and, like an idiot, I signed her contract.

Then I spent the next several hours going to about fifty galleries, looking for Antonio. But I got nothing except a broader education of art.

Afterward, I drove back to the hotel. It was almost time for an early dinner. I needed to sort things out. Something about this dry, dusty landscape and its sky, unfettered by tall buildings and smog, made me feel alive. It made me want to stay. But was that enough to quit my life in L.A.? And if, on the slim chance, I found the Picasso, would that lead to a career in art? I didn't think so. My one class in art history wasn't much of a calling card, even in the place they called the land of enchantment.

CHAPTER FOUR

"Hey! Lana Davis, want a lift?"

Oh, my God. Darlene Cocobaker, driving an old, dusty Chevy pickup, slowed down at the curb in front of the Zimoro Hotel. "Darlene? Is that you? What are you doing in Santa Fe?"

I hadn't seen Darlene since we were roommates at UCLA. Not a pleasant memory either. Darlene was fun, but a total slob. And the way she partied, it didn't surprise me when she flunked out of school, which ended our roommate status. After that, we lost contact.

"How about if I tell you over a drink and dinner?" she said.

"Okay," I called out. "I'll meet you in a half hour in the café here. I'm staying here, at the Zimoro."

Darlene looked impressed. "I'll grab us a table."

I took a shower and changed into jeans and a sweater. Maybe I should check out of this place and find something cheaper. Charley paid for the hotel and my trip by giving me a per diem as a direct deposit. He'd never know. That way if I got fired from both jobs, I'd have something stashed away.

My phone was flashing, so I called the front desk. Tyler had left me a message there. I went downstairs and retrieved it before going into the cafe. *Red barn. Can't miss it. On the way to Elamos. Party tonight. Hope to see you there, Tyler.*

Hmm. He didn't have a phone, he drank more than I liked and he lived in a barn. A free spirit living life in the moment, like the person I was about to have dinner with. I must have been a free spirit myself, or I wouldn't have accepted Carone's offer. I just wasn't sure I wanted to live in Tyler's moment, or in Darlene's.

"Lana! Over here," Darlene yelled. It was happy hour in Santa Fe. Darlene's loud voice was no louder than anyone else's, I decided, trying to brace myself. Darlene, as I remembered, could be overpowering.

I went over to her. "Crazy running into you like this."

Darlene sipped a margarita. "Sorry, I couldn't wait for you. You've come up in the world. Staying at the Zimoro Hotel?"

I laughed and sat down. "It's just temporary." I wasn't sure what to tell her. Now that I was working at the Merryweather Galleries, I figured I'd better stick with that story instead of my original one.

"So you're going to live here?"

I shrugged. "I'm just here for a while." The waitress came to take my drink order. "I'll have a mineral water."

"So what are you doing in this part of the world?" Darlene asked.

I smiled. Darlene's major in college was partying, with a minor in gossip. "I'm going to be curating an art show."

"You're kidding? I moved here because I'm an artist. I didn't know you were into art. I heard you got into insurance or something."

"That was some time ago." The waitress came with my drink. "Thank you. I haven't decided what I'm going to eat yet."

"I'm not ready either," Darlene said. "We're old friends. We've got a lot of catching up to do."

The waitress left us with more time. "I didn't know you were an artist," I said.

"I didn't know it either. After I left school, I waitressed, cashiered—any job I could get. I thought I was going to get my big break in acting." Darlene rolled her eyes. "But I couldn't fight nepotism. That industry is rank with it. Then it came to me. My talents lie in expressing emotion, raw emotion. So now I paint. I know the art world is all about who you know—don't get me wrong—but it's not the whole nepotism thing, the way it is in acting. So what gallery are you working for?"

"The Merryweather Galleries."

Darlene slapped me on the shoulder. "Get out of here. You are working at the biggest gallery in Santa Fe? You have to introduce me to Carone. I hear she's the ice princess. But if she likes you, she can make your career. She's got connections in New York."

"I'm just working there on a temporary basis. Then I go back to L.A. And I don't have anything to do with the current artists, just the—"

"Dead ones. Yeah, they're big on that. Everyone knows they don't make money on contemporary artists, not enough to cover their lifestyle anyway. But it's the local artists that tourists are interested in. Everyone wants to meet a Santa Fe artist, and you can't meet someone who's dead—even if they end up buying one of their paintings. You've got to introduce me."

I took a sip of my drink. "Okay. So how long have you been in Santa Fe? What kind of artwork are you doing?"

Darlene laughed. "I got here six months ago. I came with a guy and we broke up and then I got a job at a clothing store. It's just across the street. I was on my way home and I couldn't believe it when I saw you. I paint abstracts. They look like landscapes, in a way. But not really."

I didn't ask her for more details. I didn't want her to know how ignorant I was about art. On safer ground, over dinner, I told her about meeting Tyler.

"You got invited to Tyler's party? Everyone wants to hang with Tyler."

"He doesn't even have a phone."

"Well, I might be interested in him, if you're not. He's a catch. The old rules don't apply here. This is Santa Fe, the city different. The land of enchantment. Anything can happen here. It's not like L.A. People here drive old cars and best friends don't always know your last name, or where you live. It's all in the moment here."

"I get that. I'm not sure I'm going."

"But this is a party at Tyler's. Everyone will be there. It's Saturday night. Take me with you."

"I have to look for a cheaper place. That's really what I should be doing. I can't afford to spend like I've been spending." If I didn't find Antonio, I'd be the fall guy for Charley. Especially when I billed him for the two hundred the old man robbed me of. The job at the Merryweather Galleries might end up as my only source of income. And however generous Carone thought she was, it wasn't enough to support my apartment in L.A. and living here at the Zimoro.

"You can't be as broke as me." Darlene looked down at her plate. "This is going to set me back. Can I pay you next week for dinner?"

Friendship with Darlene used to be a one-way street, and it still was. Okay, I fronted her dinner and she talked me into going to Tyler's party. It was Saturday night—not a great time to go looking for an apartment anyway.

Although I asked Darlene not to tell anyone about my job at the Merryweather Galleries, when we got to the party, that's all she talked about.

"I thought you said you were in the insurance business?" Tyler said. "You were looking for some guy, weren't you?"

Darlene looked surprised. "Huh?"

I smoothed over the situation with, "Oh, I quit that. Only did it to make ends meet. Got to scrounge where I can. Art is my real passion." With that, I launched into a discourse about how the traffic in L.A. made me crazy and how much I liked the scenery here. Tyler and Darlene stopped asking about the insurance job, so I must have distracted them enough to forget about it. I kept talking so they wouldn't think of asking me about the art the Merryweather Galleries exhibited, or what exhibition I was curating. I knew I couldn't talk intelligently about that.

I didn't need to worry. The liquor flowed, and soon no one remembered what anyone said. The barn had a few hundred people in it. The flat acreage surrounding it, planted with junipers and non-desert shrubs, courtesy of Tyler, made it a great setting for a party. The nearest neighbor was a half mile away.

I asked a few people if they knew Lefty, as if I had a job for him, but didn't get any leads. Darlene hooked up with some guy. I drove home alone, sneaking away just as Tyler went to get another beer. It's not that I didn't like him. I did. His paintings, abstract and multi-colored, were interesting. But he drank too much. And I had my heart set on seeing Alan again.

After I left the party, I didn't go back to the hotel. Instead, because Alan lived nearby, I drove by his house. He lived in Elamos, on Argon Drive. His house, a Santa Fe version of a California ranch-style home, was set back from the road on about an acre. All the houses on the street looked like they had been built by the same developer—sprawling one-story houses with awkward-looking arches above front porches, and shrubbery limited to native plants and a few oak trees. The house was dark. It was late. I couldn't knock on the door and claim I was lost and needed directions. Oh, well, tomorrow was another day.

But not a good day. I read in the newspaper that Angelica had died from her gunshot wounds. Police were seeking any information about her killer.

I dug into my purse to find that police officer's card, but it wasn't there. Crap. I bet it fell out of my purse at Tyler's place, when I got my keys out. I was in a hurry to leave without Tyler seeing me.

I made a call to the police. They transferred me to an officer's voicemail. I left my name and number and said I had information about Angelica's murder. After I hung up, I wasn't sure I did the right thing. True, Angelica had looked strange when I mentioned Route Eighty, and a guy shot at me there. Maybe that didn't amount to anything worth telling. Then again, maybe it did.

Carone lived on a dirt road on the outskirts of town, about a mile off Canyon Road. But unlike the houses on the rural routes I had seen the day before, Carone's house sat on expensive dirt, the type shared by celebrities and other high-profile landowners.

Located on a rolling hill with native flowers and shrubs, Carone's house, three stories high, looked massive. Yet the pale red adobe exterior and the gray-blue windowsills made it charming as well. The house had a gentle, faded quality, as if it had been there for a hundred years. Just the way old money liked it.

A young, pixie-faced Hispanic maid in a black uniform answered my ring. She spoke no English. She knew who I was. I asked for Carone. *"No en casa,"* she said, or something like that.

Like Carone's office, the interior of the house was all in white except for the paintings on the walls. Although I couldn't recognize the artists, all of them, portraits, still lifes and abstracts, looked like masterpieces—executed with thick, lush painting. Not like the reproductions my aunt hung on her walls.

The maid led me upstairs into a large bedroom decorated with white, lacquered colonial-style furniture. The maid showed me to the hallway off the bedroom. In there, I saw two closets, each the size of my whole living space in L.A. Another maid was sorting clothes in one of the closets. When she wasn't looking, I glanced inside and saw menswear. I didn't remember whether Carone had worn a wedding ring.

The maid picked out some black and gray outfits and matching scarves, and left me alone in the bedroom to change. Because Carone wore her hemlines below her knees, her outfit looked like a miniskirt on me, but still in good taste. The maid came in after I finished dressing. She had a comb in her hand. Okay. I let her fix my hair. She tied my hair back with one of Carone's scarves. Then she put my old clothes, along with several more outfits of Carone's, into a small suitcase.

On my way out, I glanced in the mirror by the front door. I didn't look half-bad. Tying my hair back gave me a sophisticated air. Just like a docent at a museum, or like one of those stuck-up sales clerks in a Beverly Hills boutique. Not too shabby for a job paying only two thousand a month, especially if it included a hair appointment, free clothes and was in addition to my regular job.

When I got to the gallery, I felt like a kid on her first day at a new school. Would I fit in? Would the kids like me? I felt weird walking into the place faking my expertise, and having the boss know about it. I had never done anything like this before.

I did a certain amount of faking enthusiasm and loyalty at my real job. I didn't like working in claims. I didn't like working in insurance. I didn't think anyone in the department did, including Charley. But companies didn't want unenthusiastic, disloyal people working for them. So we played the game, knowing we were bureaucrats, a hated species. No one liked insurance workers. To get back at people for their scorn, we used rules to torment them, even though we didn't follow them ourselves.

And now I was about to enter a world where people worked

because they loved it. They had a passion for art. I wasn't blessed with a talent of some sort, so this was out of my comfort zone. I didn't want anyone to find out I was a fake. That was even worse than being a bureaucrat.

I should have looked at the file Carone gave me instead of going to Tyler's party. My one day of education on the Santa Fe art scene probably wouldn't convince any of Carone's staff I was a curator, despite looking like a Carone clone. I didn't know what a curator did.

Carone was not at the reception desk when I arrived. Instead, a redhead sat there. Her bright red hair made a sharp contrast to the gray walls and the elegant gray and black granite counter. The woman's outfit was like mine or, more accurately, like Carone's, but not as expensive. She had a stocky build and looked about twenty-five. She had no makeup on her round, translucent face, and wore her hair pulled back in a knot, similar to mine. Her raised eyebrow told me she recognized me from the day before, but I didn't remember seeing her. Her stern glance intimidated me. I felt I had lost some unnamed battle with her.

I stopped looking at her and focused on the interior of the gallery. It seemed to stretch out like a giant runway. The walls and ceiling, painted pale gray, set off the paintings better than white walls did, inviting the viewer into the works. Yet at the same time, using gray instead of white made the gallery look overwhelming and forbidding. It must have taken a severely jaded thief to steal from a place this awesome.

A door opened behind the redhead, and Rodney, again in his mustard-colored jacket, sauntered toward me. He had pale skin, sandy brown hair cut longer than most, and a mustache that drooped. He was slim but strong looking and about thirty. His large hands almost looked like those in a Michelangelo sculpture I had seen in a book. It was odd how details of my art history class, forgotten for years, materialized in my brain now that I worked for a gallery.

He leaned against the wall and gave me a bored glance. He was good-looking, and he knew it.

"Do you have an appointment?" the redhead asked. Her voice had an arrogant tone.

"Come on, love," the man said. "Must we be so formal?" He gave the redhead a slight smile, which made her blush and flutter her eyelashes.

"Don't mind her, love," he said to me. "She's a great gal when you get to know her."

The redhead smiled. "Let me do my job. Did you have an appointment?" she repeated. This time she sounded friendlier.

"Yes," I said, "it was for one o'clock. I'm Lana Davis."

"Oh. You're a few minutes early and Ms. Merryweather is in a meeting—she may be late. Why don't you sit over there?" She indicated some overstuffed gray velvet chairs across from the counter. "It may take a while," she said.

I nodded, leaving the two of them to work out their attraction for each other. I didn't mind waiting. It gave me a chance to go over the gallery floor plan Carone had given me.

On my right was the contemporary gallery, where aspiring painters in Santa Fe hoped to display their work, according to Darlene. There were three other galleries next to the contemporary one, separated by eight-foot-high partitions. The first one displayed works collectors brought in for resale. The last two galleries housed the Merryweather family collection, with one room reserved for early-twentieth-century European art and the second for post–World War II European and American art. Each gallery had a small conference room within its walls. Alongside of the galleries were separate storage rooms for the inventory not on view, accessible by a door in each gallery space. These rooms were the stacks, where Carone had found a drunken Antonio one night. The stacks were also accessible from a hallway in the administration wing, near the back door.

After I reviewed the floor plan, I glanced at the front desk, but the receptionist and Rodney had gone off somewhere. So I got up and wandered.

The contemporary gallery featured paintings by Jack Rickenfaller. His large abstracts looked like squiggly blobs of paint to me. I had to admit, I liked Tyler's work better.

The resale gallery, according to the brochure at the table in the entryway, displayed paintings by well-known contemporary artists popular in the New York art scene. Although not mentioned in the brochure, I figured these works were from collectors who either had hit hard times or had bought when prices were lower and wanted a return on their money. I didn't recognize any of the artists, though I liked some of the paintings.

I perused the two Merryweather family collection galleries. I was busy studying a collage by Braque—a world-famous artist during the nineteen-twenties—when out of the corner of my eye, I saw the door to the stacks fly open. Someone must have walked by me and I hadn't noticed.

Figuring it was my job to see who went in there, I made a dash for the door, catching it before it closed. I looked into a room crammed with paintings. They were everywhere. I had seen the stacks on the floor plan, but looking into the actual rooms was humbling. I never realized there could be so much art in one place. It was staggering, considering the total value of all this work.

I stopped feeling amazed when I heard footsteps—somewhere in the stacks. Like the public areas, the stacks had cement floors. It could have been nothing. After all, the staff used the stacks. Maybe someone needed a painting to show a potential collector. All the same, I went after the footsteps. Unfortunately, my heels clicked and clattered on the cement, and the footsteps stopped.

I waited, and the footsteps started again. They had to belong to a man because they sounded heavy and farther apart than a woman's.

I took off my shoes and tiptoed after them. The footsteps broke into a run. So did I.

A door closed and everything became quiet. The man must have gone out, but exactly where, I couldn't figure out. This place was a maze of paintings, corridors and doors.

The door to my left opened and a dark-haired man in a tweed three-piece suit and horned-rimmed glasses looked at me in surprise. "Who are you and what are you doing in here?"

CHAPTER FIVE

"I'm—the new curator Ms. Merryweather hired."

The man looked down at my shoeless feet. I realized the scarf tying my hair had become undone, because the end of it now brushed my arm. I felt hot and sticky, despite the cool temperature of the air conditioning. "My shoes hurt," I said. I felt stupid. "They're new."

"Is this your first day here?"

"Yes."

"I think you're supposed to wait in the reception area—that's usually how it's done. You're not supposed to be in here."

"Sorry, I just wanted to check things out."

"Well, you're not supposed to be in here until you have an assignment from Ms. Merryweather."

"Okay. Can you tell me how to get back to the reception area?" I was too flustered to remember the gallery floor plan.

He gave me a haughty look. "This way please."

I put on my shoes and followed him. I listened to his footsteps, but I couldn't tell whether those were the ones I had heard. When we reached the reception area, he walked to the reception desk and disappeared through the door to the office wing.

"Oh, there you are," the receptionist said. "Ms. Merryweather is waiting." She gave me a long look—my clothes must have looked as disheveled as the scarf. I patted my hair and tightened the scarf. Not much I could do about the wrinkles in the dress.

47

I followed the receptionist into the office wing. Rodney whizzed by me.

"Well, love, we meet again," he said. "Good luck with Carone."

His glance told me that despite his bored, flirting manner, he was curious about my business with Carone. I didn't see the man with the horned-rimmed glasses anywhere.

We didn't get very far when I heard a loud voice coming from Carone's office, shattering the quiet decorum of the place. A woman shouted, "No!" A man swore loudly. Afterward, I heard some muffled talking I couldn't make out.

Regardless of the ongoing commotion, the receptionist headed straight for Carone's office. Before we entered, a tall, cosmopolitan-looking man with black hair rushed out, and the arguing ceased.

Since this wing had carpeted floors, I couldn't listen for the man's footsteps. I wondered why the receptionist didn't buzz Carone on their interoffice phone to ask her if this was a good time. Every business had such a phone system. I looked at the redhead, but her face showed no emotion.

When Carone saw the receptionist and me, the existing frown on her face changed to a pleasant smile. I had a feeling the smile was more for the redhead than for me.

Carone looked stunning in a white silk suit with short sleeves. White seemed to be her color. Her elaborate turquoise necklace stood out against the stark white of her outfit and of the room.

"Ms. Davis," she said. "Good to see you." She gave my dress, or rather her dress, a brief stare. Carone didn't run in her clothes.

Carone addressed the redhead. "There will be a meeting in five minutes. I might as well introduce you two now. Marny—this is Lana Davis, the new assistant curator. Lana, Marny Jenkins."

Marny gave Carone an expectant look, as if to elicit another response from her. But Carone didn't comply. An awkward silence followed and I filled it. "Nice to meet you, Marny," I said.

"Welcome aboard," Marny replied. However, her face said otherwise. She excused herself and went to the door.

Carone asked me to take a seat and as I did, I caught a glimpse of Marny's retreating face. On it was a look of absolute hatred. Whether it was directed at me or at Carone, I didn't know. But the first chance I got, I was going to find out.

Carone wasted no time getting down to business. "I wrote down some notes about my staff and about our gallery procedures. Also, I've included pictures of the works taken from the gallery. I noted the title and artist of the work on the back. You are somewhat familiar with Picasso?"

"Somewhat. I took a class in art history in college."

Carone handed me the photos and some handwritten notes. "Please don't let anyone know you have these. I hope you can read my writing. I didn't want to type them on a computer—someone could trace that. I can't let anyone know the Picasso is missing. Put this in the folder I gave you. You can look at them later."

Carone looked composed, but I heard a note of desperation in her voice. "Of course, I understand," I said.

"I put Patty Sanders first on the list," Carone said. "Not because I suspect her, but because you shouldn't cross her. She's our office manager and bookkeeper. She's the only one who knows why you're here. She's older and set in her ways—but she can be very helpful. She's very particular about anyone wasting supplies or not having a neat office. If you respect that, you'll get along fine."

"I'll try to remember that. By the way, who's in charge of security?"

"We're all supposed to be involved with it."

I asked whether it was as easy to slip in the back door and steal something out of the stacks as it looked on the floor plan.

"No one can walk in or out of the stacks without having someone to attend to them," she said.

Thinking of my mishap with the man in the horned-rimmed glasses, I supposed she was right, most of the time. "Weren't the paintings in the stacks when they were stolen?"

Carone sighed and hunched her elegant shoulders. Her voice shook when she said, "Both the front door and the back exit connect to an alarm system. It would be a difficult thing to accomplish."

"But it did happen, didn't it?"

"Yes, I suppose. That's what happened." Admitting the security breach upset her, as did the resulting theft of the Picasso. But probably her argument with that man, most likely her husband, was why she looked so distressed.

"We also have a buzzer system," Carone said. "A plastic tag is attached to the back of each work in the gallery. If someone walks out with a locked painting, the alarm will sound. We can't have the atmosphere of an armed camp, but during our openings, someone stands at the door to make sure nothing is stolen or damaged."

"Can this tag be removed easily?"

"It's supposed to be removable only by a tool—similar to those you've seen in clothing stores."

"Who has access to this tool?"

"We have several of them and only my staff has access to them. Usually, we keep them locked in a drawer at the reception counter—but everyone has a key to the drawer—and we didn't always keep the drawer locked. We do now."

"Since you've been locking up these tag removal tools, have any paintings disappeared?"

"No."

"Could—one of your customers—clients—have used one of them to unlock a painting without anyone knowing? Where do you keep them during receptions?"

"As I told you, we don't call them customers or clients. They're collectors. Please remember that. Otherwise, no one will believe you're a curator."

"Sure. Sorry."

"The thing is, we have to have access to the removal tool—we sell paintings quite often during receptions that are in the stacks and not on exhibition. This isn't the bargain basement. We have to remove tags casually, if the collector is present. We don't want our collectors getting the impression we're worried they'll steal anything. If it's a small painting, and not part of an exhibition, sometimes a collector will take the work home that night. Naturally, we remove the tag before it leaves the gallery."

Her system didn't seem secure to me. "But someone could have removed a tag and walked out with a painting without anyone knowing it."

"Yes, but highly unlikely."

"But in a big crowd, you couldn't be watching all the time."

Carone shook her head. "That couldn't have happened."

"But somehow it did. Maybe not at a reception. Somehow someone or some people took paintings out of the gallery."

"I don't know how it happened."

"Well, how about the private lives of your staff?" I asked.

"Of that I know very little. I make it a practice not to get involved—unless it concerns the gallery. I'll leave that up to you, if you find it's necessary." The expression on Carone's face discouraged me from asking about the man in her office. Or why Marny seemed full of venom.

"What about a cleaning crew? Do you have a service?"

"Yes. They come daily, at nine—I'm here or someone from

the staff is. They don't clean the stacks. One my staff handles that. We dust and damp-mop the floors. Once a month we vacuum the racks. It's simple. With so much valuable art, we couldn't let cleaning people in."

"Hmm. I see."

"Did you have a question?" Carone said.

"A man entered the stacks while I was waiting to see you. I followed him and—he started running. I didn't see who he was. Does that sound right to you?"

"I don't know. It could have been someone on the staff—you'll have to be discreet—I can't have them thinking I suspect them of stealing. I can't imagine it's one of them."

Carone couldn't bring herself to imagine anyone she knew had stolen those paintings. But who else could, except someone familiar with the gallery? She didn't seem concerned about a man running in the stacks. Or did the very rich cover up their feelings better than the rest of us? Carone made nonchalance into an art form. Maybe a trait worth cultivating, if I wanted to find the Picasso.

Carone looked at me as if our five minutes were up, so I stuffed my notes into the file and stood up, ready to go to the staff meeting. But instead of getting up, Carone hesitated, as if she wanted to say something.

"Is there anything else?" I asked.

"No. The conference room is to the left as you walk out. I'll be there in a few minutes."

The staff had already assembled in the conference room, which was really a typical office break room with white laminate counters and cabinets and a white vinyl floor. A large rectangular mahogany table dominated the room. The staff consisted of Marny, an older woman who had to be Patty Sanders, and three men, two of whom I had already seen. When they saw me, their conversation stopped. I saw Rodney folding a newspaper.

"I'm Lana Davis. I'm the new assistant curator."

"Welcome. I'm Patty Sanders, the office manager."

"Hello. Is that today's paper?"

"No," Rodney said. "It's a week old."

Just like in my office, newspapers had a long shelf-life. People read the same one day in and day out in the break room until finally someone brought in a current edition.

No one spoke for a moment. Rodney put the paper on the counter by the sink. I caught a glimpse of the headline. *Man Killed. Shot in Alley.*

"He used to work here. He was killed," Marny said.

"Yeah. Poor Max. Hello, I'm Clyde."

Clyde was a burly, dark-haired man with a dimple on his chin. He looked about my age. "Hi, Clyde. That's really too bad," I said. "Carone told me about it."

"Yes, love," Rodney said. "Max Beely. Poor soul. Used to be the handyman."

"That's terrible," I said. "Do they have any leads on who did it?"

"Here, love, read it for yourself. Oh, I'm Rodney. Nice to meet you." He grabbed the paper and handed it to me.

"Hi. Nice to meet you."

Rodney poured himself some coffee from the pot on the counter. He whispered something to Marny. But when Carone walked in, all talking stopped.

The staff meeting lasted about twenty minutes. Aside from the staff being less than enthusiastic about its subject, the gallery's annual charity auction show for the Children's Hospital, I didn't get a chance to speak to any of them. But I observed them. The man with the horned-rimmed glasses turned out to be Bentley Orson.

The meeting reminded me of those in my office. I caught

snippets of bickering, boredom and resentment. People were the same everywhere. Still, there was something surreal about this meeting. They were planning an event that would be the talk of Santa Fe, and by some quirk of fate, I was now a part of it. I felt as if I was floating in someone else's dream. But the angry look Marny gave me brought me back to reality. That one had it in for me.

For the show and the auction, the gallery was going to remove the partitions between the viewing rooms. Considered a major social event, many celebrities attended the show and auction. Aside from helping the hospital, it was good publicity for the gallery.

The culmination of the month-long charity show was the auction, and since the gallery donated all the money to charity, the staff didn't receive commissions on sales during this month, just their regular salaries. And Carone reminded the staff that they were required to donate twenty percent of their base salaries during this month to the charity. Ouch. The staff wouldn't admit how unhappy that made them, but I could understand how they felt. I wondered if Carone expected me to donate twenty percent of my two thousand. She didn't mention that in the contract, though I would donate if asked to do so. How could I complain, when I was double dipping?

At the end of the meeting, Carone introduced me as an assistant curator for special projects. Afterward, Patty Sanders whisked me aside to show me my office.

Patty was a crusty old gal with a face as hard as a granite mountain. Her green eyes were keen but not unkind. She wore a double-breasted black suit with a red silk flower in her lapel. Judging from the sunspots on her hands, she was at least sixty—if not more. She also had a funny habit of twirling a pen behind her right ear, which messed up the short, tight waves of her otherwise neat white-blond hair.

"Your office will be next to Marny's," she said. "I'm sure if you need anything, she'll be glad to help you."

I had my doubts about that, but asking for Marny's help would be a perfect opportunity to find out what bothered her. "I thought she was the receptionist," I said.

"Marny is filling in for Ms. Merryweather's secretary, Amanda, who's out sick. Amanda usually works the front desk."

Patty led me into the supply room and picked out some pens, stationery and other office supplies for me. She made me sign for each item.

"Have you been with the gallery long?" I asked.

She gave me a quick look. "As you are aware, I'm the only one besides Ms. Merryweather who knows why you're here, so if you want to ask me any questions, I suggest we go to your office." She pursed her lips as a gentle reprimand, making me feel like a four-year-old.

With Patty sitting across from me, I stocked my desk with the office supplies she had given me. Patty regarded my efforts with approval.

My office was small and painted in the same gray as the viewing rooms. It was also the library, for on all four walls were books on floor-to-ceiling gray lacquered shelves, with no space to hang any paintings. Across from a desk, between the bookcases was a small window.

I shut the desk drawers when I finished. "So what can you tell me about the situation?"

"There have been paintings missing. That's all I know. Apparently, all but one has turned up again. Art isn't my subject. I just work on the books and keep track of things in the stacks. That's how I found out about it. I was the one to tell Ms. Merryweather about the missing paintings."

"How do you think this could have happened?"

Patty turned almost purple for a second. "The accounts and the office supply room are my departments and I keep a tight hold on everything. No personal expenses ever get by me, and I know just how many pens everyone has. If I had control of the stacks, no one would go in unless signed in by me. Then none of this would have happened. Someone had a key and came in after hours. That much I know. I have volunteered to stay late to catch the thief, but Ms. Merryweather won't hear of it."

"Well, it's a good thing you don't. Whoever it is could be dangerous and you might get hurt."

Who was I to talk? I didn't want to get hurt either. Two thousand dollars, possibly less twenty percent, wasn't enough to risk my life.

"I'm not afraid," Patty said. To emphasize that, she made an extra flourish with her pen and twirled it in her hair. "I've had worse problems to deal with. I've asked Ms. Merryweather to call the police, but she won't. Very unwise. She knows how I feel."

"Do you have any idea who the thief might be?"

I almost expected a reprimand for asking such a dumb question, but instead, for an instant, I saw a glint in Patty's eyes. She shook her head. "I don't know." She looked me in the face and opened her eyes wide.

For the zillionth time I asked myself, what in the world did I get myself into? How would working here help me find Antonio? I realized Patty was staring at me, waiting for me to focus. "Uh, what about keys?" I asked. "Who has keys to the gallery?" As I asked Patty these questions, I felt an odd sense of trepidation. What about the man in the stacks? Carone had shrugged him off, but what if that man was the thief? And what if he saw me and decided I didn't need to exist anymore? Again, I came back to the realization that two thousand a month wasn't enough to risk my life.

"Everyone has a key," Patty said. "Ms. Merryweather is entirely too slack about things. I've told her that, but she won't listen. Are you feeling all right?"

"Yes. I'm fine." But I wasn't. I was afraid of what I was getting myself into. And I didn't want to take Patty into my confidence. "Tell me, if someone comes in after hours, does that trigger an alarm?"

"It's supposed to, but it can be turned off, and we all know how to do it. We have to because we turn it off in the morning. Work schedules vary, so whoever gets here first turns it off."

"Do you think any of the gallery's customers have keys or could disengage the alarm?"

"We don't call them customers. They're collectors, because they collect art."

"Right. Carone told me that. I'll remember."

"I hope you do. We don't want the rest of them to think you're not really curating a show. I don't have much to do with the collectors of the gallery. But since Ms. Merryweather is so casual about security, I don't doubt anyone could walk right in and take everything."

I was getting nowhere so I tried a different tactic. "What seems to be bothering Marny Jenkins?"

"Oh, that girl! Nothing is right for her. All she does is complain. Her computer isn't new enough, her office isn't big enough—you name it—she complains about it. But let her try and manage my departments, and I'll see that she's fired."

She spoke with such force it surprised me. I was glad I was still on Patty's good list. "Why do you think she complains so much? Has she tried to manage your—departments?"

"Marny complains because she can't go any higher in this place. Not unless she inherits the Merryweather millions. And they do have millions. They may act down-to-earth, but they're on the list of the world's richest families. Marny isn't about to inherit any of their money, so she resents Ms. Merryweather. She grabs more supplies than she's allotted. I told Ms. Merryweather about that. Marny's up to no good. And now she's trying to tell me what to do."

"Do you think she's the one stealing from the gallery?"

"I didn't say that. I don't think she'd steal. But if you ask me, she's looking for another job, maybe even a backer to open up her own gallery. Meanwhile, she's not doing her job here. She comes in late, wastes paper, complains when she has to answer the phones—we all have to do that on occasion—and she leaves the lights on. That costs us money. But Ms. Merryweather won't do anything about it."

"I see. Will I be required to donate twenty percent of my salary to the Children's Hospital?"

"You need to take that up with Ms. Merryweather."

Maybe I didn't need to have that conversation. I was already double dipping as it was.

Patty walked to the door. "If there's nothing else, I need to get back to work."

"Oh, wait a minute. You forgot your pen."

It was an expensive pen with her initials engraved in gold script.

"Thanks," Patty said. "I would have come back for it. I never go anywhere without it. I'm the only one here who thought of bringing her own pen, instead of making the gallery supply them for me. Half the time, the staff loses them. They prefer to waste supplies."

I smiled. "I won't waste supplies. And I have my own pen. So you don't need to worry about me." But did I need to worry about Patty? With Max Beely dead and Antonio missing, I didn't want Patty snooping where she shouldn't.

Regardless of my agreement with Carone, if I did find out who the thief was, I would call the police. When Carone hired me, she didn't realize how disloyal I could be.

Chapter Six

After Patty left, I studied Carone's photos and her notes. I was going to check the stacks for those paintings, when I heard Marny come into her office. Carone's notes described Marny as a saleswoman, though in parentheses Carone had written *curator,* followed by an asterisk.

I put everything in the folder and locked it in the bottom desk drawer with the key I found inside one of the other drawers. I wondered if Patty had put it there. She probably had a master key, and planned to raid the desk the first chance she got. Patty wanted to get the jump on the thief herself. I had to make sure that didn't happen.

Marny's door was open. She sat at her desk holding a cup of coffee. "Hello! I've got the office next door—"

"Oh! Damn!" she cried. "Look what you made me do. You snuck up on me and now I've spilled coffee on my report."

"Sorry. Let me help." I grabbed some tissues from a box on her desk and mopped up the spill, in an effort to gain her confidence. As Patty might have said, I had dealt with worse—though usually I didn't suck up to them.

"Thanks," Marny said. She looked embarrassed. "I'm sorry I got so mad. It wasn't your fault. Well—I should get back to work."

"Look, please don't think I'm here to take your job. I'm a temporary consultant, that's all." I gave her a smile, hoping it looked sincere. I did feel some sympathy for her. It couldn't be too great for her ego to work as the receptionist instead of a saleswoman or a curator.

My smile must have won her over. "Would you like some coffee?" she said.

"Sure. Black's fine."

"I've got an extra mug you can use. We're supposed to bring our own cups, now that Patty isn't ordering plastic ones. She thinks it gives us a bad image. The whole going green thing, if you know what I mean. You might think of getting some nice ones, to use when you meet with collectors."

"Thanks for the tip. I'll rinse it out when I'm through."

Marny poured coffee from a pot in an electric brewer on the small cabinet behind her desk. "I can't stand the office brew so I make my own."

"Mmm. It's good coffee." We drank in silence for a moment. "By the way, who was that great-looking man who came out of Ms. Merryweather's office?"

"That is Carone's husband, Jason Nichols. But I wouldn't get any ideas about him. Rumor has it he and Amanda are quite the couple."

"Amanda—"

"Carone's secretary. You haven't met her yet. But you will."

"Oh, yes. I remember hearing her name. Was he arguing with—uh—Carone the whole time I was waiting?"

Marny hesitated for a second. "I don't know, but don't look too interested in Jason, or both Carone and Amanda will be at your throat." Marny giggled, and I managed an understanding smile.

"Does Ms.—Carone know?"

"I don't see how she can miss it, but then she's pretty dense. She must be a real dead fish to live with. I mean, she's—attractive, but so cold. I see why Jason flirts. He once tried to come on to me." Marny seemed proud of that.

"Really?"

"I admit I was tempted, I mean, he is cute, but I don't go out with married men. And at the time, I was really into this job. You know—I felt loyal to Carone. But not anymore."

Marny was hard to read. One minute she was angry and distant, and the next minute she was confiding in me. It must have been my appearance—hair tied in a scarf like a docent and Carone's expensive dress—that convinced her to accept me as a social equal. A status she didn't confer on everyone, I assumed.

"So the loyalty's gone, huh?" I said.

"Carone doesn't know how to run a gallery and I'm fed up. I'm looking for another job. Don't say anything. Not that I care. I just want to leave on my own terms."

"Don't worry. I'm here only for a short time."

"Well, don't expect her to recognize your talent. She won't take any advice. I was a curator at the Taler Museum in Boston, and I know what it takes to run a top-notch gallery. All she wants me to do is sell. So tacky! And today I don't even get to do that. Amanda's sick, so little me has to play receptionist. Carone wouldn't dream of asking the men to do that. I mean, I didn't even rate an introduction as a saleswoman when I met you. She was perfectly willing to let you think I was the receptionist."

"I understand how you feel. It might have been an oversight."

"Hah! No way. I'm too much competition for her. She wants to keep me down."

"So you were hired to be a saleswoman."

"No! She hired me to make this gallery a showplace for modern art, a private museum. Carone makes everyone sell. You'd think with her millions she wouldn't need the money, not that we ever see any of it. The pay is terrible. Oh, I bet she promised you a bonus. But you'll never get it. I was supposed to get a raise after three months. I did, but it was so much smaller than what we agreed on. And here I've been trying to turn this place into a museum, I mean, a *real* museum. She just plays with the idea."

I had to agree with Marny in one respect. Carone's idea of running a gallery seemed more fluff than substance. With her influence, she could hire the right people, but she let too many things get by her. Paintings disappeared, and if I believed Marny, her husband was having an affair right under her nose. Carone floated in a dream world the way I did at the staff meeting earlier. But I came down to earth afterward. Who in Carone's life had enough authority to help her do the same?

Patty walked by. She didn't say anything. She just looked in. Then she hurried off.

"That old witch has it in for me," Marny said. "I better get back to the reception desk or she'll tell Carone I'm not doing my job. This place is insane. They treat me like a naughty kid instead of a curator. I have to sneak back to my office to get any real work done."

"That's too bad. I hope you find a better job. Let me know where you end up. I could use a permanent job myself."

"Sure. I'd help you out. You want to have a drink after work tonight? I'm going to meet a friend who works at another gallery. Would you like to come?"

"I'd love to. Let me know when you're leaving."

I went back to my office and closed the door. Even though Marny had a motive, I didn't think she'd steal from the gallery. Marny respected art too much to steal it.

But before I started forming too many opinions, I reviewed Carone's notes about the employees. At the bottom of the page, next to the asterisk, Carone had written Marny was a promising saleswoman who was in training to curate shows of the modern masters. Carone had underlined the words *in training* twice. I wondered how Marny's employment contract read. Did Carone change her mind about Marny's abilities, or did Marny overstate them?

With the exception of Amanda, I had now met everyone. Bentley was a real suspect if I ever saw one. He acted as if I were a thief, yet Carone had told no one but Patty about the thefts. Maybe he was covering up for himself. Anyway, according to Carone, he was a painter as well as a part-time salesman. He was going to have his first show in the gallery next year.

The other part-time salesperson was the charming Rodney Bracken, who was also an artist. Rodney had studied fresco painting in Florence, and had executed several public murals for the gallery's corporate collectors, as well as some murals for its private collectors.

Clyde Posten was in charge of installations. He also assisted with sales during openings. But more importantly, he had supervised Max, and most likely Antonio. Clyde also kept the stacks clean, so he was always in there.

Amanda Talbert had a university degree. Maybe Amanda resented being a secretary. Maybe she resented Carone. But was that a reason to steal from the gallery? Of course, there was always the money angle. I wondered what Amanda was like. To have an affair right under Carone's nose—now that took nerve. If it was true.

I studied the photos of the paintings again. Each one, except for the Picasso, had been missing only for two or three days. The first time this had happened was four months ago. Then every few weeks another turned up missing.

It was odd that Patty had discovered the thefts. According to Carone's notes, it wasn't Patty's job to take care of the stacks. It was Marny's. Yet Patty told me it was her job. Of course, if Marny had to work the reception desk she wouldn't have had time to keep the stacks organized.

It might be a good idea to find out how often Amanda was

sick and whether her illnesses coincided with the dates the paintings had disappeared. The problem was, the paintings could have been missing for days or even weeks before anyone discovered they were missing. With so many paintings in the stacks, it would be impractical to take inventory except every now and then.

I wrote down the names of the paintings and locked everything in the desk drawer. I taped the key underneath the desk and went to look in the stacks. Maybe I was missing another angle altogether. It might be as simple as looking for the obvious. I just didn't know enough about the gallery business to see the obvious.

Once I entered the stacks, the layout on the map became easier to understand, now that I didn't have footsteps to confuse me. There were four rooms, and in each room were four aisles of vertical wooden racks, as well as vertical racks along all the walls. Each room was open to a long corridor, connecting all the rooms. At one end of the corridor was the entry door, accessible from the reception area. Within each room were two doors. One led to the office wing, and the one on the opposite side of the room led to the gallery pertaining to the type of work stored in that room. This made it handy for the sales and installation staff to get the paintings they needed without having to walk through the entire stacks or through the public areas.

It also made it easy for someone to get in or out of the stacks from one side without anyone seeing them enter or leave from the other side. This was because the doors in each room were not directly opposite each other, and racks of paintings blocked the view of the other door.

The rooms had charts posted of all the paintings in there, listed alphabetically by artist, as well as numbered, similar to a decimal system in a library. Each carpet-lined rack had a number. Posted at one end of the row was a list of the works in that particular rack. Large paintings were in individual racks and smaller paintings were stored two to three in a rack, one behind the other.

I pulled out a painting and looked at the small security tag on the back. It was made of heavy, inflexible plastic, but with care and patience, someone could cut it off with a hacksaw or an ordinary utility knife, as well as with the tool designed for it. Though, as Carone had said, tampering with the tag sounded an alarm.

I found the six paintings that were stolen and returned from the Merryweather collection. Three were Matisses, one was a Chagall, and two were Kandinskys. But other than being modern master paintings small enough to hide under a big coat or inside a large art portfolio, I couldn't see why someone would steal these particular paintings and not others. The Merryweather collection had many to choose from. I pulled out other paintings, coming across another Matisse and another Kandinsky. I knew those names. The Merryweather collection had to be worth more money than I could fathom. And here they were, just stacked in rows, without any real security—I didn't think much of Carone's system. *Incredible.*

I went to the resale stacks and found the spot where the missing Picasso had been. To the casual observer it seemed to be still in place. A small painting of twenty inches by sixteen, its place was supposed to be against the inside wall of the rack, with two other paintings lined up in front of it. Carone had substituted another work in its spot so nothing looked disturbed.

I took out the substituted painting. A Picasso as well, but a drawing rather than a painting. Also, like the last Picasso, this one was a portrait of a woman. Carone had thought of everything, at least on the surface. Too bad she hadn't thought of a better security system.

Other than Patty and Carone, who else knew this was not the

last Picasso? My guess was nobody—except the thief. Not every day did someone come in to buy a Picasso. And because of the number of paintings in the room, who would think to look for it? This place was a gold mine for thievery.

I put the Picasso back. I heard a noise and looked up. "Oh, hello. You're Clyde Posten, aren't you?"

"What a memory," he said. "You're the new assistant curator, aren't you? What was your name again?" He looked me up and down and then lowered his eyes when he saw me watching him.

"Lana Davis," I said.

"So, Ms. Davis, what brings you to merry Merryweather?"

"As Carone said, I'm here for a special project. Just freelancing. I won't be here that long."

"You came to the opening the other night, didn't you?"

I nodded and turned away, pretending a great interest in one of the paintings in one of the racks.

"I thought I remembered you," he said. "Are you an artist? Carone usually hires artists."

"No, I'm not an artist. I just curate."

He looked as if he didn't believe me. "Don't be embarrassed. I'm a photographer and Carone wasn't interested in my work right away either. I've been here a year and a half and I'm just now getting her interested in my real work. I'm a good photographer. You should come to my studio sometime. It's not far from here. Say—don't you write reviews for *The Reporter*?"

"No. I'm just a curator."

"You look just like that reporter. What's her name? Can't think of it."

"I can't either."

"It'll come to me. Probably when I'm ready to fall asleep tonight."

I nodded. Was he trying to catch me in a lie? Was there an art reviewer for *The Reporter* who looked like me? Did that paper even exist? I hadn't been in town long enough to know. "Well, have fun thinking about it, Clyde."

"I'll let you know if I remember her name," he said. He sauntered away.

"Wait—Clyde—"

Clyde came lumbering back, his footsteps sounding loudly on the cement floor. Could he have been the one I followed in the stacks? I didn't even hear him come in this time, though.

"What is it?" he said. His face had a hopeful expression.

"Well, a friend who works at a gallery needs a handyman— for that gallery—she mentioned that the Merryweather Galleries used to have this handyman—"

"Max," Clyde said. He looked less hopeful. "He's the one we were talking about before the meeting today. The one who was shot."

"I know. But that's not the one she meant. He was someone with the nickname of Lefty—had a finger missing on his left hand. She wondered what happened to him. They need a job done."

"That's too bad. Lefty . . . left."

"I heard he does good work. Do you know where he went?"

"I wouldn't know. Only Lefty knows. If you find him, you'll know."

"Right. The thing is, my friend's gallery hired him and he didn't show up. Kind of weird, huh?"

"Not really," he said. "They'll get someone else."

"Did this gallery find someone to replace Max?"

"I wouldn't worry about it. When it comes time to hang the show you're working on, we'll get it done."

He walked away without making a sound. I found myself shaking. Clyde gave me the willies. He kept leering at me. Did he have something to do with Antonio's disappearance? He looked like the criminal type.

I went back to what I was doing. The security tag on the Chagall was still in place. Did it come back to the gallery that way? I forgot to ask Carone that question.

I heard a sound just then. I thought it came from another aisle in the room. Was that Clyde? I didn't want to call out, so I peered down the aisles next to me. I didn't see anyone.

I wandered into the next room. No one was there. Was Clyde still in here? I went into the contemporary stacks, but I didn't find anyone. I opened the door leading to the office wing. Before I stepped out of the stacks, I glanced at the corridor and saw Bentley dash into the resale stacks as if he didn't want anyone to notice him.

I waited a while, and then tiptoed toward the resale stacks. I saw Bentley searching through the racks, but he couldn't see me because I kept hiding behind paintings while I moved closer to him. I kept moving, hoping Clyde wasn't lurking nearby. Bentley went down another aisle, out of my view. I looked down that aisle, but didn't see or hear him.

I felt a sharp pain on the back my head. I stumbled. Things got hazy and then they faded to black.

CHAPTER SEVEN

When I opened my eyes, my head was killing me and everything was still black. I fell against something wet—a pail with a mop sticking out of it. I was in a broom closet.

I panicked and screamed. I pounded on the walls. Would anyone hear? Finally, when my eyes adjusted to the dark, I saw a small beam of light on the floor. I found the door. But it was locked. I screamed again.

Someone shouted at me from the other side. I heard a squeaking sound, and the door opened.

"You—you hit me." I clutched my aching head. "Why did you lock me in here?"

"What are you talking about? I did no such thing," Bentley said. "I heard screaming and I unlocked the door."

"Well, someone knocked me out and you were the last person I saw in the stacks. You were coming in as I was leaving."

"I had nothing to do with this. I've been selecting works for a collector. I have a presentation tomorrow. If you want, I'll show you. Maybe you should sit down. Do you want me to call a doctor?"

I shook my head. I felt more angry than injured. But I allowed Bentley to help me to a chair in a corner of the resale stacks. By that time, I felt more injured than angry. The next thing I knew, most of the staff, with the notable exception of Carone, had crowded into the aisle.

"Clyde will drive you to the doctor," Patty said. I didn't want to get near Clyde, but I suddenly felt too dizzy to protest. "Marny, make her an ice pack—from the freezer—put a towel around some ice," Patty said. "Now, what happened?"

"She bumped her head on something," Bentley said.

"I did not. Someone hit me from behind and locked me in the closet."

"Who came into the gallery in the last hour?" Patty asked Bentley.

"I have no idea. I was picking out some paintings for a major presentation. I don't want to seem unconcerned, but I have a ton of work to do and I have to get back to it."

"Not until we get to the bottom of this," Patty said. Bentley opened his mouth, but changed his mind about saying anything.

Patty turned to Clyde. "Did you see anyone?"

"No, I was working in the back gallery."

I didn't understand why Patty kept asking about who had come into the gallery. Either Bentley or Clyde had knocked me out. Maybe Patty thought so too, but wanted to play it cool. Or . . . maybe . . . I couldn't think. My head hurt too much.

"Where's Rodney?" Marny asked. "I thought he was here, but now I can't find him." Marny still hadn't gone for the ice pack. Patty gave her a stern look, but Marny stayed where she was. "He must not have come back from lunch."

"Leave Rodney out of this," Bentley said. "You're always trying to blame things on people."

"I am not. I just said he wasn't around."

"I tell you she bumped her head," Bentley said. "Marny likes to cause trouble."

"I'm not blaming Rodney. I have a message for him, that's all. Smart ass."

"Enough. Stop it, both of you," Patty said. "You're behaving like kids."

"Well, I can think of several people that came into the gallery

71

this afternoon," Marny said. "If anyone cares to know."

"Good. Now go and get that ice pack," Patty said. "Clyde, you should get going."

Clyde took my arm, but I backed off.

"Hey," he said, "I'm not going to bite."

"Really, I'm okay," I said.

Patty glanced at me. "No you're not. Clyde, get the van. Drive it to the back door."

Marny came back with an ice pack, and I pressed it against my head. The cold made me shiver, so Patty wrapped a quilted throw, used for protecting paintings, around my shoulders.

Patty helped me to the van. I felt too weak to walk by myself. Clyde didn't look at me as I stepped in. The van had a running board so I didn't have to step too high. My head couldn't have taken any jarring motion.

A short ride later, we arrived at Dr. Saver's office. I almost laughed when I saw his name on the door. Dr. Saver, a small, fat man with a wide smile that showed his gums, pronounced that I had a mild concussion, but no skull fracture. Keep ice on it and get plenty of rest, he said. To be on the safe side, he wanted me to come back in a few days.

Clyde didn't talk much on the way back to the gallery. Neither did I. Now that I felt calmer, I knew I shouldn't have accused Bentley. I had no proof. But someone did this. I didn't bump into a broom closet and lock the door on myself. I hadn't eaten much, but that didn't make me bump into things.

"I guess I provided a bit of excitement for everyone," I said.

Clyde didn't respond. He pulled into the gallery parking lot.

"You know, I must have slipped or something. I forgot to eat lunch. I guess I was a little light-headed."

"I guess so."

★　★　★　★　★

Patty ushered me into her office. "Are you all right?" she asked. Her look told me she wanted in on whatever I knew. "Now what happened?" she asked.

"I don't know. Someone might have hit me on the head or I might have just slipped. Maybe I did fall into the closet. I don't feel well. I'm going home. The doctor said I needed to rest for a few days."

"I'll get Clyde to drive you home."

"No. I can drive." I didn't want Clyde to know where I was staying.

Patty stared at me, as if she wanted to tell me something. But she just said, "I made Marny give me a list of everyone who came into the gallery today. That should help."

"Thanks. What do you know about Clyde and Bentley?"

Patty's eyes opened wide. "So you think one of them did it?"

"I don't know. But what's your take on them?"

"They seem to do their jobs, but Bentley uses more supplies than he should. I'll keep an eye on them. I can watch them, when they're not looking."

I shouldn't have said anything. "No, it's okay. I don't think any of them did it. Just give me the list of people who came into the gallery. Okay?"

"I've got it here."

"I may move from the Zimoro Hotel. I haven't decided where. But probably not for a few days."

Patty gave me a quizzical look. I don't know why I mentioned that. I was just thinking aloud in my dazed state. And the thought of moving stressed me out more than the bump on my head did. In my present condition, it overwhelmed me, even though I had brought only clothes and makeup with me to Santa Fe.

With Patty's list folded up in my hand, I went back to my office, almost colliding into Bentley. "I do hope you're all right," he said. He was slightly out of breath, but his manner was friendlier than it had been. "I wanted to catch you before you left. I have a feeling Ms. Merryweather would not want you to make a major thing out of this, such as calling in the police. If you slipped and hit your head, you may have walked into the closet thinking it was the exit. That door sticks if you slam it. That's probably what happened when you entered the closet. Someone may have walked by, saw that it was unlatched and latched it."

"I suppose so. I didn't eat lunch and I must have gotten dizzy. I didn't mean to make a big deal out of it. Sorry I accused you."

He looked relieved. "If you like, I'll show you the paintings I've gathered for my presentation."

"Another time. I'm feeling weak. But thanks. I'll see you in a few days."

I waved Bentley off. I felt woozy, but I made it into my office. I managed to unlock the desk drawer and grab Carone's file. I slipped Patty's list into it and took everything with me, including the desk key.

I went to the reception desk to make sure Marny knew I wasn't going out with her after work. When I got there, Marny was engrossed in an intense conversation with Rodney. Or at least Marny looked intense. Rodney still had that amused, bored look on his face.

"Marny," I said, "I'm going home. I'll have to take a raincheck on that drink."

"God," Rodney said. "If anyone looked like she needed a drink, it would be you. I heard what happened. Did someone really hit you, love?"

"I don't know what happened."

"You must have gotten disoriented in the stacks," Marny

said. "So many paintings . . . it's okay about tonight. Hope you're feeling better."

"I am. Just need some rest. Thanks."

In my hotel room, I put some ice in a plastic bag, rolled a towel around it and got in bed, holding it against my head. I didn't think I'd ever go back to the gallery. I didn't care what Carone did about the money. I felt worn out. I'd never sustained an injury on a job before. And it had only been my first day there.

I fell asleep. I woke up and found the ice had melted. I felt better though, but a little bored. I turned on the TV. I flipped the channels. Nothing seemed of interest because I had a burning desire to figure out who hit me. I didn't just stumble into that closet.

Despite the doctor's orders, I got out Patty's list and the pictures of the paintings. But my growling stomach gave me permission to order pizza and salad from a restaurant that delivered. I waited for it to come before doing anything more constructive.

Stuffing myself with the pizza cleared my head. What I knew about art forgery was from an article I read once. The forgers developed full-sized, detailed photographs of paintings and then had skilled artists reproduce fakes from the photographs. In time, they sold the fakes on the black market and minor works in respectable galleries without anyone realizing it.

With so much art sold in the world, living artists didn't always know if someone forged their work, unless the artist happened to walk into a gallery showing the forgeries. As strange as that might seem, that did happen in a case I read about.

After I finished eating, I realized the futility of my search. Experts in the art world no doubt knew of the last painting Picasso did, and who owned it. A forgery like that couldn't sell through the normal channels. It had to be on the black market.

To accomplish such a feat required a well-connected thief, or a network of thieves. I had no idea where to look. The picture could be anywhere by now—Japan, South America, Europe.

I went to bed. Things were bound to look better in the morning.

Things didn't look better in the morning. I heard a loud ringing in my ears, and I had a terrible headache. The ringing stopped when I answered the phone, but the headache remained.

"This is Carone Merryweather. Is Lana there?"

"This is Lana. I'm a bit under the weather."

"Yes, I heard. I've gotten two conflicting reports. Bentley says you bumped your head and Patty says someone knocked you out."

"I—I'm not sure. It may have been an accident—I don't know. Has Patty looked in the stacks today?"

"She doesn't look every day, but I'll ask her."

"Maybe it's a good idea if she doesn't go back there alone. Just to play it safe."

"Why don't the three of us check the stacks together, after everyone else has gone for the day? We'll see if anything's missing."

"I'm not feeling well right now."

"We don't have to do it today. Tomorrow will be fine."

Tomorrow. Except, I wasn't coming back. I didn't say that to Carone, though. "Were the security tags on the paintings when they were returned to the gallery?" I asked. "When I looked at those paintings, they were attached."

"Hmm. I don't remember. I'll ask Patty if she installed new ones. If she didn't, maybe Marny did, if she didn't see any tags. But unless Marny happened to be looking for those paintings, she wouldn't have. I wish I could remember—well, do you have any leads on where the Picasso is?"

Carone should have known whether the paintings had tags when they reappeared. She was either stupid or not telling me the whole story. "I don't have any leads," I said. "And the doctor told me to rest and keep ice on my head. So that's what I'm doing today and tomorrow."

"Look, I'm sorry about your head, but it isn't fatal. The gallery will pay all your medical expenses and I'm paying you a salary, so I expect some progress." Then in a whisper she added, "I can't afford to lose any more paintings, especially during the auction show. I have to exhibit the Picasso at the auction. I don't have much time."

I groaned. I felt too weak to argue with her. "Was the Picasso going to be auctioned off?"

"No. The collector just wanted me to display it then. But after the auction, I was going to sell it for her, privately. I'm not donating any of the proceeds from the Picasso to charity." Carone sighed. "This is confidential. I need the money. It's a temporary situation. No one can know. I'm counting on you."

I didn't feel strong enough for her to count on me for anything. "Maybe you should hire a detective. There seems to be a lot at stake here."

"I can't hire a detective," Carone whispered. "My father would find out. Don't ask me to explain."

"Well, I can't promise anything."

"You've got three weeks."

Three weeks? That was a long time to put my life on hold. I still had to find Antonio. How was I supposed to find a world-famous Picasso, when I couldn't even find a missing heir?

I said the first thing that popped into my aching head. "I need to meet your family, relatives, anyone who's been in the gallery since the thefts."

"What does my family have to do with it?"

Carone could be so dense.

"Crimes are often committed by people you know," I said. And how I arrived at that bit of wisdom, I didn't remember. It must have been the concussion talking, though it sounded plausible. "Maybe someone you know is the thief."

"Excuse me?"

I heard the anger in her voice. "Well, it's someone who—"

"If my father found out . . ."

"Can't you . . . pass me off as an old friend of a friend? Tell them I wanted a job and you gave me this curating gig. I need to meet those collectors who have been with you since the gallery started—the important ones you told me about."

"Fine. Just be discreet. I'm having a small dinner party tonight. Be at my house at eight. And as long as you're out, you can meet me at the gallery before. So we can check the stacks with Patty."

"I thought we already talked about that—"

"It can't wait. I need to know now. Take some aspirin and you'll be fine."

She hung up before I could say anything more.

I held the ice pack to my head. I began to feel human again, until I thought about Carone. She could make anyone feel like a caged animal. Why did Carone think I could find the Picasso? I wasn't even good at figuring out who committed the crimes in the mystery books I read.

I had to call Charley, before he felt neglected. I gave him a dose of the most enthusiastic employee voice I could muster. No, I didn't have anything new to report, I told him. Yes, I was working on it.

Charley gave me two more weeks and didn't sound happy about it. Two weeks for Charley, three for Carone. Did that add up to five weeks? I had a feeling it didn't.

With the prospect of being fired from First Century Life looming, I sat in bed and wrote some notes about the Picasso situation. I wanted to cement them in my fuzzy brain before I forgot them, and searching the town for Antonio seemed too difficult right then.

Taking my own advice that people known to victims committed the crimes against them, I thought about the whereabouts of the employees just before I was hit. Rodney Bracken didn't come into the stacks with the other employees, after Bentley discovered me in the closet. Marny said he hadn't come back from lunch yet. Bentley had his excuse for being in the stacks, so that was that. I probably wouldn't get any more out of him, except to view the paintings he had selected from the stacks. Everyone, other than Carone and Rodney, ran into the stacks when Bentley called them. Amanda wasn't even there.

So much for thinking one of them did it. How would I ever prove it anyway? I took a deep breath and lay back on the pillows. Maybe I did slip and fall. Santa Fe was over a mile high. I hadn't adjusted to the altitude.

I got up for a glass of water and settled on the bed again. Patty's list might be a better place to start. I'd have to think of something to say to the people on her list besides, gee, which one of you hit me on the head while I was sneaking around the stacks? Maybe I needed to find out more about Max, the handyman. Did Max Beely's death have something to do with Antonio's disappearance? And what about Amanda? Didn't want to dig too deep there. Carone wasn't paying me to uncover her husband's infidelity.

Whew! My head was spinning. Instead of slowing me down, this concussion made me speedy. My mind couldn't stop going over everything.

Like what Carone meant when she said, "Is anybody above corruption?" I knew I wasn't. Not moonlighting on the company dollar, the way I was. And not feeling too guilty about it either. Although if I were the superstitious type I'd have to say getting bumped on the head was a not-so-gentle reminder that I should feel guilty. Petty, white-collar crime. Got to love it. But was that the type of corruption Carone meant?

For her to know, and me to find out.

Chapter Eight

It took a whack on the head to knock the lazy, slacker attitude out of me. Although never a fan of the work ethic before, I now couldn't sit idle. Despite my earlier resolve never to return, I went back to the gallery.

Rodney Bracken and Marny were at the reception desk when I got there. "That was quick," Rodney said. "I thought we wouldn't be seeing you for days. Are you all right?"

"I'm okay. I feel ridiculous. Nothing like this has ever happened to me. I guess I better look where I'm going next time."

"Hey, love. It can happen to the best of us."

"Yeah," Marny said. "And guess what's happening to me right now. Amanda has to catch up on her work because she was sick, so she can't sit here to answer phones. So I have to do it. Patty says it's more important for Amanda to work on the mailing list. Can you believe that?"

I smiled. "I guess that's how it is."

"Well, if you're feeling up to it, maybe we can go out after work."

"Oh, I'd like to but I can't. Not tonight. Maybe tomorrow."

"Oh, tomorrow I'm off."

"Maybe we can get together Wednesday." Carone had said I would be here only part time. I should have asked her what my days off were. It seemed everyone worked Saturdays and Sundays, so I assumed I did too.

"Okay. Patty's so funny," Marny said. "She insisted I give her a list of all the people in the gallery when you fell. How dumb. You don't really think anyone hit you, do you?"

Rodney and Marny both stared at me.

"No, of course not. Patty—well, she's Patty—you know." I felt my face get hot. It was easy to blame this on Patty, though I did feel a tinge of guilt. I didn't realize Marny had written the list.

Rodney laughed. "Well, my loves, I better get back to the salt mines. As I was telling Marny when you got here, I made a very important sale yesterday and I need to follow up on it." He looked at me. "And no, it isn't part of the charity show. Just squeaked by before the cutoff."

Marny gazed at him. "Lucky you. You've been doing so great since you started here."

Marny made her crush on Rodney obvious. I wasn't sure Rodney reciprocated, but he indulged it by standing close and looking soulfully into her eyes.

Rodney reminded me of my ex-husband, a born flirt and an alcoholic flake. I didn't know about the drinking part with Rodney. It wouldn't have surprised me.

Taking advantage of Marny's preoccupation with Rodney, I glanced at the sign-out log on the desk.

Rodney caught me. "See, I did sign out," he said. "Marny, you should have known that yesterday." He looked at me with mock annoyance. "She went around asking everyone where I was—because she had a message for me—getting Patty all riled up. And now she can't even find the message she was supposed to give me."

"I'll find it," she said.

"Do that, love."

Rodney turned with a graceful flourish and disappeared into the office wing. Rodney could have played a good swashbuckler in an old Hollywood movie. A real Errol Flynn, he was.

"He's so talented," Marny said. Her face beamed. "He's going to have a show here next year. I think it's going to be a sell-out."

"Really? I guess he won't be working here after his show."

"Maybe, maybe not. I think he's great, but one show doesn't make a career. He'll probably want to stay here. This is the place to make great contacts."

"Well, I've got to get to my office. I'll talk to you later about Wednesday."

As I opened the door of the office wing, I saw Darlene walking into the gallery. What in the world was she doing here?

I hurried into the office wing, hoping she didn't see me. Maybe she'd be gone by the time I left today.

When I got to my office, an attractive woman with short dark brown hair and glowing olive skin hovered over my desk. She was somewhere in her thirties.

"Oh, you must be Lana Davis," she said. "I'm Amanda Talbert, Carone's secretary. I was just making sure you had everything you need."

"Well, thanks." I moved over to the desk and sat down. "I didn't get to meet you yesterday. I heard you were sick. I hope you're feeling better."

"Yes, I am. I hope you're feeling better too. I heard what happened. Anyway, I'm not contagious, if that's what you're worried about. Patty is terribly upset that I came back. I practically had to hand her a note from a doctor. She thinks I'm going to give everybody my cold."

Amanda took out a tissue from a pocket in her dress and sniffed into it delicately. Maybe too delicately for a real cold. She didn't sound nasal.

"I guess Patty is pretty strict about some things, isn't she?" I said.

Amanda's cinnamon-colored lips smiled. "But what would

we do without her?"

I decided Amanda's snooping, since that's what it seemed to be, didn't amount to much. The woman was quick to smile. Though her black jersey dress fit her curvy figure like a plaster mold, she didn't look cheap. She had style. The fake gold necklaces and bracelets she wore enhanced her outfit rather than detracted from it.

"Is Ms. Merryweather in yet?" I asked.

"She left word that she'd be out all day."

"Oh. We were supposed to have a meeting today."

"Sorry. It must have slipped her mind. I'll tell her when she returns. Hope you're feeling better."

"Yeah. Thanks. I'm okay."

Amanda smiled and then after a quick glance around the office, she left. Well, whatever she was looking for, she didn't find it. I was glad I hadn't left anything in the drawers. Most likely, she had a key to them.

Carone was turning out to be no help. I got out of a sick bed so we could go through the stacks and she didn't even show up. How annoying.

I took out Patty's list from my purse. I had to tell Patty not to give Marny or Rodney any more information. They might not be involved, but an innocent remark said to the wrong person could kill any chance of finding the Picasso. I hoped I convinced Marny and Rodney that Patty had been just paranoid when she asked Marny to make the list.

I studied the list. It included a Mr. Chasem, a Mrs. Brown, a UPS delivery man, a Mr. Souther, and a young couple whose name Marny didn't know, but who'd been interested in one of the paintings in the contemporary gallery. Marny wrote they said Bentley talked to them the week before. The young couple I put down as a dead end, along with the UPS guy, since he actually delivered a package of office supplies Patty ordered.

Had someone knocked me out? It happened so fast I had no memory of it. Just a bad headache to remind me of what I couldn't remember.

I should have gone back to my hotel for a long nap until dinner. But I was already dressed and I had two deadlines, so I had to keep going. If Carone had shown up, we could have determined if anything was missing from the stacks. I didn't want to do this with Patty, and I didn't feel well enough to do it myself.

Instead, I pored over Marny's notes. Mr. Chasem had gone in to see the exhibit in the contemporary gallery. Marny didn't remember when he left. Mrs. Brown was a new collector who donated a Chagall drawing for the auction. She came in to see where they were going to hang it.

Mr. Souther was a steady collector. He bought one or two paintings every year and he had mentioned to Marny how excited he was about attending the auction. He happened to be in the area, and came in to look around.

I felt my next step was to find out more about Max Beely. I found two articles online in *The New Mexican* about his murder. One of them was the article I had seen the staff discussing before the office meeting. The other was the article printed when they discovered his body. That had less information. The police had no suspects and didn't have a motive. I needed to find out how Carone happened to hire him. Did anyone recommend him? Did anyone know him before he got the job?

I took the list and went into Patty's office. "Patty, where do you keep the sales files? I'd like to see what paintings the people on this list bought, or were interested in."

"Follow me," Patty said. She led me into the file room, adjacent to her office. "On the right are the sales files. We list them in two ways. First by collectors, noting what they've bought, or what they're interested in acquiring or selling, and then by the title of the works sold and who consigned it. The personnel files are in this drawer." She pointed to a filing cabinet to the left of the sales cabinets. "We also have everything on the computer, but it's not as up to date as the actual files. I insist that Amanda and Marny keep up the files, but sometimes they don't get around to updating the computer."

"Thanks. I think I have all I need to get started. Is Carone coming in? I spoke to Amanda and she said Carone would be out all day."

"That's right. She needed to see a collector and then she had a dinner party to plan."

"Okay. Oh, by the way, when was the last time you looked in the stacks?"

"A few days ago. I kept hoping whoever took that painting had returned it. But it wasn't there. I haven't had time to make a thorough check of all the paintings since that one turned up missing."

"Were the security tags attached to the other missing paintings when you found them?"

"I don't remember. I assist the sales staff in putting the paintings back in the stacks after a presentation. If they get too busy, I do it for them."

"They're all tagged now. I checked."

"Well, I know I didn't put them on. It must have been Carone, if the thief didn't." Patty twirled her pen in her hair and thought for a moment. "I hope you don't think I'm letting you down. Finding that painting and stopping more thefts is of great importance, but with this auction, we are very busy. The gallery must go on, no matter what problems we have."

"I understand." Just as well. I didn't want Patty in the stacks by herself. "One more thing, I didn't realize Marny made this list for me. I don't think it's a good idea asking her to do anything, even indirectly, because she told Rodney and they both wondered if I still thought somebody hit me."

Patty looked remorseful. "I see what you mean. It's just I had no idea who had been in the gallery. I work in the back office and I don't see who comes in."

"I understand. But we can't let anyone know what we're doing. I think I convinced them that you wanted the list because . . ."

Patty raised an eyebrow. "Because why?"

"I made it seem like you were . . . overreacting."

"Oh."

"Well, I had to do that to throw them off."

Patty nodded. "I don't mind. Blame it on me. We need to get to the bottom of this."

Patty closed the door and went back to her office, leaving me with the tedious job of sorting through the gallery's files. I became so engrossed in it, a loud, piercing sound, coming from somewhere in the gallery, startled me. I rushed to see what it was.

The noise was deafening. Everyone was in an uproar, running back and forth. Somebody screamed, "Call the fire department."

I made the call on my cell. I didn't know what was on fire, but I yelled the gallery's address into the phone. Then I began to breathe in smoke. I had to get out of there. I grabbed a fire extinguisher off the wall. I wasn't sure how to use it, but I stumbled through the hallway looking for the fire.

Clyde grabbed me and tried to drag me away. "Let go of me," I screamed.

"I'm trying to get you out of here." He tugged on the fire extinguisher, but in my fury, I refused to let go of it. I shoved him away and lumbered down the hall with the fire extinguisher. I couldn't stand the noise from the smoke alarm, but my head hurt too much to run.

Amanda staggered out of an office near the back door clutching a large black purse. Then she collapsed on the floor. Clyde ran over to her and carried her to the alley. I emptied the fire extinguisher in that office, but it did little to stop the fire. I couldn't stand the smoke any longer, so I closed the door and hurried toward the back exit.

Bentley came out of the stacks, through a door close to the exit. "Everything's all right in there. It smells a little smoky but nothing's damaged," he said.

"Is anyone in the gallery?" I asked. I wondered what happened to Darlene.

"No—I checked," Patty said.

Just then, Clyde ran back inside. "Where's Rodney?" he said.

"Oh, God," Bentley said. "He's still inside. I'll go get him."

"No, I will," Clyde said. "I'm stronger. I can carry him if I have to." He dashed into the stacks.

Bentley and I went to the parking lot in the back. Patty and Marny were already there. Amanda leaned against a car. Jason Nichols, Carone's husband, hung around her.

"How did this happen?" I asked.

"We don't know," the man said. "Aman—Miss Talbert's office was on fire."

"Did anyone call the fire department?" Patty asked.

I held up my hand.

"I closed the door to Amanda's office," I said. "I hope that keeps things from burning up."

"It won't stop the smoke," Bentley said. "It'll circulate through the air system. The whole gallery is going to have smoke damage."

A moment later, Rodney straggled out of the gallery. "We can't do any more—in there," Rodney said. He was still gasping from the smoke.

Clyde darted up to Rodney. "Where were you?" he said. "I went back in there and couldn't find you. I thought something happened to you."

"I went into my office. I had to make sure none of the—work I have to show a collector—was damaged—the smoke got to me—I tried—to grab some of the paintings—but I had to get out of there. I hope someone called the fire department."

"Lana did," Patty said. "Are you all right?"

Rodney nodded. He took a deep breath. "Just need to breathe."

We heard sirens in the distance and a few minutes later, a fire truck and an ambulance drove up. Clyde and Jason told the fire fighters where the fire was. I peered in and saw Bentley arguing with them. He didn't want them hosing the whole gallery. Jason insisted only the back office was on fire. A search of the building convinced the fire crew he was right. After extinguishing the fire in the office, the firemen left. It didn't take them long.

Amanda received first aid from the paramedics. She wasn't seriously hurt, and after declining a ride to the hospital, she sat in her car.

"What caused this?" I asked Patty.

"We aren't sure," Clyde said. "Amanda was working in that office. I think she went for some coffee, and the place caught on fire. I guess it's safe to go in there."

"Yes," Bentley said. "After all this, I still have a major presentation to give. The collector will be here any minute and the gallery is still full of smoke."

Ignoring Bentley, Patty said, "Amanda, you should take the rest of the day off."

Amanda nodded. "Okay."

"I'll drive you home," Jason said.

The rest of them piled into the gallery as Jason and Amanda drove off.

"Really," Marny shouted, "how are we supposed to work with this burnt smell everywhere?"

Patty turned to her. "By opening windows and doors and turning up the air conditioning. It will be gone soon. It's mainly in the back office."

Marny frowned. Then she whispered to me, "Notice Jason's car isn't in the lot. I bet Amanda drove him here this morning."

"Did you know he was here?" I whispered back. I was never much for company gossip, but now I viewed it as part of my job.

"No," Marny said. "But I bet that's why Amanda wasn't at the switchboard today. She and Jason wanted a private office to continue their little romance. And of course, Patty wouldn't make Amanda work the switchboard if Jason needed her."

"Wouldn't Patty say something to Carone about it?" I asked. "What about the others? Wouldn't they say something?"

"Patty's not going to say anything. All she cares about is how many pens we use and if we leave the lights on when we shouldn't. You can be sure Jason and Amanda didn't leave the lights on." Marny giggled. "And as for the others, they're not going to tell Carone. Would you? If she can't figure out her hubby's chasing the secretary, that's her problem."

"I guess I wouldn't say anything, unless Carone was a friend of mine."

"Who could be friends with Carone?"

"I see what you mean."

My head throbbed. "The smoke is really bad in here."

"How can anybody expect us to work? Well, talk to you later. It's the switchboard for me, as usual."

And it was the file room for me. I needed to get as much information as I could about everyone on Marny's list, as well as on the employees. That was all I had to go on.

The smoke wasn't that bad in there, unlike in the other offices. That's probably because it was a small room with only one air vent.

I collected what I could about the employees, Mrs. Brown, Reggie Souther and David Chasem. The missing Picasso belonged to Eleanor Peabody. I found a note written by her in the files. The writing, though legible, was jagged and awkward. She lived in California in the wealthy section of Pasadena, though she also had a home in Santa Fe.

All this digging took time. I still had a terrible headache and had to write everything by hand. I didn't want anyone catching me photocopying this stuff, especially the employee records. I didn't care if Patty saw me, but since I had accused Bentley of knocking me out, I didn't want to arouse any more suspicion than I already had.

CHAPTER NINE

I couldn't do much more in the file room. The air conditioning had diffused the smoke enough for me to use my office without gagging, so I sat there and called the people on Marny's list. Mr. Souther was out, but Mrs. Brown and Mr. Chasem were in. Mrs. Brown was delighted to know the gallery was interested in her collection for a show of local collectors in Santa Fe, something I made up when I started dialing her number.

Mr. Chasem sounded less enthusiastic. Although when I told him the gallery had plans to have the show travel to the Museum of Contemporary Art in Chicago, and they wanted something from his collection, he showed more interest. I checked the Internet while talking to Mr. Chasem, to make sure Chicago had such a museum. I could always say the Chicago connection didn't come through. Anyway, Chasem agreed to my visit, though he sounded like he'd need more convincing when I got there.

Maybe Chicago wasn't such a hot idea. I mentioned it only because it was a big city in between L.A. and New York. What if Chasem checked my story before I arrived? I probably should have told Mrs. Brown the same story, but I hadn't thought of it until I heard Mr. Chasem's voice.

Mrs. Darryl Brown lived on Paseo de Papito, several blocks from the gallery. Paseo de Papito was a busy thoroughfare, but Mrs. Brown's long driveway and adobe-walled courtyard sheltered her house from any traffic noise. Probably built in the twenties, its pale brown adobe walls had a red tiled roof and windows trimmed with the turquoise color so popular in the region. Inside the courtyard, roses grew among native chamisa plants, prickly cactus and sage. In this peaceful setting, I almost forgot the business that brought me here.

I walked up a narrow red brick path and rang the bell at the gate. A moment later, a chubby, middle-aged woman practically jumped out of the house. "Welcome. I'm so glad you called," she squealed. "I'm thrilled that the gallery is interested in my collection. Of course, it isn't very large, but we're proud of it. Do come in. The gate's open."

Mrs. Brown was in her late fifties, and had little to distinguish herself except her cheerful voice. Her hair was dull brown and her complexion was pale. Her blue dress was in good taste, but lacked any sense of style. Her stubby legs, encased in support hose and planted in sensible black flats, showed varicose veins, evidence her life had not always been easy.

"Oh, do call me Emma," she said.

I couldn't help getting caught up in her enthusiasm.

Her house, furnished in French provincial, dark woods and rich neutral fabrics, looked expensive and correct, but bland.

Mrs. Brown led me into a small gallery off the living room. "We started collecting a few years ago," she said. "I don't mind telling you, we won the lottery before we moved to New Mexico. That's how we bought everything."

"Really? How exciting. I've never met anyone who won a lottery."

"Yes. It's been something. Of course, our prize was one of the smaller ones and my Darryl and I, we still want to live a simple life. But we couldn't help splurging on buying this house—we had it professionally decorated—and then we decided to collect art. It's a marvelous investment. I'm donating a Chagall drawing to the gallery's auction. I'm thrilled that a percentage of my portion goes to charity. I've never donated to a charity auction before. It's a wonderful idea. We make money, the charity makes money and we get a tax deduction at the same time. Everybody wins. How very smart of Carone."

But not if I don't find the Picasso.

Mrs. Brown's collection consisted of ten small paintings. Three were Matisses, several others were Chagalls, and the rest looked like impressionist paintings. Even with my limited background in art, I could see they were all magnificent. Still, there was something odd here, because the Browns' winnings must have been in the triple-digit millions to afford all these paintings. At any rate, if someone had attacked me in the gallery, it could hardly have been Mrs. Brown.

"Uh, these are wonderful," I said. My art history terminology failed me. I couldn't think of anything to say about them, other than, "You must have won a very big lottery."

Mrs. Brown blushed. "I don't mind telling you, we won over two million dollars. Of course, we didn't get the whole amount. Taxes took a good portion of it."

Just what I thought. They didn't win enough to afford such expensive paintings. But Mrs. Brown didn't look like an art thief or a forger. "Do you have photographs of your collection?"

The headache dulled my brain. I should have thought to bring a camera. Something better than my cell phone, to look more professional. "Did you acquire these paintings from the gallery?" The file in the gallery had only noted that the Browns had purchased a work on paper, the Chagall Mrs. Brown had mentioned.

"We bought the Chagall drawing at the gallery. The one we're donating. We didn't buy it for that purpose, but we wanted to participate in some way. Please don't tell Carone, but the Boulange Gallery is so much more reasonable. That's where I bought these paintings. Even with a lottery in the family, we don't like being extravagant."

"Oh."

"I've had the whole collection photographed. I made extra copies, so I can give you a set. But please don't tell Carone that I didn't—uh—inherit my collection. That's what I told her. You seem like such a nice girl—"

"Of course, I won't."

"Good. Come with me. You have to see this."

I followed her into the living room. She took a magazine off the coffee table and flipped the pages until she came to the Boulange Gallery ad. "See," she said, *Fine Investment Art.* Darryl—he's my husband—we bought all this from the Boulange Gallery. They do a volume business so they can afford to sell for less. We were lucky to get all this. If I told you what we paid, you'd accuse me of stealing. The Boulange Gallery buys from special collections. Andre said most art dealers don't have those connections. Now remember, don't tell Carone."

I smiled and checked out the ad. The Boulange Gallery was in Los Angeles, on the outskirts of Beverly Hills. "Who's Andre?"

"He's the director of the Boulange Gallery."

"I'd like to write down the address and phone number."

"Just take the magazine with you. I've read it. Wait, I'll get you the pictures of our collection. You will keep my secret from Carone, won't you?"

No, I wouldn't. But not for the reasons she thought. In her absence, I studied her collection, pretending to take notes. I didn't have to pretend interest in the paintings, though. The oil finishes on the paintings were so vibrant, almost as if the paint was still wet. The Browns had labeled each painting with the title, artist name and date of execution, the way galleries did. These looked like originals, but I was no expert. Neither, I thought, were the Browns.

I loved the small Matisse still life in their collection. Its child-like flowers looked like they had been thrown together, almost like a kid painted them, yet they looked amazing. But whether Matisse painted it or not, someone did a fabulous job with it.

Was the Boulange Gallery the link I had been looking for? Did this collection contain original and forged works? Somehow, Andre's reason for having low prices didn't ring true. I didn't think Mrs. Brown lied about it. From what I understood, selling famous art at discounted prices deflated the market potential of those artists. Why would a gallery undercut the market so much?

When Mrs. Brown came back with her photos, all excited about the prospect of discussing her collection in depth, I cut her short. My head ached and I still had more places to go. "I can't promise you anything, Mrs. Brown, but the gallery may have this show go to the Contemporary Art Museum in Chicago."

"Oh, how wonderful. I can't wait to tell Darryl."

"It's not final yet. So I don't want you to get your hopes up."

"Well, of course. It's an honor to be considered, though."

I thanked the woman for the photographs and the magazine. I wondered what Carone would think of Mrs. Brown's collection. Were these copies of originals, or not?

I eased myself out of Mrs. Brown's—she did talk up a storm—and drove to Elamos, where Mr. Chasem lived, and coincidentally, so did Alan. I could see Chasem and go by Alan's house. How perfect. If only I didn't have this headache.

I took some aspirin, swallowing it with a swig of water from the bottle of water I kept in the car. I should have stayed in bed. I was in no condition to see anyone, but I had already called Chasem.

Mr. Chasem's place looked like a large and boxy tract house, in the same style as Alan's house. The same developer must have built them. Large homes, but more cookie-cutter than charming.

I rang Chasem's bell. A slow, musical chime sounded. Mr. Chasem ushered me in. His stern, tanned face looked daunting against his pale gray suit.

The house had a Southwestern motif, with white cotton couches and bleached wood accent tables. There were Indian blankets on the floor and on the walls. But when I looked for a collection of paintings, I didn't see one.

"So—you're from the gallery," Mr. Chasem said. He clasped his hands together. He was in his late forties with gray-blond hair and cold, almost sinister, blue eyes.

I could tell he didn't like me. But working at First Century had taught not to care what people thought, because in my bureaucratic status, they never thought well of me anyway.

So despite his dislike of me, I put on a bright smile. "Yes. I'm new there. I understand you stopped by the gallery yesterday."

"So I did. I wanted to take another look at the current show in the contemporary gallery."

"If I had known, I would have talked to you then about looking at your collection. I hope I haven't caught you at a bad time."

"No, not at all. I'm just surprised the gallery would want to include my collection in a show. It's a very small collection."

"Well, actually, I'm curating the show. The idea is to show the work of local collectors in Santa Fe." I thought that sounded plausible enough.

"Well, my collection, if you want to call it that, is in the dining room."

He led me into a room furnished with a large bleached wood dining set and a matching china cabinet. A sliding glass door revealed a rock garden in the back yard. Two large paintings hung on opposite walls. Both were hard-edge abstracts in the pale colors often associated with Southwestern art. I had no idea who painted them. Chasem's file listed him as having an interest in contemporary work, though he hadn't bought anything yet. So at least I knew he hadn't bought these paintings at the gallery.

I pointed to one of the paintings. "I think this one interests me the most."

"Oh, the newest Hewlett. I bought that from the gallery last year. I bought both of these from the gallery. I hear Hewlett just had a show in New York. Has his work gone up in value?" Chasem smiled at me. It was a broad smile, masking whatever he was thinking.

"After a show in New York, I would assume so. But I'm not involved with sales. Actually, I didn't realize you purchased these paintings from the gallery." I hoped I didn't sound as nervous as I felt. Chasem lied about where he got the paintings, so he could be lying about whether an artist named Hewlett painted them.

"Now that I think of it, I didn't buy them from your gallery. You had only one Hewlett and it was too big for this room. I bought these two at another gallery. I'd have to look up which one."

"That's all right. Now that I've seen it, I will keep it in mind for the show. What about the other painting? I'm not familiar with the artist."

Chasem gave me a dark look. "Really? That's from Hewlett's early period. I was lucky to find it. He destroyed much of his early work by painting over his canvases."

"Oh. I've only just started getting into his work."

"You and a lot of other people. But I was one of his first collectors. I recognized his genius early on."

"Well, that's wonderful. I will be sure to mention this in the—catalog—for the show." I threw that in to impress Chasem. I remembered seeing a catalog in my aunt's house, from a museum show. An art show had a *catalog*. I almost slipped and said a *program,* a dead giveaway that I wasn't a curator.

"Thank you for your time," I said. "I hope I didn't inconvenience you too much." I didn't want to take any pictures, not with his intimidating attitude and with just my cell phone as a camera.

He showed me out. He stood at the door while I walked to my car. I didn't turn around, but I felt his eyes boring into the back of my head.

I drove around the block and parked. I didn't like lying, and that's all I had done since I took this job. And I was still no closer to finding Antonio.

Chasem knew I was up to something other than curating a show, if I even convinced him I was a curator. No doubt, he'd call the gallery. They would verify my credentials, but the question was, how did he figure into this? He had a menacing presence. He could have attacked me, though in his expensive-looking suit, he didn't look the type to get his hands dirty. He could have hired someone for that. But stealing work from the gallery—he might have done that himself. If he had, he was intelligent enough not to hang stolen art in his house, or even hang art from the same period as the stolen work.

I looked at my watch. It was after four. Maybe Alan was home.

I drove by his place, a short distance away. I got out of the car and meandered to the house next to his. Then I walked to his house and up his driveway. All that exertion made me dizzy, but I rang his bell.

A woman came to the door. She was about my age and height, with long, straggly dark hair and a chubby, hourglass shape. Not unattractive, just unkempt looking. Her "mom" jeans and faded, blue short-sleeved knit top showed bulges I would have hidden if they were mine. Alan had left me for this? Maybe she had a good heart. Looks weren't everything.

"Hi, I'm Lana Davis. I'm an insurance administrator."

"Yes? What can I do for you?"

I had to concentrate. My head was throbbing. "I'm lost. I picked your house because it looked like someone was home. My cell phone's dead. Could I use your phone? Here's my card."

She stared at my card. "Well—"

"Who's at the door, Hun?" a man said.

And there he was. Alan in the flesh. The years had been kinder to him than they had been to his wife. He still looked like the virile, muscular man I remembered.

"This woman's lost," his wife said. "Wants to use our phone." His wife handed him my card.

"You know, you look familiar," I said. "What's your name?"

He glanced at my card. "Well, what do you know? Lana! I'm Alan, Alan Finley."

"Oh, for goodness sake," I said. "How crazy. Imagine seeing you again. I'll just take a moment. I need to use your phone."

"Sure. This is my wife Karen. Honey, I used to know Lana from school, years ago. What a coincidence. You can use the phone in the kitchen."

Their large, sprawling home was, well . . . large. That's about all anyone could say about it, since clothes, magazines and other stuff covered most of it. I had a hard time following them into the kitchen because I had to step over so much stuff. Their kitchen was the same way, cluttered with cereal boxes, trinkets, knickknacks—you name it. When they left me in there to make my fake call, I turned the ringer off on my cell. It would have been too embarrassing if I got a call on a dead cell phone.

I called the gallery, pressing my finger on the button to end the call before anyone answered, and pretended to ask for directions. Alan and Karen came back into the kitchen after I said a loud goodbye into the phone.

"Thanks so much," I said.

"Not at all," Karen said.

"I had no idea you were in New Mexico," Alan said. He checked out my clothes, admiring Carone's impeccable taste. Compared to his frumpy wife, I looked like a million bucks. Okay, I couldn't help gloating.

"I'm just here on business. Trying to find a—well, it's just business. I'm here only for a short time. What do you and Karen do here?"

"I'm in construction and Karen works part time in the office. We work for Dewey Development," he said. He slurred his words. In the time it had taken me to make my fake phone call, Alan had drunk some Scotch—quite a bit, or maybe he started before I got there and I didn't hear it in his voice before. But now I smelled it on his breath. I knew that smell. It's what my ex used to drink, when he ran out of vodka.

"Oh. How nice. Well, I'm glad you were home. Nice meeting you, Karen."

"We work an early day. Seven to three-thirty," Alan said.

I thanked them again and left.

Whew! Dreams die hard, but when they do, they're gone forever. I had no one to pine for. No one to wonder about. Maybe now I would find somebody. There was always hope.

And as they say, hope springs eternal. On my way back to town, I passed by Tyler's barn and saw him standing by the road. I slowed down and rolled down the window.

"Hey, what happened to you at the party?" he said. "You disappeared."

I got out of the car. "I wasn't feeling well. It's the altitude. It got to me."

Right then, it was my head that got to me. I felt faint and I swerved. Tyler caught me before I fell.

"Easy, darling," I heard him say. "Hold on to me. Let's get you something to drink."

I must have passed out, because the next thing I knew I was in Tyler's living room propped up on his couch—a couch upholstered with a Persian rug. I glanced around the barn. The last time I had been at Tyler's, it was crowded with so many people I hadn't noticed his furniture. It had a masculine, rustic feel and none of it looked cheap. Next to the couch, he had an armchair covered with another Persian rug.

"Here you go, darling," he said. He handed me a mug. "Careful, it's hot."

"What is it?"

"Herbal tea. It will do you good."

I sipped the tea. It made me feel better.

"Maybe you should see a doctor," he said.

"I think I'm okay now. Thanks. I like your furniture. It goes with your artwork."

Tyler smiled. "My sister works at this store in town and that's where I got them."

I drank the last of the tea. "I really have to go. I'm supposed to have dinner somewhere. But thanks."

"I'll walk you to your car."

He helped me up and put his arm around my waist. When we got to the car, he opened the door for me. "You sure you'll be okay?"

I nodded.

He touched my chin. "I'll see you. I'll call you." He watched me drive off. I looked back and waved to him.

I drove back to the gallery. Now that my head felt better, I had to know if there was an artist named Hewlett. But I didn't get there until after five and the gallery had already closed. Carone should have given me a key.

As I drove past the gallery, I noticed a black car following me. It was an old Mercedes. I couldn't see its license number because, unlike California, cars in New Mexico didn't have front plates.

I drove faster. In the rearview mirror, I still saw the black Mercedes behind me. When the road dipped in front, I turned on a side street and lost sight of the Mercedes. Maybe it was nothing. Other than Carone, only Patty knew my real reason for working at the gallery. And she distrusted most, if not all, the staff too much to take them into her confidence.

With a few hours to kill before dinner, I went back to the hotel. I kicked off my shoes and relaxed on the bed. Tyler had been nice, nicer than I remembered. Except, I couldn't think about him now. I had to maintain my focus. I took out the ad for the Boulange Gallery.

If the Boulange Gallery sold forgeries, would they be bold enough to sell the Picasso? Was there even a connection? Just because one of their customers lived in Santa Fe didn't mean they knew anything about Carone's gallery. I should have asked Mrs. Brown how she found out about the Boulange Gallery. The ad didn't state they sold art at a discount.

I called Mrs. Brown, but got her voicemail. I didn't want to leave a message. I'd call her tomorrow. Maybe Chasem, and not the Boulange Gallery, was the player in this scenario. He could have had an accomplice who somehow didn't get on Marny's list. He saw me as a fake and that's why he had a nasty attitude. But even if he *had* told the truth about Hewlett and his importance in the art world, Chasem behaved with more suspicion than the situation warranted. An important gallery wanted to see his collection, regardless of its size. He should have felt honored. His reluctance qualified him as a suspect, in my book.

I went over possible scenarios. Did Chasem kill Max Beely to silence him? Had Max caught him in the stacks? Or was he in on the crime? Carone didn't say Max drank, but maybe he did. Not to stereotype, but didn't most handymen drink? Maybe

Max stayed late one night after everyone left and had a few. And Chasem, realizing Max saw him in the stacks, waited for him to leave the gallery. When Max came out, Chasem followed him and shot him.

I took a deep breath and exhaled with a laugh. What was I thinking of? Max could have been a teetotaler, for all I knew. I had no evidence linking him to Chasem, or to the thefts in the gallery. Looking sinister wasn't a crime. It didn't make Chasem a murderer, or a thief.

But it helped. Especially when I searched for Hewlett on the Internet and found attorneys, doctors, engineers and other professionals with that name, but no artists.

CHAPTER TEN

Jason Nichols, in tennis clothes, opened the door when I arrived at the Merryweather residence. His angry expression detracted from his good looks. "Why didn't Rothwell get this?" he said. "They're in the living room. I don't have time for this."

His face revealed no recollection of seeing me outside his wife's office that day in the gallery, or after the fire. Without introducing himself, he rushed upstairs.

Well, I didn't like Jason either, not that he cared. I took my bruised ego into the living room.

Since no one realized my presence for a moment, I studied them. I picked out Rothwell easily enough, because he wore formal butler attire and was serving drinks. Carone sat next to a stout, older man with white hair—I assumed her father—who wore a tweed jacket over a starched open-necked white shirt without a tie and black slacks. An older couple sat next to him, along with a man who had a pipe in his mouth. I saw two younger men and a woman somewhat younger than either of them, seated at the far end of the room. I recognized Rodney Bracken as one of them. I didn't realize he ranked so high in Carone's circle.

Carone rose when she noticed me. She looked lovely in a white chiffon hostess gown. I felt like her poor relation in her business suit.

"I'm so glad you could make it," Carone said. "Father, this is Lana Davis, an old friend. She's working at the gallery now, on a special project."

Mr. Merryweather grasped my hand. He looked too tired to make it out of the overstuffed wing chair he sat on. He coughed, and in a raspy voice spoke to his daughter rather than to me. "Was she at the university with you?"

"Yes. I hadn't seen her for ages and she came in the gallery one day."

"Humph." That was the extent of Mr. Merryweather's interest in me.

"Where is that husband of yours?" he said. "I'm hungry. It's time we got on with dinner."

Carone looked nervous. Even her hands shook. "It's just eight," she said. "Jason's had a busy day."

Carone seemed more stressed about her father's impatience with her husband's tardiness than she had been about the loss of the Picasso. Then Carone remembered her manners and offered me a seat on one of the couches.

"Busy, my foot," Mr. Merryweather said.

An old argument seemed afoot, to coin a pun. When you had money like Carone, you had a tennis player for a husband. But not without the usual consequences, as Mr. Merryweather's not so subtle reprimand implied.

"Alfred," the older woman said, "did I hear right that you sold the old Cotswell place?"

"Yes, Vinnie, so what if I did? I got tired of it. Too much trouble to rent it out."

"I told you that ten years ago."

"Enough with this argument," said the older man seated next to Alfred Merryweather. "Carone, introduce us to your young friend."

"I'm sorry," Carone said, "this is Lana Davis. Lana, this is Vinnie and Stuart Goodwin."

The Goodwins, a portly couple, had dressed formally. He

wore a black silk suit, and she had on a gray chiffon gown that matched her gray hair. They spoke with a faint British accent. "So nice to meet one of Carone's friends," Vinnie Goodwin said. Mr. Goodwin nodded with a pleasant smile. I smiled back and murmured an appropriate response.

Carone continued her introductions. "Lana, you know Rodney from the gallery. He's here with Jane Goodwin, the Goodwins' granddaughter."

Jane, petite, thin and drab with mousy brown hair, looked about eighteen. Compared to the cosmopolitan appearance and attitude of Rodney, she seemed naive. Anyway, that's how I saw her.

Jane and Rodney gestured to me. Rodney had on his usual mustard-colored jacket, worn now with a black T-shirt underneath—forever the poor artist—and Jane wore a pale green silk mini-dress. I wasn't sure Rodney believed Carone's story of my being an old friend, but it didn't matter. Rodney had none of the swashbuckler in him tonight. With his arm around Jane, he seemed bent on being the proper guest.

"And this is dear Eddy Hansen," Carone said.

The man with the pipe smiled. Eddy Hansen, in his sixties, had graying hair at the temples. Thank goodness, he didn't light his pipe. I hoped he had it for effect only. Some men liked holding pipes. Nothing like pipe smoke to ruin a meal. Maybe that's how the rest of them felt, which was why he didn't smoke it.

"Eddy's been great," Carone said. "If it wasn't for him, the gallery never would have gotten off the ground."

"Now Carone," he said, "I merely introduced you to a few of my friends. You've done a wonderful job of building the business. Hasn't she, Alfred?"

Mr. Merryweather gave him a benign smile, and Carone looked relieved. But Rodney turned away with a smirk on his face. I wondered what he thought of Mr. Merryweather and

Carone. Did he like or admire them? Although he played the poor, charming artist with ease, did he secretly resent them? Or I was projecting too much? I didn't know him well, and he did seem to be in Carone's circle. He was dating the granddaughter of the Goodwins. But he also flirted with Marny. Loyalty didn't seem to be his strong point.

I caught Mr. Hansen looking at me. I must have missed something he said.

"And don't forget young Herbie here," he said. He motioned toward the other man sitting with Jane and Rodney.

Young Herbie, who was not exactly young, came up to me. He was at least forty-five, maybe more. It was difficult to say how tall he was because he slouched, giving the impression he was too intellectual to care whether he was attractive or not. His unmanageable black hair hung over his ears, and he wore a jacket similar to Rodney's, though in a copper color. His lower teeth protruded slightly, making him look determined to get his way.

"Oh, yes," I said. "Hello, Herbie."

"Actually it's Herbert," he said. He shook my hand. "Herbert Sloan. Pleased to meet you, Lana."

"Nice to meet you."

"Young Herbie's going to have a show at the gallery, isn't he, Carone?" Mr. Hansen said.

"Well, yes," Carone said. "As soon as I can find a break in the schedule." Although she smiled at Herbie, I could tell she hoped that break never came.

Herbie sat next to me. It didn't take him long to inform me about his artistic genius and his significant connections in the art world. "More important," he whispered, "than Carone's."

A half hour later, Mr. Nichols finally made his appearance in a black tuxedo. I had to admit, he was the type I used to dream about when I was seventeen—good-looking, tall, athletic, and tan, with blue eyes and jet black hair. But his self-absorbed attitude made him appear shallow. He looked more like a cardboard cutout than a real person.

Okay, I judged him without mercy, knowing what Marny thought about him and because he was rude when I arrived. Even good looks couldn't hide his flaws.

Mr. Merryweather made a comment about how late Jason was, but Carone hushed him. Now, however, we could eat, so we marched into the dining room, with Herbie taking my arm.

Dinner was a feast worth waiting for. No home cooking here, but several main courses fit for a fancy French restaurant, as well as appetizers, soup and salad. They served a different wine with each course. I didn't see how Carone stayed so thin with food like this.

I sat between Jason and Herbie. Halfway through dinner, after Alfred Merryweather had dozed off in his chair, Jason became interested in me. His earlier rudeness to me didn't stop him from putting on the charm. "I thought I recognized you," he said. He gave me an intimate smile. "How do you like working at the gallery?"

I put my ego aside. "It's great," I said. "I love the gallery's collection. It's high quality." I had sense enough not to bring up the fire.

After that exchange, anything Jason said at dinner, to Jane or to me, came off as flirtatious. He never looked at Carone or acknowledged her presence. I glanced at Carone, but she was busy discussing something with Eddy. She seemed oblivious to her husband's flirting.

"So what's this I hear that you're from L.A?" Jason said. "Or so the gallery grapevine goes. What gallery did you work for there?"

Vinnie Goodwin happened to overhear his remark and her sparse eyebrows rose in displeasure. "L.A., as in Los Angeles?"

"Actually, I—"

"She worked at the new museum in Newport Beach," Carone said. "Cataloging exhibitions and working with the docents."

Vinnie nodded with approval. "Oh. The docents."

I knew Newport Beach. Some said it had more old money than Beverly Hills and more class than L.A. That settled it for Vinnie. She whispered something to her husband and smiled at me.

Jason leaned over and put his hand on my arm. "So what do you do for fun?"

I hesitated, not sure what to do about this overture. *Keep your hands to yourself, Mr. Nichols.*

"I like photography and nature," I managed to say.

"A photographer?" Herbie cut in. He grabbed my other arm. "Why didn't you say so before? You have to see my work."

Now I found myself in a deep, one-sided discussion with Herbie about his work. Meanwhile, Jason, prevented from talking to me by Herbie's nonstop verbiage, tried getting my attention by rubbing his foot against my ankles. A subtle action on his part, but there was no mistaking his intent. How outrageous. I kept moving my legs to avoid him, but he always managed to find them. Later, when I thought of it, I put him on my list of suspects. The creep.

But I eliminated Herbie from that list. He almost never came into the gallery, except for opening-night receptions. He connected with Carone only at her dinner parties, with Mr. Hansen acting as his champion.

Whether Herbie was as talented as Mr. Hansen said, I didn't know. Mr. Hansen appeared to have a large collection of modern masters, as he referred to them. From the way he talked, he seemed to have a lot of money too. He also considered himself an authority on contemporary art, including photography. He had known Herbie since he was a kid and behaved like an uncle to him. Several times, though, while Herbie was telling me the story of his life, I caught Hansen staring at me. I didn't think he believed the introduction Carone gave about me. And I didn't think he liked me.

I cornered Carone on her way out of the dining room after dinner, and before dessert. "I suppose you heard about the fire," I whispered.

"I don't want to discuss it here. Let's go down the hall."

Carone led me into a small office just off the living room. "So what have you found out?" she said.

"Well, the fire—"

"I already know about that. Fortunately, according to Clyde, the smoke damage didn't reach the stacks. And the paintings for Bentley's presentation were also fine. So we're okay."

Except we almost choked to death. But never mind that. I told her about Chasem, the Boulange Gallery and the black Mercedes following me. "Do you know of an artist named Hewlett? Chasem said the two paintings in his collection were Hewletts. I couldn't find any artist named Hewlett on the Internet."

"I don't recall that name."

"According to Chasem, Hewlett had a show in New York."

"Why is that important?"

"Because if there isn't an artist named Hewlett, Chasem was just trying to trick me. He didn't believe I was curating a show for you. He said the Hewlett from your gallery wasn't the right size, so he bought two Hewletts at another gallery."

"He probably thought you were lying about being a curator. I vaguely remember him. Never buys anything, but acts like he knows more about art than anyone."

"It might be helpful if you gave me a key to the gallery, so I

111

could check the gallery records to see if you have a Hewlett. I could get there in the morning before everyone."

"All right."

Carone opened a drawer from a cabinet in the room and handed me a key. She told me how to disengage the alarm. "You know," she said, "in a way I hope it is David Chasem. I'd hate to think it was somebody close to me. Chasem's not an important collector, and everyone else has been so loyal."

"I don't know for certain he had anything to do with it. And even if he has the Picasso, how would I get it back from him?"

"Leave that to me. Just find it."

"But how? I think the Boulange Gallery is a better lead. I think I should go there."

"That's a wild goose chase."

"I don't think so. The Browns had so many major paintings. Even with lottery money, they couldn't afford them. Maybe we should go back there together. Would you be able to tell if they were fakes?"

Carone looked at me as though I were a child. "You don't know very much about art. They could have been minor works by these artists. Those tend to be less expensive."

"Why are you reluctant to have me check out the Boulange Gallery?"

I couldn't believe the expense of sending me to L.A. held Carone back. It didn't cost that much to fly. Maybe she thought I wouldn't return. But I'd have to. I couldn't show my face to Charley without finding Antonio. Of course, Carone didn't know that.

"I'm not reluctant," Carone said. "I just think you should eliminate every suspect here before you go off somewhere, and Chasem could be our man. He played along with your story and then lied about the paintings—unless you can find a Hewlett in our records. It doesn't sound familiar to me. We handle so many artists. Maybe it was something Marny picked up. I had her working on something . . . and you thought someone followed you. It could have been Chasem. I don't know what he drives. I can't think of anyone who drives a black Mercedes. No one on my staff does."

Carone had a point. But one way or another, I was going to the Boulange Gallery. "By the way, I thought we were going to meet in the stacks this afternoon."

"You were injured. I had to spend time with my father and Eddy. You have to find the Picasso. You have three weeks. I can probably get Eddy to bail me out if you don't, but then he'll own the gallery." She bit her lip and looked worried. "He'll keep quiet and pay the collector for the Picasso, but I'll end up working for him. Oh, he wouldn't expect me to—he's such a dear—but I'd have to. I couldn't let him take that burden alone. Do you know how much the Picasso is worth?"

I didn't want to know.

"Well, it would kill my father if he found out. He never wanted me to open the gallery in the first place. Eddy convinced him I could do it."

"That was nice of him."

"It was more than that. He and my father have some kind of rivalry going on. Eddy always likes to prove my father wrong. The Goodwins are the same way. It's all in fun and my father puts up with it. They're dear friends. That's how they relate to each other. I don't understand it, but I've grown up with it."

"I hope I find out something from Chasem, but maybe you should hire an art investigator. In all honesty—"

"I've already told you I can't. My father looks at every invoice—and if I start taking cash withdrawals—he'd find out what I was spending it on. He's terrified someone will take me for my money or that I'll waste it. The only reason he doesn't know the gallery's in trouble is—I've adjusted the books—a temporary solution. I have to fix it before we have our annual audit." Carone crossed her arms. "This is between you and me."

People tell me the damnedest things. Must have been my honest face. Little did they know, I couldn't be trusted. "Sure," I said. "But why is the gallery in trouble?"

"I made some bad investments. I took out a short-term loan to cover them. I had to pay it back. I used the gallery's money."

"Couldn't you pay for it out of your own money, and not the gallery's?"

Carone looked angry. "I don't expect you to understand. I don't have any of my own money—everything is from my family. I can't go into this with you."

"Of course. I just thought—"

"You have to find the Picasso."

"I know. But aside from getting the painting back, how will that help you get out of the financial hole you're in?"

"The collector wants to sell it. That should pay back what I took from the gallery. That's why it's a short-term problem."

But if I didn't find the Picasso, it would be a long-term problem. Talk about putting on the pressure. What if I failed?

"I—well, tell me this, does your husband work at the gallery?"

"What's that got to do with anything?"

"I just wondered."

"No, he doesn't. He plays tennis."

"Professionally?"

"No. He doesn't need to work. My father gives him an allowance, the same as he gives me. But we have this house to keep up and expenses. What's left wouldn't cover what I owe. Jason doesn't get involved in the business."

"Does your father monitor how he spends his money?"

"No. It's only me he worries about." She gave me a cold

stare. "Oh, I know you think it's unusual, but I don't mind Jason not working. He doesn't have the same drive as I. What's wrong with that?"

"I didn't think anything of it—really."

"Actually, we complement each other." She smiled, almost daring me to contradict her.

I smiled back. I wouldn't be the one to tell her about Jason and Amanda being together in the gallery today. Not when Carone had confided in me, treating me like the friend she had introduced to her father and his cronies. I needed Carone to keep up that pretense—and believe in it—if I was going to find the Picasso.

CHAPTER ELEVEN

Was Carone blind when it came to Jason? Or did it suit her to ignore his womanizing? I didn't get to analyze that further because Rothwell appeared in the doorway.

"Ms. Merryweather," he said, "I need to confer with you about the dessert."

Out of politeness, I smiled at him. He returned my smile with a frosty look. I must have committed some sort of social gaffe.

Carone nodded to Rothwell. To me, she said, "We'll talk later." She walked off with Rothwell.

Now I understood what Carone meant. I had assumed this was Carone's house, but it really belonged to her father. And so did Rothwell. Servant though he might be, I had the feeling he was also the eyes and ears of Mr. Merryweather.

Yes, the rich were different, and at that moment, I was glad I wasn't one of them. I didn't think I could live like Carone. But now I had seen another side of her. The side Carone revealed to a friend. Yet I sensed Carone still hid something from me. When she had said, "Is anybody ever above corruption," was she feeling guilty about doctoring the gallery's books? Something didn't fit here. Was this a game to her, like the game the Goodwins and Eddy Hansen played with Mr. Merryweather?

Since Carone and Rothwell left me alone in her office, I did a little snooping, though I didn't know what to look for. If I had been a real investigator, would I be investigating my own client?

Nevertheless, I opened a drawer of one of the cabinets in the room. I didn't find anything of interest, just miscellaneous invoices. It would take some time to figure out what they were for. I put them back. Nothing with the gallery logo on them. I peeked into the closet.

"May I assist you with something?"

I almost jumped. Eddy Hansen stood in the doorway. "I—I—uh—nothing. I wanted a shawl for my shoulders. The air conditioning made me cold."

"Well, you won't find it in here. This is Alfred's study. I'll have Rothwell bring you one."

"No—no, that's okay." I didn't want to deal with Rothwell again.

"Come along then. I'll ask Rothwell to turn it down. It is a bit chilly." He took my arm to make sure I went with him. He ushered me back to the living room.

I wanted to leave after that, but as a polite guest, I had to stay for dessert. Rothwell served it informally in the living room. He rolled in a sterling silver cart laden with pastries, pies and cakes. He poured everyone coffee from a large silver decanter, and we helped ourselves to the sweets. I picked out a large piece of rich chocolate cake and savored every bite.

After a suitable time passed, Jane and Rodney excused themselves. I wanted to follow Rodney, not only to see where he went—everyone was a suspect—but also to see whether he drove a black Mercedes. Except Herbie kept talking to me, and I couldn't get out of the conversation without being rude.

An hour later, Herbie stopped to sip some coffee and I had my opportunity. I got up and said my goodbyes. I didn't get off so easily. Herbie also stood and took my arm.

"I can't wait to hear about the new project you're working on," he said. "Anyway, you can't leave now. I want to show you my work. I'm just down the street—a mile or so."

"Yes," Eddy Hansen said. "That's a wonderful idea. Herbie has some great paintings. He combines them with photography. They are amazing. Don't you think so, Carone?"

Carone gave him a bland smile.

I was surprised that Hansen acted so enthusiastic about me going over to Herbie's. He made no mention of finding me in Alfred's office, but I didn't forget how he looked at me at dinner. Did he suspect I had never been a friend of Carone's?

"Herbie doesn't know many artists, except Rodney," Hansen said. "He works in that big studio all day and doesn't get to talk to anyone."

Maybe that's why he talked nonstop tonight. So what was Hansen's angle? He didn't seem to like me, yet he encouraged Herbie. Maybe he thought I would convince Carone to give him a show—that must have been it. At any rate, unless I thought of an excuse, I was in for a long, boring night.

"I'd like to, but I can't. I've been in New Mexico less than a week and the altitude makes me tired." That seemed to convince everyone.

But I had to give Herbie a ride home. He wanted to get up early to work on a painting and Eddy showed no signs of wanting to leave, though he had driven Herbie here. So that left only me.

When we got into the car, Herbie picked up the magazine I left on the seat, the one Mrs. Brown had given me, an issue of *Country Home Décor*. "Do you read this stuff?" he said. "Silly chintz and lace curtains for old ladies. That's about all they show. Even the art . . . well, don't get me wrong, I know Carone loves the impressionists and her Matisses. I'm just thankful she has an eye for contemporary work."

"A collector of the gallery gave it to me."

"You know it's all going back to the minimalist movement again. And black is the color. I'm doing everything in black. Are you into black too?"

"Uh, yes."

"I hope so girl, because otherwise no one will take you seriously as a curator. Black—that's what's in."

Maybe when I was sixty, if someone called me "girl" I'd relish it, but now I felt like throwing Herbie out of the car.

Herbie rattled on, unaware of the annoyance that must have shown on my face. "I haven't told Carone yet," he said, "but this gallery in New York keeps calling me—night and day—about a show. So far I've put them off—I owe Carone that much, to give her first choice—but I'm going to have to make a decision soon. My work takes so much energy I can't come up with enough work for two shows—at least not right away. I want to give Carone every opportunity to get in there first—but what else can I do? It's hard to say no to New York."

I kept driving, feigning an interest in what he had to say. Carone and her group seemed to dwell in fantasies beyond my comprehension. I was glad Herbie said he lived only down the road.

"You know," he continued, "lots of people are going to stick their necks out for me. Lots of people. It's a good thing I've got lots of connections because so many artists have been destroyed by the art world. The great ones, that is. I'm not going to let that happen to me. No, lots of people are going to stick their necks out for me, and even when you have talent as I have, it all depends on who you know. Yes, lots of people are going to stick their necks out for me. They believe in me. I see it out there for me. I'm a heavy, heavy artist. I see the success. It's there for me. New York, London, Berlin—they're waiting for me."

He droned on like that for some time. His mile or so down the road turned into five. But I tuned him out, barely conscious of what he said.

"Well, here it is," Herbie announced. "Just pull into the drive where the white fence is. Come in. See my work. I promise I won't keep you. I just want your opinion of what paintings I should include in my show."

But instead of doing that, I parked at the curb. "Herbie, it's been *lots* of fun, but it's taken *a lot* longer to get to your house than I realized, and I'm exhausted. Some other time."

For a moment, he didn't speak and I used that to my advantage. I put the car in drive and lurched away from the curb. "Out!" I said.

In a panic, he opened the door and jumped out before I could get too much farther from the curb. I looked in the rearview mirror as I drove off. Poor Herbie. He stood in the street, staring at my car. I knew it was mean of me, but I couldn't stand him any longer. Well, at least he didn't try to shoot my tires.

I drove to the gallery and let myself in the back door. I turned off the alarm and went into the file room.

Mr. Chasem was on to me all right. The gallery had no Hewlett listed in any of their consignment or sale files. So now what? It still didn't mean he had the Picasso, or drove a black Mercedes.

I went into the stacks. It took two hours to discover the Merryweather family collection was all there. I thought about searching the resale stacks to see if anything was missing, but I decided to finish later, since morning had already arrived. I needed to get some sleep.

I was about to leave when I saw something on a chair near the phone in the stacks. Patty's pen. The one she always twirled in her hair.

She had been fiddling with it the last time I saw her. Although that seemed like eons ago, it had just been this morning. I should have known Patty would search the place herself. She got me to believe she didn't have the time or the interest to search the stacks. She outsmarted me. But why leave her pen, when she made such a big deal out of always having it with her?

I put it in my briefcase, so I could surprise her with it tomorrow. I imagined the mortification on her face when I gave it to her. She wouldn't be caught dead without it.

Oh, God. No. Perish the thought. Patty was okay. She was absent-minded. She almost left her pen that day in my office. Damn that woman. I never should have confided in her. It was one thing for me to investigate. A bump on the head might knock me out, but I could always bounce back. But something like that could kill Patty. I had to tell Carone to keep Patty out of this. Despite what Carone believed, someone wanted to hurt people.

I looked up Patty's home number in the files. I'd call her in the morning. I locked up and went to the parking lot. And whom did I see coming out of the restaurant across from the parking lot, but David Chasem. Did he follow me, or was this a coincidence?

I crouched behind a dumpster. I didn't think he saw me. He must have heard my footsteps, because he turned in my direction. Then he walked toward the restaurant's parking lot, adjacent to the gallery's lot.

I made a dash for my car, but I tripped on an aluminum can somebody left in the alley. It made a loud, crunching sound.

I ran behind the dumpster again. This time, Chasem didn't turn around. He ran in the opposite direction. To his car, most likely. What was he so afraid of?

With so many cars in the parking lot, I couldn't see which one was his. I heard a car drive off, its tires screeching.

If that was Chasem, I had a feeling he wasn't rushing back to his place. To test my hunch I drove to his house. When I got there, the lights were off.

I parked down the road. I crept to a neighbor's side yard and went through that yard to Chasem's side yard. Overgrown with junipers and other plants, dead leaves covered the ground there as well. I cringed with every leaf I stepped on, hoping I didn't make too much noise. He had the blinds closed. I remembered his back sliding door had transparent curtains, so I went around the back.

The gate was locked. A man called out, "Who's there? Dave, is that you?"

I ducked down, afraid to move. Then I lost my balance and fell against a fence, scrunching more leaves before I steadied myself.

The man came outside. I saw his silhouette under the porch light. He carried a shotgun. It looked like one of those semi-automatics. I held my breath.

He didn't see me. He stayed on the back patio for a minute and then went inside.

Knowing one little sound could end my life, I swept the leaves from my path, inch by inch, with my fingers, as I crawled toward the front yard. My skirt would probably need dry cleaning, maybe even repairs, but I didn't care.

What had I stumbled onto? And how would I get the Picasso out of there, if Chasem had it?

CHAPTER TWELVE

People liked their guns in New Mexico, and they used them when they saw fit. Were drugs mixed up in this? Or was that my L.A. mentality showing? In New Mexico, pointing a gun could mean a guy was just protecting his property.

I reached Carone on her cell and told her what happened. "I think I should at least call the police and report that I saw a guy come out of his house with a shotgun."

"No. They might wonder what you were doing there in the first place. And if they have the Picasso, you'll ruin it for me. They'll find it and the press will have a field day. I don't have enough influence or money to keep that quiet."

"But if they do have the Picasso, what should I do?"

"Go back there during the day. Maybe you can look in the windows."

And risk getting shot? No thanks. "Even if I see it, how will I get it out of there?"

"You'll think of something."

Right. I'll think of something. The last time we talked, Carone assured me *she* would think of something. Well, she did. She got *me* to think of it.

So I did. I called the police and gave an anonymous tip about a man carrying a shotgun outside his house. Then I went to my room and slept until the maid knocked on my door. I forgot to put the do-not-disturb sign out.

My head didn't ache as much as yesterday. While the maid

tidied my room, I called the hotel café and ordered breakfast. I'd never ordered room service before, and since I was probably going to be fired from both jobs soon, I might as well live it up. French toast and hash browns, ordered like a condemned prisoner for her last meal, never tasted so good.

I had just finished my first cup of the coffee when Charley called. "I'm on it," I said. "I may have a new lead. I'll know more tomorrow."

And when tomorrow came, I'd tell him the lead didn't pan out, but I was working on a new one. I could probably milk that for a while. Maybe by then, I'd have something. Or not.

Carone's way of smoothing things over with a dose of unreality had rubbed off on me. I sat reading the hotel's complimentary copy of *The New Mexican* as if I hadn't a care in the world. How nice to be just a well-off tourist.

On the obituary page, I glanced at Angelica Ortiz's obituary. Of her survivors, the article listed her parents and a brother Jesse. That had to be the bellhop. I hadn't seen him around since Angelica's death.

I felt bad about Angelica, wishing I had made the last hour of her life more pleasant. Instead, I'd annoyed her with my map request. That must have been all there was to it. She didn't know anything about Antonio Chavez, or about the weird man at the house on Calle Fernando.

Then I saw what had eluded me. The second to the last paragraph of the obituary stated Angelica belonged to the Suique tribe. Oh, my God. Was she Antonio's girlfriend? The funeral was today at Saint Francis Church. Three o'clock. But what would I learn if I went there? I couldn't exactly strike up a conversation. Or could I?

I got dressed. I had hours to kill before the funeral. Although I had time to search the resale stacks, I didn't want to exert myself. Lunch, in a few hours, seemed a more important option. Having a concussion made me both sleepy and constantly hungry.

To pass the time, I got ambitious and looked at the list of employees Carone had copied for me. I had everyone's Social Security number. I knew just whom to call. "Sandra, I need a favor. It's Lana. Don't tell Charley I called." Sandra worked in the benefits department of First Century. Unlike me, she had no scruples about doing unauthorized credit checks.

"What are you doing?" Sandra asked. "I heard you went to find some beneficiary. Since when do you get to be a detective?"

"Since Charley decided he needed someone to take the blame for not finding the beneficiary. This is something different, though. I need some background checks on a few people. Credit, arrests, employment—the works. It would be a big help if you could. I don't want Charley to know. I don't want him to think I'm not working at my job."

"Okay. Give me the info."

I didn't feel bad. I wasn't doing anything wrong. Sandra had no scruples, so she didn't feel bad either. Besides, after reading the employee contracts, Carone had the right to pull their credit scores and perform background checks, but nothing in her records indicated she ever did.

An hour later, I had my reports. Clyde was busted four years ago for shoplifting. He got off with three years' probation. Since then, he had two traffic tickets and a termination from a job as a waiter. His job prior to working for the gallery was at a photography studio. Although he behaved admirably during the fire—making sure everyone got out—I didn't like the way he leered at me when I first met him.

Bentley lived in the same neighborhood as Carone, in a house he owned. He didn't always pay his credit card bills on time. He also had an old debt of six hundred dollars that went to collections. Recently, he charged large amounts on his cards, but paid them off in full. He also drove a BMW. Since he lived in Carone's neighborhood, he probably could afford his lifestyle. But did the gallery support that, or did Bentley have another source of income? A search of his assets would take longer, and I didn't want to ask Sandra for more favors. She wouldn't hesitate to tell on me if she got caught. No honor among thieves, not at First Century anyway.

Marny lived in an apartment near the gallery, in a somewhat expensive neighborhood, at least according to an Internet map search. Not significant in itself. Educated in Switzerland, she could have come from a wealthy family. But for her to knock me out and drag me into the broom closet, she needed an accomplice. She didn't look strong enough. I was about ninety-nine point ninety-nine percent positive I didn't accidentally bump my head and end up in the closet.

Amanda had a college degree from a state college in Colorado and resided close to David Chasem. In fact, several blocks away. Did they know each other? She lived in a house she got as part of a divorce settlement three years earlier. Four years before her divorce, she and her husband adopted a boy named Theodore. After the divorce, Theodore went to live with the ex-husband in Texas. Amanda wasn't a big spender and had no criminal record. But her son didn't live with her. That seemed unusual.

Rodney spent one year on an honor farm when he was eighteen for selling cocaine. Did Jane Goodwin's grandparents know that? Since then, he had a clean record. Not even a traffic ticket. He paid his bills on time and his part-time job at the gallery, along with sales of his paintings, supported him. He rented a house near the College of Santa Fe. He owned an older Ferrari and a Dodge pickup—no black Mercedes. An online search of his house showed a large, sprawling hacienda on several acres. He didn't own it, but it looked expensive. Maybe he had roommates, helping him pay the rent. Or maybe his coke connection kicked in, if he was still dealing. Or was I being too cynical?

The phone rang. It was Lieutenant Seastrom from the Santa Fe police. "I understand you may have information about the death of Angelica Ortiz," he said.

"I don't know if it's important, but I asked her for directions an hour or so before she was killed. I thought she knew the house I was trying to find, but she acted as if she didn't. The thing is, that's the place I think her boyfriend rented. I'm in Santa Fe to find him. He's a beneficiary—I work for a life insurance company in California."

I told him about the old man at Calle Fernando. "I didn't file a police report because I didn't want to deal with it at the time. But now that Angelica Ortiz was murdered, the fact that she pretended not to know her boyfriend rented an apartment there—"

"Thanks, ma'am. If we find a connection, we'll investigate. And we can talk to that individual who shot at you. Sometimes these old-timers get a little rambunctious."

"Do I need to press charges first?"

"No. We'll check it out. We don't want to send any senior citizen to jail if we can help it."

From the sound of the detective's voice, I gathered he didn't think much of my information. That surprised me. I had found a connection between my case with what seemed like a random murder. How could that not be important? But if he did talk to the old man, maybe that would stop him from shooting me if I went there again. If I were crazy enough to do that.

I studied the newspaper again. Nothing in it about the fire. That was strange. It was a newsworthy story about a prominent gallery.

The phone rang. It was Carone. "I thought you would have been here, checking the stacks," she said.

"I did that yesterday—your family's collection. I need some time off. I'm still recuperating from that bump on my head."

"You were able to make it to dinner. Your head can't hurt that much. I expect results. You don't have much time."

"Then let me go to the Boulange Gallery in L.A."

"You just want to go home."

"No, I don't. I think it's an important lead."

"Did you learn anything at dinner last night?"

"Just that you don't want to give Herbie a show."

"Well, you could have been nicer to him. Eddy's upset. And I need him on my side. Just what did you say to Herbie?"

"Nothing. I was tired. I dropped him off at his house."

"Well, you have three weeks."

How could I forget, with Carone reminding me every second? "By the way, I didn't see anything in the paper about the fire."

"Naturally. I have a few friends here. I didn't want my father to know. He wanted to close the gallery when our handyman was killed. And he would have, if not for Eddy. If my father finds out about the fire—anyway, thanks for not mentioning it at dinner."

The lady knew enough to say thanks, but not enough to show sympathy for the bump on my head. "Did they find out what caused the fire?" I asked.

"The insurance adjuster said it was from a cigarette thrown into a wastebasket. No one smokes except Marny. I don't allow it in the gallery, but she admitted going in there with a cigarette. She said she put it out before throwing it in the wastebasket, but obviously, she didn't. The insurance company is going to pay. The damage was mainly to an office I was planning to redecorate—when things get better. I told Marny I'd have to let her go if she ever smoked in the gallery again. I consider the matter closed. With the auction coming up, I need her. She can be very good with collectors."

I wondered whether the thief set the fire to create a diversion, with the motive of sneaking into the stacks to steal something else. But if Marny was the thief, she wouldn't have admitted starting the fire. Why did she admit it? She was looking for another job, and that wouldn't look good on her record.

I didn't have time to waste on the matter. I had a funeral to go to—later. I showered. I took a short nap and when I woke up, I puttered around, watching TV and not doing much until one o'clock. Oh, the life of the idle rich.

The café downstairs was crowded for lunch. I had to wait until a table was ready. I could have gone somewhere else, but it was easy to charge it to my room.

"Hey, I thought I'd find you here."

I looked up from the menu to see Darlene smiling at me. Just in time for lunch. How convenient for her.

"We really have to stop meeting like this," I said.

Darlene laughed, probably thinking I was joking.

I wasn't.

She sat across from me. "I stopped by the gallery the other day, but you weren't there," she said.

"I'm not there all the time."

"I'm hungry. You wouldn't mind splitting a salad with me? I'm broke till payday."

"You haven't paid me back for the last time," I said.

"I will. As soon as I get paid. Say, what's happening at the gallery? Are you working on the auction? I would love to get an invitation."

"I'm not working on that. I've got a different project."

"How many invitations are you getting?"

"I don't know. They haven't talked about it. Everyone has to work that night, I think."

I split the salad with her, and we filled up on sourdough rolls and butter. Darlene had to get back to her job, so I didn't need to make excuses to ditch her. But I had to stop eating lunch at the café, or I'd go broke feeding her. Or Charley would.

Impressive, like all Romanesque churches, Saint Francis Basilica had a large courtyard surrounding it. The earliest version of the church dated back to the sixteen hundreds. This updated version, built in the eighteen hundreds, didn't have the grace of a Gothic cathedral, but it had a quaint charm all its own.

I was early for the ceremony and I sat in the back. There was an open casket, but I didn't view the body. I felt too guilty for whatever part I played in her death. I wasn't even sure what I was doing here.

The organist played softly while people trickled in. A short, Hispanic man came in through a side door. He crossed himself. He viewed the deceased for a moment. When he leaned into the casket, seemly overwhelmed with grief, he stumbled. He regained his balance by grabbing the side of the casket. His left hand had only four fingers.

Antonio—Lefty—Chavez.

I jumped out of my seat and hurried toward him. Too bad I didn't know Angelica was his girlfriend before she died. Maybe I could have convinced her to let me see him—why wouldn't she tell me she knew him? I had money to give him. Why didn't she believe me?

A crowd of mourners entered the church, blocking my way. I darted through them, murmuring apologies for pushing anyone. "Antonio Chavez," I called out. "I need to speak to you."

At the sound of his name, Antonio turned. I tried to get closer to him, but more people streamed in from the side door near him. "Antonio, I have good news from your great-aunt." That didn't come out right. "Antonio, wait."

Antonio glanced at the crowd to see who called his name. He looked afraid and he fled out the side door. I rushed through the crowd and chased him, again making apologies as I bumped into people.

The side door led to the street, but when I got outside, I didn't see him. There were so many people coming into the church by then. I ran to the alley up the street. I thought I saw him. "Antonio Chavez, I have news for you, about your inheritance," I shouted.

He disappeared. He must have gone inside a building or the backyard of a house. For the next forty minutes, I searched the alley, calling Antonio's name. Good thing I came early or I would have missed the funeral.

I went back to the church. I was about to enter the side door when I saw a familiar face.

"Hello, love," Rodney said. "There's a funeral in there. Maybe you should go sightseeing another time."

"Oh, I knew her. I'm staying at the Zimoro Hotel, where she worked. Did you know Angelica Ortiz?"

Rodney gave me a long look. "I did. Such a sad business. She referred several collectors to the gallery and one of them bought a painting of mine."

"Oh, I see. Terrible that she died. Her boyfriend worked at the gallery—Lefty Chavez. He was the handyman for a while, wasn't he? Did you realize they knew each other?" All this time I had concentrated on finding Antonio from what Carone knew, which was nothing. I should have asked her staff, except I couldn't. I was a curator to them, not an insurance administrator.

Rodney shrugged. "I guess. I never thought of it. Hey, I'd sit with you, but I need to pay my respects to her family. Take care, love."

Rodney slipped through the crowd and went inside the church. I stood at the door, peering in. I didn't see Antonio or Rodney.

I saw a police officer enter. He looked familiar. *Of course.* He was the officer who interviewed me when they took Angelica away. He recognized me too. He was there to check out the mourners. Maybe he suspected someone. I hoped he didn't think I was that someone.

I turned and found myself face-to-face with Bentley. "Oh, hi, Bentley. I guess you knew Angelica Ortiz. I just saw Rodney. So sad how she died."

"Yes, it is. She referred people to the gallery. I'm here on Carone's behalf. She couldn't make it. What brings you here?"

"Uh, she was the concierge at the hotel where I'm staying. I met her briefly. Did you know the handyman the gallery hired—the one called Lefty—was going with her?"

Bentley looked blank. "Really? I don't keep up on those things. Well, see you in there."

I nodded, but I hung out by the door, waiting until Bentley went inside. I didn't want to sit with him. But I figured I should stay.

Bentley said he didn't keep up with Antonio's love life and Rodney implied he couldn't care less about it. That seemed odd. They had to have known Angelica and Antonio—Lefty—were at least acquainted. Angelica was somewhat important to the gallery, referring people who bought paintings. Or maybe Angelica didn't go to the gallery. She just sent people there.

I went to the alley again, looking for Antonio. I didn't find him.

I called Charley on my cell. "Antonio is alive. I saw him. He was at a funeral, but when I tried to talk to him, he ran away. Something spooked him. I don't think it was me."

"How could you lose him?" Charley said. "You have to find him. Put an ad in the newspaper."

"I don't think that's going to work. The thing is, his girlfriend was shot and killed. That's the funeral he went to."

"Talk to his girlfriend's family. They'll know where he is."

"They're having a funeral. I don't think they're going to be in a talking mood."

"Money always talks. Tell them about the inheritance. You have to find him."

"Okay."

I went back to the church. I sat in the back. The service had already started, and I didn't want to draw attention to myself.

I cried. I barely knew her. I didn't even like her. But I cried. All these people loved her. Though maybe love was too strong a word to describe what Rodney and Bentley felt.

People from the Suique tribe spoke about Angelica. They made me cry even more. She was just over thirty and now she was dead. Not from disease, but from violence. That was horrible. I was one of the last people to see her alive. The enormity of it overwhelmed me.

At the end of the service, everyone walked by the casket and offered condolences to her family. I couldn't avoid the open casket without looking offensive. When I said my condolences, I asked them about Antonio, though to their faces, I called him Lefty. I said I was a friend of his and knew his great-aunt, who had left him an inheritance. I told them how important it was to find him.

"Come to the house afterward. I will give you his address," an old woman in funeral black said. "I'm Esther, Angelica's great-aunt. I saw Antonio earlier, but I don't see him now. He always said he would take care of Angelica—my angel." She sobbed. "Come to the house."

"Thank you."

I didn't go to the grave site. That would have meant I had sunk to a new low. I already felt like slime, taking advantage of a family's grief to get a job done. Then again, if Antonio's vow to take care of Angelica included using an inheritance to help her family, maybe I had redeeming qualities after all.

The Ortiz house was in Los Rios, in what looked like the poorer section of the town. Their small, old adobe was crowded with fake, early American furniture and shabby upholstered couches and chairs—the type you would have seen in a Sears or a J.C. Penney catalog of some bygone era. Heavy, deep purple velvet drapes covered the windows.

I met Angelica's half-brother Jesse—the bellhop. He didn't stay long. Rodney and Bentley didn't come, which was good. I stayed long enough to be polite. Before I left, I spoke to Esther.

"Lefty will help us," she said. "He was so good to Angelica. Let me write his address. Angelica supported us—her mother and me. Always came home with her paycheck. We don't know who did this. The hotel don't want to pay anything for Angelica's death. They say she already left work. But she still had her uniform on. They have their nerve."

"If I find Lefty, maybe he can help you," I said.

The address Esther wrote was for the house on Calle Fernando. "I've been there," I said. "He doesn't live there. And the older man who does shot at me."

"Oh, I know who you mean. Don't pay attention to him. He thinks he's the manager, but he's just a caretaker. So Lefty's great-aunt passed on. Is there much money?"

"I don't know how much there is. I was just told to get in touch with him."

CHAPTER THIRTEEN

I didn't think the man at Calle Fernando lied when he said Antonio moved. But Frank Ortiz, Esther's nineteen-year-old grandson, offered to take me there to make sure. We went in his old white Chevy pickup. He drove up the dirt driveway and honked. The man came out. He didn't have his gun with him this time. Frank got out of the truck. I got out, but kept my distance from the man.

Frank was a tall, husky guy, and he yelled at the man. "Where's Lefty? What's this I hear you were shooting at this woman? What are you doing? Lefty's great-aunt sent her to find him."

The man cowered. "I'm sorry. I didn't know who she was. I have to guard the place."

"Guard, my ass. Stop hassling this woman. You took money from her. Give it back. You don't collect the rent here. You just take care of the grounds."

"I don't have it."

"You better have it. You stole it from her. I'll call the police."

"Okay. Okay. I'll get it." The man went into the house, through a door on the left side of the building.

The man came back. "I only have a hundred left. I'll pay you the rest next week."

Frank all but growled at him. "We'll be back next week, and you better have it."

"I will. I don't need the police again."

"What are you talking about?" he said.

"I called the police," I said. "They told me they would talk to him."

"They did," the man said. "They came out today. I didn't mean to shoot you. I'm sorry."

So Lieutenant Seastrom believed at least some of what I said. I stepped away from the truck and took the hundred the man offered. "I'm Lana Davis."

"Just call me George."

"George, we just want to know if Lefty came back here. I saw him earlier today."

"He's not here. And he did owe the rent. But he didn't come back to pay it. The owner is mad."

"I'd like to see his room," I said.

"Okay. But you won't find nothing."

"Which one is his place?" Frank demanded.

"Here. Follow me." He led us to a door on the right end of the house.

Now that I looked at the house, I saw the two smaller, attached guest wings. Antonio had rented one of them.

George took out a ring of keys from a pocket in his faded jeans and opened the door. Antonio had a studio apartment with the kitchen on one side of the unit and a bed and nightstand on the other. In the middle of the room was a small card table with two wooden chairs. A rack on the wall with a few hooks on it served as a closet. The place was bare of personal effects.

"Is this his furniture?" I asked.

"No. It comes with the place. See, I told you. He moved out. I'm trying to rent it."

"You're not going to get it rented if you keep shooting at everyone," Frank said.

"I'm sorry."

I checked under the bed. Nothing there. "Did you clean out this place, or did Lefty leave it this way?" I asked.

"He cleaned it. The girlfriend helped him. That was a week or two ago."

"That girlfriend was my cousin. Now she's dead. Did you shoot her?"

George shuddered and shook his head. "No. I would never shoot her. Even if Lefty owed the rent."

"Well, where did he go?" I said.

"I don't know."

"What about his other friends?" I asked. "Did anyone ever visit him?"

"I think he had friends. I didn't pay no attention."

"Who lives in the other units?" I said.

"I live in one and the other one, someone rents it. They don't come here too much. They use it for storage. Things like that."

"Did Lefty know them?"

"Maybe."

"Who are they?"

"It's a guy. His name is Arby. That's all I know. Everyone pays the owner."

"Do you have a key to Arby's apartment?" Frank asked.

"Yes. But I can't let you in. He rents it."

"Just remember, we're coming here next Monday and you better have the other hundred," Frank said.

Frank brought me back to the Ortiz house. Everyone had left, except the family. Jesse had returned. He sat on one of the couches, his eyes downcast. Frank told Esther we didn't find Lefty.

I turned to Jesse. "Do you know any of Lefty's friends?"

He shook his head. He looked drunk.

"What time on Monday do you want to go back?" Frank asked.

"Do you really think he'll have the money?"

"He better. Or I'll beat the shit out of him."

"Frank! Don't be so disrespectful to Angelica's memory," Esther said.

"Sorry. Did you tell the police about the money?"

"No. I guess we could go there Monday afternoon," I said. "If you don't mind." The extra hundred would come in handy if Charley and/or Carone fired me. Or I'd give it to Esther. I didn't think she faked her sob story. They had lost a dear family member and their breadwinner.

"I don't mind," I said. "I usually can get off early on Mondays."

I had no real schedule at the gallery. But if I didn't work there on Monday, I worked for First Century. Since this concerned Antonio, this would be on their time.

I went back to the hotel. I was hungry again. I hadn't eaten anything at the Ortiz house, though they had plenty of food. I didn't think it was right to eat their food. I wasn't there because of Angelica.

This time I didn't go down to the café. I went across the Plaza to a little Mexican restaurant called Taxco. It felt good to have another hundred in my wallet. After a great meal, I called it an early night.

In the morning, I contacted Reggie Souther, the other collector who had been in the gallery when I got hurt.

"Oh, how nice of you to think of me," he said. "Of course, I'd be delighted to show you my collection." He spoke with a slight twang, as if he'd been born in Texas but had worked on his accent.

But before I saw Reggie, I drove to Albuquerque to see

Clyde's former employer, Southwest Photography. But rather than look like a Carone clone, I tousled my hair and wore a brown pants suit. I didn't put on any makeup and wore an older pair of sunglasses. For all I knew, Clyde and his former employer talked to each other. I didn't want him telling Clyde I stopped in.

Southwest Photography, located in a small beige stucco building next to an outdoor newsstand, didn't look like much from the outside—a little rundown, in fact. But it had a slick interior, decorated with white designer furniture, black granite countertops and oversized photographs of high desert landscapes, portraits of families and weddings. A young woman with blond spiked hair in a very short skirt greeted me.

"I'd like to talk to the owner," I said.

"Do you have an appointment?"

"This will take only a minute. I need to ask him some questions about a former employee."

"Oh, all right," she said. "Malc!"

A tall, thin man darted in from a back room. He was out of breath. He wore a pale pink shirt, a black-and-white checkered tie and gray slacks. His hair, groomed into a pompadour and very un-New Mexican, made him look like a New Yorker, or a hairdresser from West Hollywood. He held some photographs in his long, slender hands.

"Yes, yes. I'm Malcolm Courtney. What can I help you with?"

I handed him a business card with the name of one of my coworkers. "I'm Madeline Neihouse from First Century Insurance. We're doing a confidential background check on one of your former employees. He gave you as a reference. I just need to ask you a few questions. It won't take long."

Malcolm agreed, after telling me he was in a rush to finish a job. We went into his back office. He offered me a seat on a pink and green couch with fake leopard skin cushions.

"We're doing a background check on Clyde Posten. Was he a conscientious employee?"

"Uh . . . Clyde. He worked here for a short time. About six months. I don't know why he gave me as a reference. I can't give him a good recommendation. He wasn't dependable or even a hard worker. But he knew what he was doing, when he cared to show up."

"Was he honest? Did he ever steal?"

Malcolm pondered this. "There was one time I thought he took some equipment from the studio. I never accused him of it. After that, he got sick a lot. Didn't come in when he should have. But that's off the record. Forget I said that."

"Sure. Did you fire him?"

"No. People know when things aren't working out. He got another job and didn't give notice. So if you're asking me if I'd rehire him, the answer is no. That's all you can put me down for."

"Of course. Did his next employer get in touch with you?"

"No."

"Was it a lot of equipment you thought was missing?"

Malcolm picked up several photographs of vegetable center-pieces from a desk near him. "I really can't say. I'm sorry I can't be more help, but I need to finish a job."

I thanked Malcolm and went to my car. I knew better than to ask him the details. Legally, all he could say was Clyde wasn't someone he'd rehire. But Malcolm's comments added to the bad feeling I had about Clyde. Why did Carone hire him? He didn't seem the type she'd want around. But then neither did Rodney. Bentley was a better fit, with his arrogant attitude and business-like manner. He looked like someone who would work in a gallery.

I drove back to see Reggie Souther. He lived near the College of Santa Fe, off Saint Francis Drive, on a dirt road. His large house, a traditional Santa Fe adobe-style with bright turquoise-trimmed windows, had some acreage and a view of the city.

Before getting out of the car, I pulled my hair into a bun with some bobby pins. I still had on my somewhat rumpled brown suit. Okay, I didn't look as pulled together as I had in Carone's clothes, but I thought I looked enough like a curator to fool this guy.

Reggie let me in and showed me around. He had a large collection of paintings, hung in every room of his house. I didn't know one artist from the other, but the paintings were large with lush coloration. Judging from the size of Reggie's house and property, I had to assume they cost him plenty. He didn't let me hang around too long in any one place. "Come," he said. "I have quite a bit to show you." He took my elbow and steered me into room after room filled with contemporary art.

As I studied Reggie's collection, I also studied him. He was a tall, lanky man and he looked at ease in his faded jeans and blue open-necked work shirt. He had the charm of a Texan but the sophistication of a New Yorker. I noticed the wide glass sliding doors in the living room opened to a brick patio scattered with children's toys.

"I'm excited about the auction," he said. "I've got my eye on one painting. I saw it in the catalog the gallery sent me."

"Which one would that be?"

"I'm not telling. I want it all to myself. Maybe no one else will bid on it."

I laughed. "It's wonderful that you want to add to your collection. You have a large one already."

"I've got my boys with me now. Their mother moved back here from New York. I used to live there, now I get to see them more often. I want them to grow up with art. That's my motivation. You can't have too much art."

I commended him on his philosophy. And myself, on zeroing

in on his New York background.

"I work in the financial field," he said. "Great income, but very dry stuff. I need art to make me feel alive. Come, I've got some more work in my office."

His office was in another wing of his house. It was light and airy with white walls and pale gray carpeting. One wall was devoted to a large figurative mural.

"You recognize that, of course," he said.

I nodded, though I didn't.

"Rodney and I are great friends. I commissioned him to paint it when I bought the house last year."

So that was what Rodney Bracken did. Even to my untrained eye, it looked good. I liked the strong colors and vibrant movement of the figures. I walked up to it and noticed his signature in the bottom right corner.

"And here, behind my desk, is my latest prize," Reggie said. He held up a small landscape. "I'm going to hang it over my desk."

"Oh. Well. That's something. One of my favorite artists," I said. I hoped he believed me. I had no idea who painted it.

We talked for a few minutes and then I found myself led to the front door. It was time for Reggie to end his break and get back to work. I didn't seem to realize I'd never made a list of his collection or taken any photos of it.

Before I got to my car, Carone called. "I just saw Reggie Souther," I said. "He seems to be on the level. I think he loves art too much to steal it."

"Okay. You want to go to L.A. and see about that gallery—"

"The Boulange Gallery."

"Find a flight and I'll pay for it. Do it now and you can be back here by tomorrow, late morning. That should give you enough time."

In whose world? But I took my laptop out and found a flight.

Carone called the airline and I drove to Albuquerque. If I had known I was going there, I wouldn't have gone to see Reggie. Well, at least, unlike L.A., Albuquerque didn't have horrible traffic jams. And again, unlike L.A., even though I didn't get to the boarding gate two hours ahead of schedule, they let me on the plane. I didn't need to pack. I had plenty of clothes at my apartment.

When I landed, the one thing I didn't have was my car. I had taken a taxi to the airport when I flew from LAX to Albuquerque. So I had to pay for a ride in a taxi to get to my car, still parked at my apartment. I couldn't ask Carone to pay for that, not when I was moonlighting on Charley's dollar. I couldn't ask Charley to pay for it either. I just had to eat it.

I didn't stop to see what mail I had, or whether the woman I hired to water my plants had done a good job. I needed to get to the Boulange Gallery. It was on Beverly Drive in Beverly Hills, a good ten or twelve miles from me. Driving two miles in L.A. could take forever, and getting into Beverly Hills would take that and then some.

The Boulange Gallery occupied a white two-story building with large display windows. A sign on top announced, in bold, red letters, the gallery sold fine art investments at affordable prices. The window displays looked schlocky, for lack of a better word. The gallery displayed paintings stacked in multiple rows, crowded together on the walls. Below each piece was a hanging price tag. Even with my limited knowledge of art, I realized this place was a total sham.

I didn't know much about fine art prints, but I remembered an article I read about Salvador Dali, the famous surrealist artist. He signed hundreds of blank papers, later used to make prints of his earlier editions. Unscrupulous art dealers numbered these later issues as if they had been part of the earlier original print editions. The art world considered these later editions reproductions and not original prints. Reproductions, however fine, didn't command the same prices as originals. When people discovered this deception, the market for Dali prints collapsed.

Before I went into the Boulange Gallery, I took out an old business card an interior designer had given me. She worked in a furniture store offering design services for its customers. I was going to use her services to help decorate my living room, but I didn't like the selection the store had. I crossed out her phone number and put in my own. Why not? People changed phone numbers. I messed up my hair so I looked artsy and eccentric.

An energetic salesman met me at the door. He wore a blue suit and his hair plastered to his head with hair wax. "May I help you?" he said.

"Yes. I'd like to see some Picassos."

"We have some very fine original prints I can show you."

"No. I was thinking of a painting. Either a Picasso or a Matisse."

"Ah. Of course. This way, please."

I followed him down a wide aisle. It led to another room crowded with art.

"Here," he said. "This is our Picasso collection. And over on that far wall, we have a few Matisses."

I didn't see anything that looked familiar. "I'm scouting for a client of mine." I handed him the designer's card. "I'm decorating her home office. Do you mind if I take some photos?"

That seemed to annoy him, but he said, "Of course. If you wish."

"Also, a catalog would be helpful," I added.

"Oh, I'm sorry. We don't print catalogs. Work comes in so quickly and even more quickly it goes out."

"I see. Well, I think I'll have a look around. I'll let you know if I find anything suitable."

"If you need me, I'm Andre Cavin." He left me to my own devices.

I took some photos with my cell phone. Then I wandered through the gallery, trying to figure out how I could get a look at their client list, when I spotted a familiar shape.

She wore a blond wig, but I knew it was her. What was Amanda Talbert doing in the Boulange Gallery in Beverly Hills in a blond wig? Was this how she spent her sick days?

CHAPTER FOURTEEN

Amanda didn't see me. I put my head down and scurried to another aisle. This place reminded me of what the stacks might look like after an earthquake. Paintings and prints were crammed on walls, in bins and even on counters. But in this case, the clutter served as a good cover, allowing me to spy on Amanda without her seeing me. I hid behind a large bin of prints and snapped a picture of her talking to Andre.

Although Amanda didn't notice me, a salesman did. He approached me after I had just snapped another picture of Amanda, one from a better angle. He was a short man with a bald, pointed head. "Would you like some assistance?" he said. He spoke with a European accent.

"No, I'm just browsing. Thank you."

He nodded and then approached a couple who seemed interested in a painting. I spotted Amanda walking out the door. I went after her, when something caught my eye. In the next room, I saw a Chagall. It looked like the one taken from the gallery in Santa Fe.

I stopped chasing Amanda and whipped out the pictures of the paintings stolen from the gallery. I took a deep breath. Sure enough. I had found the Chagall. I put the pictures back into my purse. My heart thumped. My hands shook. I had just discovered an art forgery.

I snapped a picture of the reproduction. Then I looked for the bald salesman. Of course, he was nowhere in sight.

Whenever you needed a salesperson, they made themselves scarce.

I went into the main room and flagged down Andre. "I'd like some information on a Chagall I saw in the next room." I could hardly contain my excitement.

"Certainly. I believe I know which one you mean."

I rushed over to the Chagall, with him following me. We stood before it in silence, as if he wanted to give me a moment to bask in its magnificence. After a moment, he said, "You have made an excellent choice."

"It is beautiful." I tried to remain calm.

What should I do? Yell, this is a fake?

I decided on a more subtle approach. "Can you tell me something about this painting?"

"Please, allow me to show it to you properly." He took the painting from the wall. "It should be displayed separately from all the rest." He led me to the back of the gallery and into a private viewing room. He put the painting on an easel and offered me a chair across from it. I was getting the royal treatment.

He started to explain the symbolism and the wonderful brushstrokes in the work, but I stopped him. "That is something I am well versed in. My client needs to know the date of execution and its provenance. I assume it's an original."

"Of course it's an original. No question about that," he bristled.

I smiled. "I have to ask. There is so much . . ." I gestured with my hands. "My client is interested in its investment quality as well as its aesthetic value."

"Of course," he said. "Let me get the paperwork on this piece." Rather than leave me alone with the painting, he called his secretary on the phone next to him. "Mimi, please bring me all the documentation on number x-one-two-ninety-three."

Mimi appeared a few minutes later, a fiftyish woman, with blond bouffant hair and large pink-tinted glasses. Her purple knit dress hugged her curvy figure. Mimi handed Andre a manila folder and left the room. I could see Amanda looking like that in twenty years, albeit with a little more style.

"Here it is," Andre said. "The painting was done in nineteen-fifty-three, a very prolific year for Chagall."

"Really. And who were the prior owners?"

"Ah. Here's the list of those who once owned this painting."

I didn't see the Merryweather name on it. "May I view the back of the painting?"

He obliged, and I saw a Chagall signature on the back, along with the date of nineteen-fifty-three. The Chagall I saw in the stacks had a date on the back, but no signature. Chagall had signed it on the front. He must have considered that enough. Whoever painted this signed it on the back first, for practice maybe.

Before Andre put the painting back on the easel, I took a picture of the back of the painting with my cell phone. "Isn't it interesting? He also signed the back of the painting," I said. I now had the proof of the discrepancy between the fake and the real painting.

Andre put the Chagall back on the easel. "The title of this work is *The Sleeping Cow*. As you can see from the list of past owners, the artist Leon Stravinsky, a great friend of Chagall, once owned it. Then it was sold to the Broder family."

Who was Leon Stravinsky, if he had existed at all? I didn't want to ask and expose my ignorance. Was Andre knowingly conning me? And when did the Merryweather family get it? I'd have to ask Carone that. "Broder," I said. "Where are they from?"

"Beverly Hills," he said. "They have a wonderful collection. They may even bring in a Matisse soon."

"If they do, please let me know. My client is also interested in Matisse. And in Picasso as well. Also Kandinsky."

His eyebrows shot up. "The Broders have a Kandinsky. They just aren't sure they can part with it. But with the economy the way it is, they may bring it in yet."

"Definitely, let me know. Better yet, if you could send me a snapshot, I could show it to my client."

"Of course."

He was about to close the file when I leaned over and dropped my briefcase—on purpose. Some papers fell out and he bent over to retrieve them. I had just enough time to glance at the Broders' address before he got back to his seat. They lived on Almont Drive, in the flats of Beverly Hills. Not far from the gallery.

I apologized for being clumsy and thanked him for all his help. I took his card and said I would be in touch, after I talked to my client.

As soon as I left the gallery, I called Carone's house, blocking my number first. It was after five in New Mexico and Carone answered. Disguising my voice, I asked for Mr. Nichols.

"I'm sorry, he isn't here," Carone said. "Do you want to leave a message?"

I said I was from the cleaners, mumbling the name because I really didn't know the names of any cleaners. "Mr. Nichols never picked up his sports jackets and it's been over a month."

Carone offered to have it picked up, but I said I needed to speak to him about an alteration he ordered for one of them. "When do you expect him?" I asked.

"I don't know. He's not going to be in until later. I'll give him the message."

I probably shouldn't have called. I didn't want Jason to get suspicious. But I wanted to know if he had gone to California with Amanda. But the phone call didn't resolve that.

I had a gut feeling Mr. and Mrs. Broder were Jason and Amanda. And they had taken the works out of the gallery in order to make reproductions of them. But what about the Picasso? It didn't belong to the Merryweather collection. Somehow, I felt Jason and Amanda needed a better connection than the Boulange Gallery to sell off the last Picasso. A well-known painting like that had a traceable history.

But if Jason and Amanda had taken it, why hadn't they returned it? Was I underestimating them? The Merryweather Galleries attracted important, influential people. Would one or more of them help Amanda and Jason sell stolen paintings, under Carone's nose? It had been a daring feat for Jason and Amanda to enlist the Boulange Gallery in the sale of forged paintings in the first place. Yet if they had accomplished the more dangerous job of selling the Picasso, what were they sticking around for?

I drove to the Broder house. I parked half a block away, on a side street where I had a view of the place. It was on a corner. They lived in a muted brown, Grecian-style home. According to the title on the property, the house belonged to Norma Talbert. Whether that was a sister or her mother, someone in the family had money. A house in the flats of Beverly Hills cost a ton of it.

I got out of the car, wearing sunglasses and an old, wide-brimmed sun hat I kept in the back seat. A glance in my side mirror showed a woman who looked too casual to have been Lana Davis, freelance gallery curator. Still, I wasn't about to knock on the Broders' door. Instead, I strolled past the house. It didn't look like anyone was home.

I went to the house next door and knocked. A fat, older man with white bushy eyebrows answered. I told him I was selling magazine subscriptions, and when he didn't want any, I said, "Your next-door neighbors, the Broders, told me to come back today, but they aren't home. I collected too much money for their subscription and my manager gave me a refund check for them. Do you know when they're coming home?"

"I think they left for the weekend already. They aren't here very often. He works up in San Francisco. I'll take it and see that they get it."

"Well, they have to sign for it."

"I don't think they'll be back for a week or so. Her mother used to live there. I guess she gave it to her daughter when she married."

"She's the blonde, isn't she?"

He gave me a sharp look. "I don't think so. You sure you got the right address?"

I looked at the numbers on his house. "Oh, my. I'm on the wrong street. I mixed up the names. I already gave them their refund. Thank you for your time." I hurried away.

I went to my car, contemplating what to do next. Amanda had to be Mrs. Broder. She wore the wig when she set up deals with the Boulange Gallery, and not where she lived. I had to hand it to her. That took nerve. I didn't think she had it in her. Was Jason as competent as that? Well, he knew how to flirt. Maybe he sold the Picasso to a woman. An older woman, perhaps?

There was just one problem. Jason and Amanda had a good thing going already with the Boulange Gallery, assuming the Boulange Gallery had already sold some of the forgeries, or was about to sell them. Why ruin it by taking the Picasso?

Maybe they didn't realize how stupid it was to steal the Picasso until they had already done it. So why not give it back and focus on another painting? Maybe they didn't steal it. Maybe Chasem did—working alone. Or with Amanda? No. I couldn't see her working with Chasem. They lived near each other, but that didn't mean anything.

Whatever the case, I couldn't see Amanda working alone in

this gig. Someone had knocked me out and shoved me into that closet. Amanda and Marny didn't look strong enough for that. And Jason, well, he probably would sooner flirt than fight. But I couldn't say that about Chasem. If looks could kill, I'd be dead already.

But what about Bentley, Rodney and creepy Clyde? They all had access to the gallery and at least some knowledge of the resale market in the art world. Well, maybe not so much for Clyde. Of course, they could all be in it together.

No. Dumb idea. Bentley didn't seem the type to get his hands dirty. He would have thought of a less messy way to get rid of me. And Rodney was even more of a charmer than Jason was. I couldn't see him knocking anyone out, especially a woman.

But someone was afraid I would discover something in the stacks. I kept coming back to Clyde. With him, anything seemed possible. He saw me in the stacks, poking around. And Southwest Photography gave him a bad reference.

Too many suspects. How could I zero in on the right one? It made me dizzy just thinking about it. Never should have gotten into this. The lure of easy money in a weak moment. But not so easy now, with this concussion.

Wasting time sitting in the car paid off. The Broders hadn't left for the weekend, as their neighbor had thought. Amanda drove up in a white minivan, handy for transporting paintings. A moment later, Jason arrived in a cab. He tipped the cabby and got out about the same time as Amanda did. I snapped a picture of the two of them embracing. Then I snapped another one that revealed their faces. A little sleazy of me, but now I had something to show for my efforts. I felt like a real detective, though I still couldn't eliminate the other suspects. I had no proof Amanda and Jason stole the Picasso.

Since this was Beverly Hills, hiding in the bushes and peeking in windows wasn't an option. Not unless I wanted a Beverly Hills cop to arrest me. I had earned some time off anyway. I went to my apartment, ordered pizza—my favorite comfort food—and crashed on the couch. It was good to be home, though I missed having a maid throw the pizza box out and turn down the bed.

Poor Charley. I left him hanging. Just insisting Antonio was alive wasn't going to get Miguel Rivera off our backs. But my headache told me to forget it for the night.

I ate and spaced out on some TV reruns. Before I went to bed, I loaded the pictures I took onto my laptop. Carone wasn't going to be happy with the ones of Jason and Amanda. I just hoped she wouldn't kill the messenger.

Things were in an uproar at the gallery when I got back. Patty hadn't shown up for two days. They called her home, but she didn't answer. Meanwhile, Amanda, who must have flown in the night before, slaved on things Patty was supposed to complete. Carone recruited Clyde to help as well.

Marny had to pitch in too. She made sure everyone within hearing distance knew how unhappy that made her. "I wasn't hired to do clerical work. If I had wanted to work in the mailroom, I wouldn't have bothered to get my degrees."

"Come on, Marny," Amanda said. "We all need to help now and then." Amanda turned to me. "It's so unlike Patty to desert us at a time like this." She looked as if she wanted to ask me to help, but unsure of my status in the gallery's hierarchy, she didn't.

I nodded and at the same time avoided looking at her. Not that I didn't want to help. I just didn't want my suspicions about her to show. I walked past everyone and went to Carone's office.

Patty's pen was beginning to burn a hole in my briefcase. I

hoped that horrible feeling in my stomach was a hunger pang and not some premonition.

Carone gave me only a few moments of her time. She was expecting an important collector. "Can you believe Patty never called?" she said. "I left messages. I thought for sure, by now, she would have called."

"Maybe she had an accident. Have you called the hospitals?"

"I never thought of that."

"I'll follow up on it," I said.

"No, I'll have Marny do that. What did you learn in L.A.?"

"I have some pictures to show you." I turned on my laptop and opened the photos.

"This is the Chagall. They showed me the list of people who had owned it. Your family's name wasn't on it. When did your family buy it?"

"My father bought it in Paris in the nineteen-fifties, from the gallery that represented Chagall. No one else has owned it."

"Well, they had a long list of people who had owned it. And this is Amanda in a blond wig."

Carone studied the photos of Amanda. "It doesn't look like her. That could be anyone."

I didn't show her the ones of Jason and Amanda. I didn't think I had the nerve. "You should call the police."

"Not yet. We don't have the Picasso. And we don't know who is behind this. What about David Chasem?"

"I'd have to go back there. I'm a little reluctant to do that." *I wonder why?*

"And you really think Reggie Souther had nothing to do with it?"

"He didn't do it. He has kids, two little boys. He wouldn't have time. You have to face the facts. You already suspect it's someone with firsthand knowledge of the gallery. Who else, other than Amanda, has that kind of access to the gallery?"

For the first time, as far as I could tell, Carone gave this idea a minute of her time.

"You've met the Goodwins. I've known them all my life. There's no way they could be involved. They're somewhat elderly. You've met Eddy Hansen. He's been such a great help to me, so he's not involved. And then there's Jason. But we're married. It has to be someone else. Those pictures . . . that's not Amanda. It's not her."

"Okay. Let me ask you, what would Hansen gain if your collector found out her Picasso was missing?"

"That's an odd way to put it. He wouldn't gain anything. As I told you, I'd have to ask him to pay the collector. The work in the gallery is insured, but not for mysterious disappearance, as they call it. You must know that. You work in the insurance industry."

I understood that. The exclusion for mysterious disappearance or loss prevented people from stealing their own stuff to collect on a claim.

"Even if the insurance company paid, which they won't, a claim that large would close the gallery. We'd never get insurance again. And without insurance, none of our resale collectors would consign works to the gallery. Income from resale sales is a large part of the gallery's profit. If I had to ask Eddy to pay the collector for her portion of the sale of the Picasso, well, I don't think I could face that. I don't know if he has money enough for that. It's in the millions."

"Would he want to see the gallery close?"

"No. Absolutely not."

"How about your husband? Does he get involved with the operations of the gallery?"

"Why do you ask?"

"Do you get along?"

She gave me a hard look. "Yes. We do."

"I mention it only as an alternative you might have to face. Do you have a prenuptial agreement?"

Carone looked down at her desk. Her hands twitched. "My father insisted on it. Jason doesn't get any of my family's money. Of course, everything the gallery earns is part his, as part of his allowance . . . from my father. So you see, he would want the gallery to do well. He wouldn't steal from it."

"Not unless he planned on selling forged paintings."

"Really! Jason doesn't know anything about art, let alone how to forge it. And—he can have whatever money he needs."

"I need you to look at two other pictures." I opened the ones of Amanda and Jason.

"Where did you get these?" Carone said.

"At the house owned by Norma Talbert, Amanda's mother or sister. Jason and Amanda are posing as Mr. and Mrs. Broder, who brought the copy of the Chagall into the Boulange Gallery. I talked to the neighbor next door and he said Amanda was married to a man named Broder. They don't stay at the house very often. Seems Mr. Broder works in San Francisco and Amanda is rarely home—that's because they're here. I got the address from the Boulange Gallery when the salesman I talked to wasn't looking."

Carone turned her back to me and stood by the window. She didn't say anything for a moment. When she faced me, her eyes had teared up. "You were hired to find the Picasso, not find dirt on my husband. I no longer need your services. Your employment is terminated."

"But what about the Picasso?"

"You're fired. Get out."

CHAPTER FIFTEEN

I stomped out of Carone's office. My face burned. My head ached. My mind raged. The nerve of her! No one had ever fired me before. And no one would ever again, if I could help it.

I removed my belongings from the desk in my office, thankful I got Carone to pay for the round-trip ticket before I left for L.A. Getting reimbursed for it now would have been next to impossible.

I marched down the hall, rushing past the group still working in Patty's office. They were arguing about whose turn it was to do something. They didn't see me open the file room door. I had one last thing to do.

I was about to step inside the file room when the switchboard buzzed. Marny looked up. "Oh, for God's sake. I don't have time to answer that."

"Neither do I," Amanda said.

"Lana," Marny said, "could you please get that?"

"Uh, sure." No reason to tell them Carone had fired me.

I ran to the front desk. I picked up the phone and heard a loud, angry male voice on the other end.

"You broke my contract," he shouted. "I'm going to sue you for . . . ten million dollars. Do you hear me?"

"Who is this?"

"This is Sergio Serrano. You won't get away with this. My lawyers are going to contact your lawyers. I will ruin you. Do you hear me? Ten million dollars. That's what you will pay me.

I'll see to it that—"

"Wait a minute," I yelled. "I don't know what you're talking about. With whom did you wish to speak?"

"You bastards. I'm going to sue you."

I hung up. Who could reason with people like that? Not with the mood I was in.

I went back to the group in Patty's office. "Who in the world is Sergio Serrano?" I asked.

The three of them groaned. "Not him again," Marny said.

"I hung up on him—he started swearing."

"Good for you," Marny said. "He calls every week, threatening to sue us. Carone was going to give him a show, but when she went to his studio to pick out the work, all he had were these sick paintings of gangs torturing and murdering people. Those weren't the paintings he originally showed Carone. She didn't like them and cancelled his show. He couldn't get a show anywhere, so he threatened to get the ACLU on our backs. Why them, I'll never know. Carone wouldn't budge. They weren't the paintings he submitted in his portfolio review, and she didn't want to show them."

"I'll tell Carone he called again," Amanda said. "We're keeping a record. Maybe we can drum up a case of harassment."

"Don't count on it," Clyde said. "He's a nut. I wouldn't want to deal with him, but his work is good. I hope he gets a show somewhere. I don't believe in censorship."

Marny grimaced. "You would say that. Your work has a violent streak in it."

"No, it doesn't. I show reality. Life is violent. And anyway, Carone is putting me in a group show, so she likes my work."

"Censorship has nothing to do with this," Marny said. "Sergio is just after controversy. He thinks it'll make him famous. That's the only reason he painted those things."

I didn't have the time or the inclination to get involved in this discussion. I had more important things to think about. I went to the file room and closed the door. I wrote down Patty's address and phone number, something I should have done earlier. I hoped she was all right.

On my way out of the gallery, I ran into Rodney Bracken. More out of curiosity than anything, I struck up a conversation. "That was a great dinner the other night," I said. I didn't want to use Angelica's funeral as a topic of conversation.

"If you think so," Rodney replied. He seemed anxious to be off.

Still the detective to the end, I didn't want to let him go so fast. I tried again. "I was over at Reggie Souther's the other day. I saw your mural in his office. It was really great."

He brightened a little. "Thanks," he said. "Sorry, I've got to run, love. I'm late for a meeting."

So much for Rodney. It didn't matter. But I had to find out what happened to Patty. If I hadn't told her we were going to look in the stacks together, she wouldn't have gone there by herself—hoping to figure things out before I had a chance to. Because that's what she did. It was too much of a coincidence she left her pen there.

Patty lived on the first floor of a beige, four-unit stucco apartment off Paseo de Papito. Although close to Mrs. Brown's house, Patty lived in a more modest neighborhood. No stately mansions or expensive cars here.

I rang her bell. There was no answer, so I banged on the door. I was about to peek in the front window when the door to the apartment next to Patty's opened. An older lady in a long green velour housecoat stood in the doorway. She was thin and had pink plastic curlers in her gray hair.

"You looking for Patty?" she asked.

"Yes. She didn't show up for work today. She didn't call in

sick. That's not like her."

"No, she wouldn't do that. I'm Cerise, her landlady."

"I'm Lana Davis," I said. "I worked with her at the gallery. Do you suppose we could see if she's all right?"

"Wait. I'll get my keys. I haven't seen her for a few days myself."

Cerise left her door open and went to get her keys. A long delay followed. Finally, she returned.

"Sorry to take so long," Cerise said. "I'm always losing the keys."

She turned the key in Patty's lock. The door was stuck. I pushed on it a little and it opened. "I told the handyman to fix this door," Cerise said. "I hope Patty isn't upset about it."

We found Patty's decomposing body in the bedroom, slumped on the floor, still wearing the clothes I last saw her in. It looked like she dragged herself there. Or someone did. I saw dried blood on her blouse.

"Oh, my God!" Cerise cried. She kept repeating that, like a broken record.

I opened the windows. The smell of rotting flesh overpowered us. I put my arm around Cerise and led her back to her unit.

Cerise went into her bedroom and cried. From her kitchen, I called the police on my cell, speaking softly so Cerise wouldn't hear. "I think she's been shot," I said to the dispatch officer.

Cerise came into the kitchen after I hung up. "Oh, my God," she moaned. "It was the same with old man Halpern. He lived upstairs. I was the one who found him. Poor Patty. I wonder if it was her heart. The way she worked. At her age. She should have retired, but she said the gallery needed her."

I didn't tell her about the dried blood on Patty's blouse. I didn't want her to get hysterical. "Did you hear her come in?"

"No. I have the TV on. I mind my own business. That's why I have tenants. I never give them a reason to leave. I get respectable tenants, so I don't have to check up on them. Such a shame. Makes you think how fragile life is. One minute you're here, the next minute you're not."

I noticed some tins of tea on a shelf above the sink. "Could I make you some tea? How about if I make us both a cup?"

"Oh, I forget myself," Cerise said. "Let me do it. I need to occupy my mind." She picked up two of the tins. "What'll you have?"

"I'll have the herbal, no sugar. Thanks."

"Good for you. Sugar is bad for you."

We drank our tea and waited for the police and the coroner.

Twenty minutes later, a police officer came to the door. I unlocked Patty's apartment. Cerise wasn't up to it. I stood outside, while several officers and others in white coats went in. Sometime after, they took Patty's body out in a body bag. By then, the whole neighborhood stood around to see what had happened.

Detective Seastrom of Homicide was the one who questioned me. "Your name sounds familiar," he said. "So you work at the same place?" His blue-gray eyes scrutinized my face, as if he expected me to lie to him. He was about my age and good-looking in a rugged kind of way. His dour expression told me daily contact with crime and tragedy had left its mark on him.

"Yes, I do. I told you about Angelica Ortiz—that I believed she pretended not to know the address I was looking for. I'm a guest at the Zimoro Hotel where she worked."

"You also reported a man shot at you on Calle Fernando. And now you found Patty Sanders. Do you make it a habit to find crime?"

"No. It just—look, Patty is someone I happened to work with at the Merryweather Galleries. Angelica Ortiz was the concierge at the hotel where I'm staying. I'm from L.A. I'm here on a temporary job."

"Weren't you looking for a missing heir too, for an inheritance? How many jobs do you have?"

"I came here to find Antonio Chavez. He's the missing heir, also known as Lefty Chavez. And he was Angelica Ortiz's boyfriend. I saw him at the funeral, but he ran away when I called his name. Her murder and the fact that he ran away—I think they're connected."

Lieutenant Seastrom stared at me. "So how many jobs do you have?" he asked.

"I had two, but now just one. I don't work at the gallery anymore. They were both part-time." Concurrently, but he needn't know that. "I think Antonio Chavez knew something about his girlfriend's murder. Angelica Ortiz referred customers to the Merryweather Galleries. They're all connected."

The lieutenant nodded. "Santa Fe is a small town, so I'm not surprised. Do you know who might want to shoot Patty Sanders?"

"No. But I found her pen in the gallery's stacks—where they store the paintings in the gallery. Some paintings were missing from the gallery. Carone Merryweather hired me to figure out who took them. You'll have to talk to Carone for more information because, as I said, I don't work there anymore. I think Patty Sanders was killed because she caught someone stealing another painting."

"Oh. And what painting was this?"

"I don't know."

"And why do you think Ms. Ortiz was killed?"

"All I know is when they put her in the ambulance, I noticed the diamond locket she wore was missing. I told the police that when they took her to the hospital. Maybe she was killed for that."

"Thank you, ma'am."

"I think Patty's death is related to the thefts in the gallery," I said. "If we can find the missing painting, we can find her killer."

His quick stare made it clear he didn't appreciate my advice. "You need to let us handle this, ma'am."

"I just think you should find out if anything is missing from the gallery."

"Thanks. I may do that." He turned around and went into Cerise's apartment. I followed him in and said goodbye to Cerise. She had started crying again and managed only a feeble wave to me.

Detective Seastrom stopped me as I left Cerise's apartment. He asked me for my address and phone number, though the police already had it. "If you think of anything else, call me." He handed me his card.

Once I was back in my car, my calm demeanor gave way. I put my head on the steering wheel, overwhelmed with grief, but I couldn't cry. It was my fault Patty had died. I never should have told her anything.

I must have been sitting there for a long time because Detective Seastrom tapped on the window. "Ms. Davis, are you all right?"

I don't remember how I made it back to the hotel, but the next day I woke up at eleven. The maid had come. I forgot to put the do not disturb sign on the door. The only thing she didn't change was the bed, because I was in it.

I jumped into the shower, feeling like I had a giant hangover. Patty was dead and I was to blame. How could I have let this happen? I should have been there for her. I made such a big deal about not going through the stacks alone. But that's what we both did, only she ended up dead.

I got dressed and made myself a cup of coffee. I opened my door and grabbed my complimentary copy of *The New Mexican*.

Patty's murder was a small article on the third page. She'd

been shot in the chest. She was sixty-seven years old. The police had no suspects. The article mentioned the gallery and Cerise. It didn't mention me, or any stolen painting or possible motive for her murder.

I flipped through the paper. One article almost floored me. Chasem was bad news, but not in the way I had thought. The police had seized almost a half a million, street value, of cocaine from Chasem's house. The police shot Chasem and another man in a gun battle. Chasem sustained minor injuries, but the other man died. No wonder Chasem was annoyed with my visit. He must have decided to go along with my hoax rather than risk exposure by telling me to leave. I was lucky to get out of his house alive.

If I had watched the news on TV, something I rarely did, I could have already told Lieutenant Seastrom about Chasem's connection to the gallery. Now when I called him I got his voice mail. I left a message, saying I had important news.

With nothing else to do, I stayed in my room. I didn't have any leads on Antonio. Everything had reached a dead end. Around two o'clock I ordered lunch from room service. I didn't want to run into Darlene. Thirty minutes later, I munched on romaine and tuna salad. The food had a way of making things better, but it couldn't fix Patty's death.

I finished eating and turned on the TV. Then I turned it off. I didn't know what to do with myself. The phone rang. I grabbed it on the first ring. I thought it was Detective Seastrom.

It was Carone.

"I just found out about Patty. The police have been over here, asking questions. Just what did you tell them?"

I told her what I said to the detective.

"Well, don't volunteer any more information. I don't want the gallery hurt by this."

"Don't you care what happened to Patty? Maybe she was

killed because she found out who was stealing from the gallery."

"Amanda and my husband aren't murderers, if that's what you're thinking."

"I'm not talking about them. I don't think they stole the Picasso. I think it was someone else. I think Patty figured out who."

"You don't know that. And there's nothing to link Patty's death with the gallery."

"There will be when I tell the police about David Chasem." I read her the article about his arrest and told her I found Patty's pen in the stacks. "Chasem may have put her body in his car and brought her back to her apartment."

"How would he have known where she lived?"

"Maybe he didn't kill her until he took her out of the gallery—drove her home and killed her."

"You're making this up. Her death has nothing to do with the gallery. When are you coming in?"

"I'll pick up my check tomorrow. I think you were supposed to pay me on the spot, when you fired me."

"That's not what I mean, but I have your check. I'm sorry I blew up at you. I've been under a lot of pressure with the auction and—the Picasso. The collector wants to see the painting when we install the show. We're showing it during the auction, even though it's not part of it. I have to hang it by opening night. I need you to keep working on finding it."

"You fired me."

"I'm sorry. I need you to come back."

"Well, if you're going to hire me back, you can't withhold information from me. That includes information about Eddy Hansen or your husband."

"Amanda no longer works here. I fired her. What do you want to know about Eddy?"

"I'm not sure. Just don't hold back. What about your husband?"

"He doesn't know anything."

"But he and Amanda are the Broders. They took the Chagall."

"That's no longer an issue. I need to find the Picasso. Jason doesn't know anything."

"All right. But why didn't you tell me you knew Angelica Ortiz and Lefty Chavez were seeing each other? Now she's dead."

Carone didn't answer. "Are you still there?" I said.

"Yes. I'm here. So they knew each other. I don't get involved in the private lives of my staff. When are you coming in?"

"I'll let you know."

CHAPTER SIXTEEN

I called Detective Seastrom again. This time he was in. "I got your message," he said. "How can I help you?"

I told him about Chasem. Seastrom thanked me for the information, but didn't seem impressed by it.

"Aren't you going to question him?" I asked. "He may have killed Patty Sanders and stolen a painting."

"We have no evidence the victim was anywhere near the Merryweather Galleries when she was killed. Most likely, where she worked had nothing to do with her death. But thank you for your information."

I sensed rather than heard the sarcasm in his voice. What did he know? And what was it about this town that made everyone so dense? Even if Chasem didn't kill Patty, I knew her death had something to do with the gallery. I just couldn't prove it.

So what else could I work on, now that Carone had hired me back? I looked into Clyde's background and observed Rodney at Carone's house. And nothing came up. Maybe it was time to zero in on Bentley. I wouldn't have picked him as the criminal type, but the most unlikely people committed crimes.

I drove to the gallery, parked in the adjacent lot of the Mexican restaurant and waited. I didn't want to go into the gallery and deal with Carone right then. I wanted her to think I wasn't coming back. To make her sweat a little.

I'd get my check from her later—maybe put some of it in a bank. Getting fired, when it actually happened, freaked me out—like a wake-up call. I lived too close to the edge. Other than the small retirement account I had at First Century, if *they* fired me, I had few resources to fall back on. So finding Antonio was my first priority. But without leads, I didn't know where to turn. Carone's job would have to keep me busy until I did.

At five, Bentley came out the back door of the gallery. I had no trouble following him because he drove his BMW as if in slow motion. I had to stop several times to let him get ahead of me.

Bentley went straight home. He had a large two-story house, built in the Santa Fe style, which meant it had a wooden, flat roof with exposed wood beams. Since coming here, I discovered the great distinction between an adobe house made of adobe bricks, and one made of stucco to look like adobe. People frowned on stucco in Santa Fe. They considered an adobe house as the more authentic version of the Santa Fe style. Only mass-produced houses were made of stucco—and untrendy people lived in them. Bentley's house made the grade. Like Carone's, it was a real adobe.

In the next two hours, I learned Bentley led a boring life after work. Through his open window blinds, I observed him watching TV and eating something from a bowl. It looked like leftover pasta. None of that proved anything. Many a thief lived in boredom and ate on the cheap before committing his next crime. Where I got that bit of wisdom, I didn't know. I'd never investigated any thieves before. It just seemed to fit.

I didn't want to eliminate Bentley as a suspect, but I did get tired of waiting for something to happen. So I drove to the gallery to look up his income. I went in the back door and disengaged the alarm.

His file showed he made forty thousand dollars at the gallery last year and his year-to-date income was thirty-five thousand. Since this was the end of July, if he continued making sales with the same momentum, he would do better this year. But on an income like this, could Bentley afford such a grand house? His background report didn't state his marital status. Maybe he had a rich wife. Next time I saw him, I'd look at his ring finger.

After I put Bentley's file back in the file cabinet, I thought I heard a noise. It sounded like it came from the stacks—as if a painting fell over. The place had seemed empty when I came in. I should have made sure of that. Not very smart of me.

I grabbed a metal letter opener, to use if I needed to defend myself, and tiptoed into the stacks. I switched on the lights, but I didn't see anyone. I started to go through the rooms when I heard someone running. I ducked into the broom closet, holding the door open a crack.

A moment later, someone shoved that door against me. I heard the bolt sliding across the latch, locking me in. I was stuck in here—again. I didn't know whether to scream or pretend I wasn't here.

Not to worry. A loud noise startled me into keeping quiet. Scuffling noises and things knocking about followed. A man grunted. A shot rang out. I heard a faint moan.

Someone came by the closet and rattled the latch. I held my breath. The rattling stopped and the person walked away. A door slammed, and then silence.

I waited until the quiet seemed normal. Then I grabbed a mop and pounded the door with the end of it. The door flew open, almost coming off its hinges. In my haste to free myself, I almost tripped over something. I looked down and screamed

Clyde Posten lay on the floor in a puddle of blood, dead. He had been one of my prime suspects, and now he had a bullet in his chest.

I called the police. Soon the place swarmed with them. The paramedics covered Clyde with a sheet and zipped him into a body bag. An officer escorted me out of the gallery. I was in a daze. I knew Patty better than I knew Clyde. But Clyde's death devastated me even more than Patty's.

I didn't like Clyde. He once told me he minded his own business, inferring I should do the same. So why did he come to the gallery after hours? People always gave advice they never took themselves. This was one time he should have heeded his own words.

Although I hated to admit it—it seemed inhuman—but in dying, Clyde had left me with fewer suspects to choose from, and, in this case, that wasn't a good thing. I didn't have anyone else. Other than Chasem, who was now in jail, Clyde fit the description of a criminal better than Bentley or Rodney did. Clyde had a creepy side. He had leered at me, a past employer had suspicions about him, and he didn't mind violence, at least in art, according to what he said about Sergio Serrano's paintings.

In the parking lot, I saw Detective Seastrom. "Well, look who's here. You seem to have a knack for finding dead bodies," he said.

If he meant to inject humor into this situation, I didn't laugh. "They were all people I knew." I started to say more, but my brain froze and I couldn't speak.

The detective's stern look softened. "You've got to admit it's a strange coincidence. Didn't you say you no longer worked here?"

I found my voice. "The owner asked me to come back."

"What were you doing here after hours? Doesn't this place close at five?"

"I needed to look something up in the files. I heard a noise in the back—I went to see what it was."

"What was it you needed to look up in the files?"

"Something about one of the employees. As I once told you, Carone Merryweather hired me to help find a stolen painting.

That's why I'm working here."

"We don't have a report on any stolen paintings. The owner of the gallery never referred to them when we questioned her. She said you were a part-time employee. That's all."

"I'm not supposed to say anything. But two people have been murdered."

"Just don't leave town. We may need to ask you for more information."

"I want to help, if I can. Whoever killed Clyde Posten had a key to the gallery."

"And did the victim know you were going to be here?"

"No. I just decided to come here. But someone on the staff, or someone who knows them, killed Clyde. You might want to look at the personnel files."

With reluctance, the detective let me show him the employee files. "That should do it," Detective Seastrom said. "We can take it from here. You should go home now."

I didn't realize how exhausted I was. "What about Carone Merryweather?" I didn't want to break the news of Clyde's death to her.

"As I said, we'll take it from here. Thank you for your co-operation. And by the way, next time don't stick around after hours. You might get hurt."

I wished Clyde had been here to get that same advice. "Thanks, I'll remember that." Despite Detective Seastrom's mockery, I knew he was right.

Marny and Rodney were at the front desk when I came in. They looked downcast. I had read the article in *The New Mexican* this morning. In a police statement, Carone claimed Clyde associated with unsavory people and that she had warned him not to have them in the gallery. While expressing sorrow for Clyde's death, Carone insisted his murder had nothing to do with the gallery. Damage control was in full swing here. The article didn't mention me by name, just that a part-time employee had found the body. I was safe. Charley would never know, but I didn't feel like celebrating.

"I guess you heard about Clyde," I said.

Rodney's eyes were red. "Really sad, love. I liked him."

"Yeah," Marny said. "It's shocking."

"Nobody knew he was hanging around addicts," Rodney said.

"Is that what it was?" I said.

Marny nodded. "Carone said she warned him. She gave him another chance, but I guess he didn't listen. We didn't know anything about it."

"I thought I knew him, but I guess I didn't," Rodney said. "Well, I'm handling the funeral arrangements, since there's no one else."

"What about Patty's funeral?" I asked.

"Her family is having her body sent to Florida. They're going to have the funeral there," Marny said.

"So sad," Rodney murmured. "I don't care what anyone says, I always liked Patty. Well, my lovelies, I guess I'll be off."

"Rodney," Marny said. "If you need some help . . ."

"I'll be all right, love. By the way, what happened? Carone said you found him."

"I—don't—exactly know," I stammered. "I heard a noise and called out, but no one answered. I got scared—I was alone—I hid in the broom closet. Then someone locked me in. It may have been Clyde . . . before he was killed. I thought I heard fighting. Maybe Clyde saw me and locked me in—to protect me."

It sounded plausible. Otherwise, why lock a closet door? Unless the killer did that, to make sure Clyde didn't have a hiding place. I didn't know what to believe. Poor Clyde.

Marny and Rodney stared at me.

"Wow," Marny said. "What made you come to the gallery at that time?"

"Yes, love. Why were you here? You could have gotten yourself killed."

"I know that . . . now. I forgot some files I was working on . . . I heard a noise in the stacks and peeked in. Uh, is Carone here?"

"This isn't a good time to see her," Rodney said. "After Clyde . . ."

"I'm not going to bother her. I just need a few minutes."

A few minutes to find out what happened to . . . my mind went blank. What was I supposed to do? Okay, I could ask her about Amanda and Jason. If Amanda was no longer working here, did that mean Jason was no longer with Carone?

"I've got to be going," Rodney said. "Take care, my lovelies."

Rodney left by the front door. He must not have planned to stay long, or he would have parked in the back.

"If Carone isn't in her office, she and Bentley are probably in the stacks. That's where she said to transfer her calls," Marny said. She leaned forward on the reception counter. "Are you here to pick up your last check? Did you quit already?"

"No, why?" Did she hear Carone talk me into staying?

"I know if I quit, I'll have Carone mail my last paycheck. The way things go around here, I don't think it's safe to stay around for it. You must be horrified. I would be if I found someone dead. I mean, I didn't like Patty or Clyde, but—"

"I feel terrible about both of them. I did like Patty. It's hard to believe they're both . . . dead."

"I'm sorry. I shouldn't have brought it up," Marny said. "But at a time like this, you've got to think of yourself, Lana." She gave me a conspiring look. "Don't tell anyone, but I'm not going to be here much longer."

"You found something else? Where?"

"I can't say yet. I'll let you know."

"Is Carone going to put the fire on your record?"

"That wasn't my fault. Someone took one of my cigarettes and stuffed it in that wastebasket. I put my cigarette out."

"But you did walk into that room, didn't you?"

"Bentley saw me go in there with a cigarette, so I couldn't deny it. I know there's no smoking here, but I didn't start any fire."

"Why did you go in there?"

"I was just curious. Amanda complained that the front desk was too noisy for her to get any work done. Of course, she and Jason just wanted a room to themselves. And Patty . . . let her get away with it."

"It's hard to believe Patty would put up with that."

"Jason told her he needed to dictate some letters to Amanda—some new project he wanted to start for the gallery. That's a lie. He never works in the gallery. But what could Patty say? Jason's married to the boss."

"So what did you find out?"

"Nothing. They weren't in the room when I walked in. It would have looked strange if they locked the door, so they didn't. But someone stole my silver cigarette case out of my desk drawer. It was expensive too. Art Deco—I bought it in an antique shop. Someone must have taken it when I walked into the back office. It's no use accusing anyone. Everyone thinks I started the fire because I'm the only one who smokes. The firemen found traces of a cigarette in the wastebasket. It *was* my cigarette. But I *never* smoked it."

"Someone wanted to make it look like you started the fire. But why?"

Marny snickered. "Someone who didn't want me to find out something."

"Amanda and Jason?" I whispered.

"You didn't hear it from me."

"How long were you in the back office?"

"I wasn't in there very long, before everyone smelled the fire, maybe ten, fifteen minutes later. I didn't smell smoke when I was in there. And I didn't light my cigarette. I was on my way out to smoke it in the alley. I smoked it and went back inside."

"But you left your cigarette case in your drawer?"

"I did. I didn't think anyone would take it."

"So you went straight back to your office after you came in?"

"No, I—why are you asking me these questions? I feel like I'm getting the third degree."

"I'm just trying to be helpful. Two people have been murdered. Maybe if you go over everything, you'll remember something that could be important. It sounds like someone took one of your cigarettes and set the back office on fire."

"I guess you're right. I think I went into the break room to make a call—I didn't want anyone to hear me. I didn't want to talk in the parking lot. Too noisy out there. I never knew when Patty would walk into my office. She was always checking up on me. It's weird to think she's dead. She was never nice to me. But I didn't want her to die."

"I know. Did you see her when you went into the break room?"

"No. I didn't see anyone. If I were you, I'd get out before—"

"I hear you. Well, let me know where you end up."

"I will. You're brave to want to talk to Carone today. I'm staying out of her way. What do you think she and Bentley are looking for?"

"It could have been a robbery. Maybe there's a painting missing."

"Somehow I doubt that. I don't think drug addicts are into art."

I shrugged. "You never know."

"I wouldn't go into the stacks. Wandering around this place makes me nervous."

"Carone and Bentley are there. Nothing can happen."

"I guess. Safety in numbers."

But Marny's recollections got me wondering. Had Amanda or Jason set the fire to cover up their real activities—like stealing another painting? If so, why didn't they take anything? Did Amanda fake her reaction to the smoke? She didn't want to go to a hospital. Well, regardless, I didn't think Marny started the fire.

On my way to the stacks, I noticed Carone's door was open. She wasn't there, so I went in and looked around. I clicked her computer mouse, taking it out of the screensaver mode. An image of an amazing-looking realistic landscape painting displayed on the monitor, done in a style similar to the old master painters of the Renaissance. I scrolled the mouse on the image. Donald Walker was the artist.

"Lana?"

I looked up to see Carone staring at me. I moved away from her desk. "I wanted to talk to you. I noticed the paintings on your screen. What an incredible artist. I just—"

"I didn't know we were meeting today. I have to run an errand."

Somehow, I couldn't picture Carone running errands. It must have showed on my face.

"I need to put some money in the account—for the gallery. I make those deposits myself, Lana."

"Oh. I'm sorry about Clyde."

"Yes. The police told me you were there."

"The newspaper article said—"

"That was a cover. Marny and Rodney—"

"I know. They told me. Clyde was into drugs. Poor Clyde."

"I had to say that. I can't have anyone thinking the gallery is involved. Now tell me what happened."

"I don't know. I think Clyde locked me into the broom closet. I heard fighting and a shot. When I got out, he was on the floor. Dead. What about Amanda? You said she no longer works for you."

"She's . . . I don't want to discuss it. Amanda had nothing to do with it. I fired her. Insubordination. I caught her rifling through my desk."

Insubordination? Carone believed what she wanted to believe, regardless of the truth staring at her in the face. "Carone, two people are dead. Maybe more. Max Beely could have been killed for the same reason as Clyde and Patty—"

"It's not your concern. Max—he was a handyman. He didn't know anything about art."

Or maybe he just found himself in the wrong place at the wrong time.

"When I get back," Carone continued, "you can help Bentley and me check the stacks. We need to make sure nothing is missing. And don't come into my office when I'm not here. In the meantime, sit in your office and look busy."

Look busy. I laughed to myself. How many times had I sat at my desk at First Century Life, trying to look busy when I was daydreaming about something else? If Charley could see me now.

CHAPTER SEVENTEEN

Fifteen minutes into my look-busy assignment, I got bored. Having someone tell me to look busy, instead of thinking of that on my own, took the fun out of it. I got so bored I dozed off.

My office phone rang, jolting me from my nap.

"Lana. How've you been?"

"Darlene. Hi. Hey, I'm kind of busy right now. I'll have to call you back."

"Please, just tell me you got me an invitation to the auction."

"Darlene, haven't you heard the news?"

"About the guy getting shot? Yeah, I heard. But the gallery is still having the auction. It would be great if you could introduce me to Carone. Come over tonight. I'll show you my work. We can go to El Casita afterward. It's a great club. Maybe Tyler will be there."

"I—"

"Come on. After ten, you can get in for free. They have a good band tonight. I want you to see my work. It's perfect for Carone."

Maybe I did need some fun, and the music would drown out Darlene's constant demand for an auction ticket. I didn't know whether I'd even be here for the auction. But with my concussion, was I up for loud music? I'd have to see, minute by minute. I hadn't thought of Tyler in a while. After the deaths of Patty and Clyde, I hadn't thought of much else.

Carone stopped in, having come back from the bank. "I need

you in the stacks," she said.

I hung up from Darlene, cutting her off in mid-sentence because she kept talking even when I said I had to go, and followed Carone.

Carone, Bentley and I picked through the stacks. A very slow process the way they did it. At the rate we were going, we'd be here all night.

Suddenly, Bentley called out, "What have we here? The Modigliani is in the wrong spot. Someone screwed up. They put it where a Zalez should have been."

"Well, that's great," Carone said. She took the painting from him. "The number on the back corresponds to the right number on the chart, but it's the wrong painting. You're right. It should have been the Zalez."

Carone held up the Modigliani, and we paused to admire it. The elegant woman in the painting, with her elongated neck and almond-shaped eyes, looked back at us as if surprised by the fuss we made over her. I once saw a movie about Modigliani. Considered one of the greats, he didn't live long. His paintings were rare, especially since, as the story went, he destroyed many of them before his death.

Carone checked where the Modigliani should have been and found a Klatzen. She found the Zalez where the Klatzen should have been. "What a big mess this is," she said.

"I'm sure Marny is responsible for this one," Bentley said. "She screwed me up last week on a painting I needed. She had it misplaced."

"I did not." Marny stood in the doorway. "And I didn't put the Modigliani back. Patty insisted on doing that. So if it's not in the right place, it's not my fault."

"I thought you were at the front desk," Carone said.

"I was, but I went to my office for another cup of coffee. I thought maybe you could use some help. Anyway, I always put everything back in its rightful place. I'm a professional."

"Oh, I forgot," Bentley said. "You're the professional around here."

"Please, let's not argue about it. Marny, I need you at the front desk. I don't like leaving the gallery unattended."

Marny left. But the smirk on her face showed she thought she had won this argument. So much for her being too nervous to wander around this place. Had she shown up to make sure no one discovered any of her thefts? Or to find out whether we found the Modigliani, because she tried and couldn't? Or maybe Patty had put it in the wrong spot.

We didn't discover any other misplaced paintings, or missing ones. After we finished in the stacks, Carone let us go home. She closed the gallery for the rest of the day. Whether to give her employees time to mourn, or because staying open after an employee died here made her look uncaring, I didn't know.

Poor Clyde. He didn't have the best reputation, and his death further soiled it. Just like Carone to make him the fall guy.

Carone laughed. "Lana, you've got to be kidding. Bentley's harmless. Go home, already. Come on, I want to lock my office."

Maybe, or maybe not. Other than the tiff with Marny and the misplaced Modigliani, Bentley hadn't said much while we worked in the stacks. He never said anything about Patty or Clyde. Carone did, murmuring how sorry she was. Even Marny talked about it, and she hadn't been at the gallery as long as Bentley had. Yet Bentley had worked with them for some time and seemed to get along with them.

Maybe I quit my surveillance of Bentley too soon. While I was looking up his records in the file room, he could have driven to the gallery. It wouldn't have taken him long. Did Bentley overpower Clyde and shoot him? Did he knock me out and push me into the closet the day I started working here? He was the first person I saw when I came out. But would he have told us where the Modigliani was if he was the killer? Was it a co-incidence that Marny appeared just when Bentley discovered where the Modigliani was? Bentley and Marny didn't get along, but was that a ruse?

"Well, how does he afford such an expensive house? Not on the salary he earns here, I bet."

"Lana, he's an artist. His paintings do quite well. He could exist on those sales alone if he lived in a less expensive place."

I hadn't thought of that. Both he and Rodney made only part of their incomes from the gallery.

Although I didn't expect Carone to put stock into anything I said, I gave her my take on the Modigliani. "It could be the next painting stolen."

"How did you come to that conclusion?"

"It's valuable and rare."

"I'm having a security company install another alarm system tomorrow. It's not going to be a problem."

"But Carone, who else knows you have a Modigliani? Does it belong to you, or to someone else?"

This time Carone considered what I said. "A collector brought it in the week before you got here. I showed it in the resale gallery for a few days."

That did it for me. Money or not, Carone was either too lax or too stupid for me to work for. "I hope your new security system works out," I said. "But I can't do this. I'm sorry. You fired me and now I quit."

"What? We have a contract. You can't quit."

"Then sue me. Three people are dead."

"Only two."

"I can't believe you said that. Even one person killed is one too many. And yes, three people are dead. Angelica Ortiz knew

Lefty Chavez. He disappeared—I saw him at her funeral and he ran off—too scared to show his face after his girlfriend was killed. He has a connection to your gallery. She was his girlfriend and she referred people here. So yes, three people are dead. This job isn't worth my life."

"Please," Carone pleaded. "Just hold on. I've got to find the Picasso."

"You need to tell the police the truth."

"I will. Just give me a little more time."

"All right. I guess the gallery is safe until you install the new security system. I wouldn't think the killer would come back today. Not with the police watching this place."

"Yes. They've been all over here this morning. Why can't they figure out who killed Patty and Clyde?"

"Because you won't tell them what's going on. You're giving them false leads."

"I've given them as much information as they need. I can't destroy everything I've worked for."

"But Carone—" A noise at the front door startled me. "Shh."

"What was that? I thought Marny locked up," Carone whispered.

The apologetic face of Herbie Sloan appeared in the doorway of Carone's office. "Knock, knock," he said. "I hope I'm not interrupting."

I took a deep breath, thankful Herbie and not someone more sinister had walked in.

"I just wanted to say how sorry I was about Clyde. Is there anything I can do?" Herbie said.

"No, but thank you, Herbie," Carone said. "Actually, uh—"

"I understand a Modigliani was misplaced. I didn't know you had one. Lucky the murderer didn't find it. I mean, that would have made things worse. A murder and a theft. A murder is bad enough. It's sad about Clyde—I didn't know him, but a theft on top of—"

Carone sighed. "Yes, yes. I understand."

"How did you know about the Modigliani?" I asked.

Herbie didn't acknowledge me. Well, I supposed I deserved that.

"Imagine, a Modigliani," he exclaimed. "They're so rare. I'd like to see it. Is it going—"

"Yes, how did you know about it?" Carone said.

"Marny told me. I saw Bentley and her in the parking lot. Was it something I wasn't supposed to know? I didn't mean to say anything."

"It doesn't matter," Carone said. "But I'd appreciate it if you didn't mention it to anyone else."

I left the gallery after Herbie trapped Carone into looking at the small portfolio he had under his arm. I almost wanted to see what kind of work he did, but I hated to think he could be talented.

I saw Rodney in the parking lot, sitting in his car.

"Carone closed the gallery for the day," I said.

"I know. I talked to Marny before she left. I made the arrangements. Clyde didn't have a family. How awful that must have been for you—to find him. I'm having a hard time with this," Rodney said.

"I'm so sorry."

Rodney looked like he had lost a good friend. Clyde even went into the stacks to rescue him from the fire. I was wrong about Rodney, the way I was wrong about Clyde.

Although the memory of Clyde's blood on the floor made me queasy, talking about him might help us both. I didn't know much about Rodney and this would be an opportunity to find out what I didn't know. I hadn't seen this side of him before.

He valued his friends more than he valued his love interests.

"I guess I should have broken the closet door down sooner—it's amazing what strength you can have—but I was terrified. The paramedics thought Clyde died almost instantly. They couldn't have saved him no matter how soon they got there."

"He was like a brother to me. You must have some idea of who did it. I'd like to go after the bastard myself. Did you see anyone? Did you hear him call out a name?"

"No," I said. "I wouldn't try to avenge Clyde's death, if I were you. Let the police handle it. You don't want to end up like Clyde."

"I know. But the police—humph. You can wait forever for them. It's weird. Patty and Clyde murdered within days of each other." He stared at me and then looked away, as if his emotions got the better of him.

"I don't know if their deaths are related."

Rodney looked thoughtful. "Maybe they are. I wish I knew. I'd like to get my hands on the guy who did this. Do you think there was more than one person?"

"I don't know. I was so freaked out I didn't hear how many people were in the gallery—when it happened."

"Do you think it's safe to work in the gallery after this? I hate to desert Carone—I'm going to have a show here soon . . . I don't know what to do."

"I can't help you there. Do what you think is best."

"Well, take care, love." As an afterthought, he added, "I hate to leave Carone with Herbie—I saw him drive in—but I have to be going."

"Is Herbie always like this?"

"He has his good side," he said. "Unfortunately, it rarely shows."

CHAPTER EIGHTEEN

And after getting fired and quitting, I was still working for Carone. No matter what she said, I didn't see her going to the police with the truth. If I threatened to tell her father and Eddy about her bad investments and the missing Picasso, they'd close ranks around her and oust me. I had to find another angle.

But not tonight. Darlene caught me in a weak moment when I agreed to see her work and go to El Casita with her. In the meantime, an early dinner awaited me. One without Darlene.

I went to Taxco, fast becoming my favorite place. I needed quiet, and this place provided it. I stretched my legs and spaced out. After the waitress took my order, someone tapped me on the shoulder. "Oh, Lieutenant Seastrom. What a surprise." He was in jeans and a T-shirt.

"Even cops get time off. Find any more dead bodies today?"

"No. And that's not funny. Is this an official visit, or can I ask you to leave?"

Seastrom smiled. "I'm sorry. Don't get mad, Davis."

"Davis? Should I take that as a sign of friendship?" Seastrom didn't put much stock in anything I said, and now he wanted to be friends. What a smart aleck.

"We keep running into each other, and Ms. Davis sounds so formal. I'm Mike."

"You already know, I'm Lana."

"Aren't you going to ask me to sit down?" he said.

"Go ahead. Ruin my day." I said it with a smile, but I meant it.

He sat across from me. "I'm out for a nice evening meal. I'm friendly."

He called the waitress and asked for a menu. We sat in silence while he looked it over. He signaled the waitress and she took his order. "Would you like a beer?" he said.

"No, thanks. I'll stick to my diet soda."

"So, are you still working at the Merryweather Galleries?" he asked. "Did you ever find the painting you were looking for?"

"Well, you finally believe me then."

Mike smiled. He didn't look too bad when he did that. "I never said I didn't believe you. I just didn't want you mixed up in anything dangerous. Did you find your missing heir?"

"Not yet." I had a horde of questions I wanted to ask him. Did he know who killed Patty and Clyde? Was Angelica's murder linked to theirs? But I didn't ask them, knowing he wouldn't give me any answers, even if he had them.

The waitress came with our dinners. "This place is a find," I said.

"The locals like it. Good food."

We ate and talked. He wasn't bad company.

"What puzzles me," he said, "is how you got involved with a place like the Merryweather Galleries. You don't act like the rest of them."

I laughed. "You mean, what's a nice person like me doing in a place like that?" I laughed again. "I ask myself that every day."

"It's just they all seem so superficial."

I took that as a compliment. "I guess they can't help it. Art is a strange business, I'm finding out. So tell me, why did you become a police officer?"

"It runs in the family. My family came from Detroit, where my father was a cop. My uncle was a cop too. He was killed on

duty when I was a kid. I guess I wanted to be in law enforce-
ment like them."

"I'm sorry about your uncle."

"Thanks."

"Were you the officer who went to Calle Fernando and talked
to George, the caretaker there? He's the old man who shot at
me. If so, thanks. He changed his attitude after that."

Seastrom smiled. "I assigned that to another officer. But I'm
glad we could help."

When we finished eating, he left some money on the table for
his tab. "Remember, if you need help, call me."

"Sure. But why the change of heart? When I've called you
before, you thought of me as more of a pest than anything."

"How can you say that? You seem like someone who could
use a little help. If you're looking into a problem at the gallery,
we want to know about it."

"I'll keep that in mind."

He walked me out of the restaurant. In fact, he walked me to
the hotel. Then he said goodnight.

Did he think this was a date? The idea didn't entirely repel
me. But dating a cop? I had to think about that.

I didn't want to deal with Darlene's paintings. I had learned
about symbolism and composition in my art appreciation class,
but my brain forgot most of it.

"Darlene, can I come over another time to see your work? I'd
love to, but my mind is on overload—with all the work at the
gallery. I'd rather see it when I'm fresh. Besides, my specialty
isn't uh . . . contemporary art. It's uh . . . well, it's not contemporary."

I knew from reading the gallery's literature that contemporary
meant the work of living artists. At least I got that right. I didn't
remember what kind of art my specialty was. Carone never told

me. But I was supposed to be working on a show of the modern masters. Those were the dead ones, as Darlene put it. So maybe that was it. Another reason not to see Darlene's work. She was bound to ask about the show I was working on. And I didn't have a clue.

"I understand," Darlene said. "Just introduce me to Carone. She's going to love my work."

"Sure. I'll introduce you." Why not? One way to get back at Carone for firing me. Sic Darlene on her.

I arrived at El Casita at ten, and looked for Darlene in the crowd. I hadn't done any serious socializing since Tyler's party. He never called to see how I was. That kind of fit. A Santa Fe flake. He drank too much anyway.

I saw Darlene across the room, already engaged in conversation with a few people. The band had taken a break, so I called out her name. But the idea of traipsing through the crowd to get to her gave my sore head a bigger headache.

She didn't hear me. Then I spotted Tyler. He was talking to somebody.

Rodney.

Oh, no. How did Tyler know Rodney? Then again, why wouldn't he? They were both artists. And in Santa Fe, everyone knew everyone. But I didn't remember seeing Rodney at Tyler's party.

I had to get out of here. I wanted to grab Darlene and get her out too. I didn't want her asking Tyler about me, with Rodney standing next to him.

But so far, so good. The place was packed and Darlene seemed too busy to notice Tyler. The band started playing. Loud, but not bad. If I didn't have a headache, I might have enjoyed it.

Darlene drifted off with a few people. She never said anything about Rodney when I told her I worked for the Merryweather

Galleries. Tyler knew I was looking for Antonio, if he remembered. Maybe it was nothing. Tyler drank a lot, and he had no reason to mention Antonio's name to Rodney, if he even remembered it.

All the same, I left El Casita. Maybe I was just paranoid. It wasn't that big a deal to have another job unrelated to my work as a curator. Freelance curating didn't pay a lot. And why not apply for a job at the gallery where I thought the missing heir worked? That seemed reasonable. Or maybe, like Carone, I wanted to believe what suited me.

I learned I could wake up with a hangover without having had a drink the night before. Concussions were like that. I texted Darlene the next morning, saying I had gone home because I felt sick. She didn't know about my concussion. An hour later, I got a text back. She had a great time. She saw Tyler there, but didn't get to talk to him. She met a guy named Drake.

Rodney didn't make it into the text. I wondered what Rodney and Tyler talked about. Since Tyler never followed up with me, I wanted to assume he had other things to contemplate.

I went to my follow-up appointment with Dr. Saver. So much had happened since I saw him last. Three murders. I wondered what he'd think of that.

I didn't tell Dr. Saver my woes. And he didn't tell me anything I didn't already know. Take it easy. Don't strain yourself, and get plenty of rest. Not bad advice. If I had been in L.A., I wouldn't have needed a concussion to follow those orders. Being the slacker I was, it came naturally. But in Santa Fe, despite a concussion and the high altitude, which Dr. Saver said contributed to my headache, I couldn't sit idle anymore. Maybe a conk on the head and finding murder victims had changed me.

On my way out of the doctor's office, I saw Jason Nichols

walking to his car. He carried a shopping bag under his arm from some store. There he was, spending more of his allowance from Carone's family, or from his divorce settlement. I didn't know which.

He didn't see me. So, as they said in classic films, follow that car.

He drove a maroon Mercedes. Would I ever find out who drove the black one?

I tailed Jason to a modest neighborhood. A little too funky for his tastes, I thought. Was this a trip down memory lane for him? Had he come from humble beginnings? Most of the houses were small, on tiny lots and clustered together, with weeds separating their yards.

Jason parked behind an old blue VW van. I parked a half a block behind that. He got out without the shopping bag and went to one of the houses. I skulked after him.

He made his way through a yard littered with junked cars. I crouched behind one of the cars and saw him knock on the front door of the house. Someone let him in.

I crept closer to the house. Through the windows, I saw him talking to a guy with a beer belly and a handlebar mustache. The guy wore an old T-shirt full of oil stains, a pair of paint-splattered jeans and his brown hair was tied in a short ponytail. His place looked as squalid as he did. What a contrast from Jason's crisp, blue polo shirt, khakis and expensive haircut. The guy looked like a biker, but I didn't see a motorcycle in the yard. He could have been an artist, because the splatters on his jeans looked too colorful for a house painter. I took a picture of the two of them with my cell phone.

They disappeared into the next room. I moved to the side of the house where I thought they went. I ducked into some junipers growing along the wall. Their needle-like leaves scratched my bare arms, but I peeked in the window without them seeing me. This guy must be an artist because I saw the backside of a canvas on an easel.

I took another picture of them. Jason and the guy had a few more words and then Jason left. I was about to follow Jason when the guy came out with a portable radio, blasting heavy metal music. I rushed back to the junipers for cover. The guy didn't look like someone who'd appreciate my snooping.

The guy took out a toolbox from a wooden shed at the end of the yard. He started tinkering with one of the cars. While he tinkered, I tried to get another look at that painting. But no matter where I stood, I couldn't see the front of it.

I wanted to leave. The hot July weather made me thirsty. And I couldn't stand another minute of his music.

Just when I felt I had reached my limit, a white-haired, older lady stuck her face over the fence. She yelled for the guy to turn off his radio. He didn't hear her, but she spotted me hiding in the junipers. "Will you tell him to turn that music off?" she shouted.

I held up my hand, as if to concur with her demand.

"I've had enough of this noise he calls music," she shouted.

I bobbed my head in agreement.

"So tell him," she screamed. "I'm waiting."

I pointed to my throat.

"You got a sore throat?"

I nodded.

The woman shook her head. She gave me an angry look. "Look at you. Sitting in the dirt. What are you, some kind of nut?"

Why didn't she go away? The guy's music blended in with her screams, so he didn't seem to hear her. But if he turned off the music while she was yelling at me—I didn't want to be here then. Not when the guy had a crowbar in his hands.

The guy didn't turn down the music. He went inside. Probably to get a drink, since the sweat dripped from his forehead. Taking my chance, I dashed to the street and ran to my car.

"You're all crazy," I heard the neighbor shout.

I didn't care. I got out of there before the guy came back and the neighbor told on me.

CHAPTER NINETEEN

Despite his loud music, I had to talk to the guy. I changed my clothes, and, with a clipboard, some paper and my camera, I went back to his house an hour later.

The neighbor had gone inside her house. But the guy must have gotten her message because he didn't have the radio on. Instead, he sat on his porch, drinking beer. I figured if the neighbor came out and accused me of hiding in the bushes, I'd deny it. I looked too respectable for anyone to believe that.

"Hi. I'm with the New Mexico Artist Commission and we're doing a survey of artists in the community. This is a new grants program for individual artists. We're gathering profiles of artists and their portfolios. Are you listed with any of the arts organizations?"

"Sure. I was. I haven't sent them any new images yet." For a big guy, he had a mild voice.

"If I could see them?" I said. "Do you have any work here?"

"Excuse me." He set his beer can on the porch. "I just stopped to take a break. What was your name? What organization did you say you were from?"

I gave my name as Olivia Thompson and repeated my story. "Is this your house?" I asked.

"Nah. I just rent. I had a big studio in town, but they tore it down to build a restaurant. Come in. I've got some work I can show you."

He opened the door to his small, unkempt house. It came as

no surprise, since I had seen some of it from the window. The Saltillo floors wore paint splatters and dust. He didn't have much furniture. Just a faded red couch, an old television he put on a stack of bricks and some books stored in a corner. His kitchen had dishes piled up in the sink.

We went down a short hallway, into the room where he kept the painting on the easel. Before I entered, he took the painting down and faced it to the wall. "This is just some commercial work I'm doing for a decorator. My gallery closed down last year. I've got to survive."

"Well, we're hoping these grants will assist artists, as many as possible, to pay their expenses."

"How much of a grant are they giving?"

"I'm not sure yet. This program is so new. I don't even have forms for you to fill out. I'll be sending one to you as soon as they're printed."

He took a few canvases from a closet and lined them against the walls. These landscapes looked similar to the one I had seen on Carone's monitor. Leonardo Da Vinci couldn't have done better if he tried, at least in my opinion.

"I have other work in the shed outside," he said. "I can get them if you like."

"Sure. These are fantastic. Do you have a resumé—a biography?" The gallery didn't call them resumés, I remembered.

"Uh, it isn't up to date."

"That's fine. We just need something to go by. Do you mind if I take some pictures? I need something now to show the committee."

"No, go right ahead."

I snapped a few photos of his work, along with one of him. "Why don't you get me your biography? It doesn't matter if it needs updating."

"I've got the file in the kitchen. I'll be right back."

I heard him rummaging in the kitchen, so I grabbed the painting he removed from the easel. Just as I thought. Jason was paying him to forge a Matisse. I recognized it from the ones taken from the gallery. He didn't have it finished yet. But I saw enough to know it would turn out to be a decent copy.

I included a few of his other works along with the Matisse copy in the picture I took. I put the painting back before he returned.

"Here," he said. "I've been in two more shows since I printed this."

"Thanks." I glanced at it. Yep—Donald Walker. I had the right guy. Did Carone already know what Jason was up to? Or was Carone interested in Donald's work because she liked it?

"You said your gallery closed. Are any other galleries interested in your work?" I asked.

He hesitated. "Do I have to have a gallery to apply for this grant?"

"Oh, no. We just want to know if you're going to have an exhibition soon."

He brightened. "I hope to. I sent images to a few galleries, but so far I don't have a gallery."

So Carone hadn't contacted him yet. "Well," I said, "I have a few more artists I need to see today. But thank you so much. I'll send you an application as soon as they're ready."

"Don't you want to see the rest of my work?" He looked disappointed. Not every day did someone approach him about his work, I thought.

"For now, this is fine. I have a good idea of what you do. Your work is fabulous. I'm sure you'll have no trouble getting a grant."

That seemed to cheer him. When I left, he waved and went back to drinking his beer. I hated to lie to him. If anyone needed a grant, he did. From the looks of his place, Jason wasn't paying him much. It wasn't a crime to copy a painting. But marketing the copy as the original was. Was Donald Walker an innocent artist, paid for his skills, who didn't know Jason had planned to pass the work off as an original Matisse? I hoped so, even if I didn't care for his music.

I didn't think Carone had thrown Jason out. After the murder of Clyde in the gallery, Alfred Merryweather must have had a fit. Carone was smart enough not to let her marital issues upset him further, I should think.

I followed my hunch to Amanda's house, a one-story duplex. I caught a glimpse of Amanda and Jason together, embracing. They didn't see me and I got close enough to snap a picture of them.

After their embrace, they parted ways. Jason drove off. Amanda went inside and came out with her purse. She opened the garage door next to her place, to get her car. That gave me time enough to run to my car.

By now, the route had become familiar. So had the junipers. Next time, I'd wear jeans and a long-sleeved top. Amanda didn't bother to put on her blond wig. Donald had opened his windows and I heard them arguing. I shot a video of them and their heated discussion.

"You were supposed to have it done last week," Amanda shouted. "What's your problem? You have to finish it now."

"What's the rush?" Donald said. "I said I'd get it done. You want it right, don't you?"

Amanda's tough demeanor shocked me. I would have picked Jason as the heavy in this situation. Amanda must have had some connection with Donald, other than business, making it okay for her to push him around.

Donald was a big guy. Yet he almost cowered before Amanda. Unlike Antonio Chavez, Donald was a *big* guy with a *little* guy complex. Had poverty and uncertainty made him that way?

Amanda crossed her arms. "I don't intend to leave without it."

Donald's expression changed. He stopped cowering. "I hope you brought dinner and then some, 'cause you're going to be here for a while. Important people are interested in me and I need to finish my real work. Not copy stuff. What do you and Jason plan to do with it anyway?"

"I told you. It's for one of our collectors. She likes to impress her friends. She's rich enough to indulge her fantasies, but not rich enough to buy originals. She's having a party and we need to get them finished in time to frame them. So hurry up."

"It's not going to be tonight. You're not paying me enough to jeopardize my real career. I'm expecting a big arts commission group to come over to see my work and I want to be ready. It's going to be done by the first of the week, so stop hassling me."

My scam worked on Donald. I wished I could give him a grant. He didn't deserve to be copying great paintings for jerks like Amanda and Jason. But would my evidence convince Carone to tell the police everything?

Chapter Twenty

Carone agreed to meet me the next day at the gallery, after hours. She didn't want to stay late, with a murderer loose, but I told her it wouldn't take long. I got there at five-twenty. My key to the back door still worked. I would have thought she'd put a new lock on the door, instead of installing only a new alarm system. I hoped she was standing by the door, because I didn't know how to turn off the new alarm.

I didn't need to know, because it never went on. I flipped the lights on, since they were off, and called her name. She didn't answer back. She knew I was coming. Where was she?

I checked the offices. I didn't see her. With some trepidation, I walked into the stacks. Carone had installed a Masonite door on the broom closet with a new latch. It still needed painting. I opened it, scared of what I might find. But it contained only cleaning supplies.

I went back into the office wing. I was going to give Carone another five minutes. While I waited, I considered the idea of showing the video and the photos to Lieutenant Seastrom.

The back door opened. I held my breath, hoping that was Carone.

No such luck. Eddy Hansen walked in. "Why are you here?" he asked. His eyes darted around me, as if looking for something I might have stolen.

"I'm supposed to meet Carone now."

"She's getting out of the car. Who let you in?"

"I have a key."

"I fail to see why someone working on a freelance project needs a key to the gallery. Who are you anyway? You're no friend of Carone's, that's for sure."

"I most certainly am." I scowled at him. How dare he question my lies? Anyway, with Carone's wardrobe, I looked enough like a curator to be one of Carone's friends.

"I have work to do," I said. "Tell Carone I'll be in my office."

With my heart pounding, I ran to my office. Eddy Hansen scared the hell out of me. I felt any minute he'd drag me into the alley and shake the truth . . . or the life . . . out of me. He had a lot to gain if Carone didn't find the Picasso. Was he the killer?

Eddy Hansen wanted to get rid of me. He made that clear. So I didn't like Herbie. Big deal. If he didn't think I was an old friend of Carone's, he had to think Carone lied about it.

Did Eddy want me out of the way in order to steal the Modigliani? Jason and Amanda had stolen at least the Matisse and the Chagall. Was Eddy working with them, against Carone? Did he have the Picasso?

I had to leave my thoughts on the back burner because Carone finally made an appearance.

"I hope Eddy wasn't too hard on you," she said. She looked upset. "I had to rush to the printers before they closed. We needed new invitations for the auction. The original ones listed Patty and Clyde on the staff. I had to change that. I dedicated the auction to their memory. But I can't have the auction if you don't find the Picasso. Come to my office, where we can talk."

I had the foresight to upload copies of the video and my photos on my laptop before I showed them to Carone. I didn't know how she would react, but in the event she stomped on my cell phone, I wanted to preserve the evidence.

Before I showed her anything, I asked what had ticked off

Eddy. "Does he know why you hired me?"

"Eddy. Dear Eddy. He thinks you're after my money. And somehow, you'll talk me into giving it to you, even though he knows my father controls everything. He noticed the suit you wore at dinner belonged to me. That's what sparked it. He doesn't suspect anything. He knows about the fire and, of course . . . about Clyde and Patty." She gave me a stern look. "I'm not going to tell him about the Picasso, unless I have to."

I didn't feel as sure about Eddy as she did, but I didn't say so. "I thought you said you were getting a new security system. I didn't hear an alarm when I came in."

Carone sighed. "That was the strangest thing. The old alarm broke and Alarmco didn't show up to install the new one. When I called to complain, they insisted I cancelled the installation. But they're coming tomorrow."

"Did they say who cancelled it?"

"No. But whoever called knew when the appointment was, or so they said."

"Did they say it was a man or a woman who cancelled it?"

"I think it was a mix-up in their office. So what did you have to show me?"

"Just a video and a few pictures." I laid out the pictures first, fresh from the one-hour photo store in town. "The guy with Jason is Donald Walker. He's the artist whose paintings you had on your monitor the other day."

"So?"

"I came back later and told him he was in line for a grant. He let me in and, as you can see, he was in the process of making a copy of the Matisse—here's his biography." I put the paper on her desk, letting my words sink in.

I showed her the other pictures. "Here's a few of Amanda, at Donald Walker's house. I followed her there—" I turned on the video, holding the camera closer to me than to Carone.

Carone listened and shook her head. "Well, what does that prove?" Carone said. "She doesn't work here anymore. So Amanda has a side business. You heard her. She has a collector who likes fakes. It doesn't mean she took the Matisse out of the gallery. She could have taken a picture of it. That's all someone like Donald Walker would need to make a decent copy. They haven't done anything illegal."

"So why is she working with Jason on this?" Working was an understatement. Working didn't mean hugging one's coworker. But I decided not to show Carone the one of Amanda and Jason at her house. She had already seen the one of them at the Broder house, and that didn't get a rise out of her.

"Don't you think I know all about Jason? If he isn't with Amanda, he's with someone else. I made a mistake marrying him. In the beginning, I thought he took the Picasso. But he's not that clever. I hoped you'd be smart enough to look beyond the obvious. I already knew about the Boulange Gallery. Jason had something on his desk at home about it. He doesn't have the Picasso. Yes, he may have taken the paintings out, to have them forged. Petty crime, that's all. He put everything back."

"Why didn't you tell me? Why let me go to the Boulange Gallery?"

"I thought by some miracle you'd find the Picasso there—the original. As you can see, I'm not that clever either."

"Well, what about Mrs. Brown? She bought her paintings there. She could be looking at the Chagall."

"Maybe she knows they're fake. She's not going to tell you that. She could be the collector Amanda talked about."

I couldn't believe what I was hearing. We were talking about a major forgery scheme, and Carone didn't care. Mrs. Brown didn't strike me as a devious person. She believed she had the originals. "So you knew Donald was making fakes?"

"Yes. I knew. Do you have more pictures to show me?"

"Just another one of Amanda and Jason hugging."

"Don't bring me garbage. Bring me the Picasso."

Even if Carone didn't press charges against Amanda or Jason, they were the Broders who consigned a forged Chagall to the Boulange Gallery. That was a crime. And a bigger one if the Boulange Gallery knew about it. But tell that to Carone. . . .

"Lana, I don't care about the truth. I want the gallery to prevail. My father wants me to close it. If I put on the auction and it goes well, he'll change his mind. That's all I care about—the gallery."

She stared out the window with her back to me. "All right. You have enough evidence to go to the police, so do it. Just leave the Picasso out of it. It'll give me an excuse to get rid of Jason. No one will fault me for that, not even my father. He won't blame me for not realizing Jason's a thief. A lazy womanizer, yes. But not a thief."

"Okay. I'm sorry—"

"No need—just find the Picasso."

I grabbed all my stuff and got out of there before she changed her mind.

I called Lieutenant Seastrom and told him I had new information on the gallery murders.

"I wasn't aware there was more than one," he said. "But come in."

I didn't argue the point on the phone. I felt the murders were connected. What connected them eluded me. I wondered why the police didn't understand that. They were the experts.

Maybe they did. The lieutenant wasn't obliged to tell me everything. For all I knew, he suspected me—because I kept finding dead bodies.

At the police station, the dispatch officer showed me to Lieutenant Seastrom's office. He sat behind a worn gray metal desk, talking on the phone. He motioned for me to sit, but he wasn't the smiling lieutenant I remembered from my last meeting with him. He was on duty and serious. When he hung up, I showed him my pictures and the video, filling him in on the details.

"So, this is it?" he said.

Why did I always get this response? First Carone, and now him. I had an important case here.

"All right. I'll turn this over to the proper department. I handle homicides only. This doesn't pertain to the murder in the gallery. Thanks for coming in."

"But what about Patty Sanders? Don't you think there's a connection? And Max Beely—he worked as a handyman at the gallery. And he's dead."

The lieutenant leaned toward me. "What do you know about him?"

"Nothing. But he worked for the gallery."

"Well, thanks for coming in. Just fill out this form, explaining what you told me. You can attach the pictures. Ask the dispatch officer where to email a copy of the video. Now if you'll excuse me, I've got a busy night ahead of me."

CHAPTER TWENTY-ONE

So much for reporting my big scoop. I had to get back to solving my real problem, finding Antonio. Charley hadn't threatened to cut off funds yet, but if I took too long, I'd be out on a limb.

I called Frank Ortiz. No, Antonio hadn't shown up to see them. But now they had a lawyer, agreeing to take their case against the hotel. The lawyer felt they had a good chance of winning. Frank repeated his offer to make George pay the hundred he owed me, but Monday was out because Frank had to work late and I had Clyde's funeral to attend. We settled on Tuesday. Probably a better choice. Frank thought George would skip out on Monday to avoid us.

I didn't know what I hoped to do at the house on Calle Fernando, other than maybe getting the hundred from George. Although the place had three units, according to the title information, the county still considered the property a single-family residence. Zoning permitted a guesthouse, but not three units. Well, illegal units existed everywhere. I didn't come here to report building violations. I came here to find Antonio.

With no new leads on Antonio, I had to go back to the Picasso problem. That led me to Marny. Maybe I needed to have that drink with her, with mine being nonalcoholic. I didn't like advertising my aversion to alcohol. But a concussion was my excuse not to drink.

I wondered whether the concussion had clouded my thinking more than I realized. I got bopped on the head, and before I fell, someone pushed me into a narrow closet too small to lie down in. It wouldn't take more than a tap on the shoulders to tip an unconscious person forward and shut the door on them. Marny, who hated Carone and her job, could have managed that. Although I made certain she didn't see me as a threat to her job, maybe she thought I saw her take a painting from the stacks.

Marny had a reputation as a nuisance and a troublemaker. No one took her seriously. Even when they thought she started the fire, Carone didn't accuse her of doing it on purpose. She was the employee who screwed up, complained or didn't put things back where they belonged. Even with those shortcomings, Carone didn't fire Marny because she was good at her job.

Marny said someone took her cigarette case. But maybe she started the fire in an effort to divert attention away from the stacks, so she could look for the Modigliani. It might have been true that Patty misplaced it. But now Marny and Bentley knew where it was. Everyone did, including Hansen, if Carone chose to confide in him. If it should turn up missing again, Marny would escape blame because no one considered her dishonest, just inept. If she was the murderer and had stolen the Picasso, she set up a perfect cover. Likewise for Bentley. No one considered him a dangerous person either.

Marny could have forced Patty to go with her. With Marny pointing a gun at her, Patty wouldn't think to retrieve her favorite pen. Marny could have shot Clyde as well. Although I heard sounds of a fight, that could have been Clyde trying to get the gun out of the Marny's hands. It didn't take much strength to shoot a gun.

I didn't call Marny first. I just drove there. She lived on the west side of town on the ground floor of a small apartment complex. In typical Santa Fe style, this place had a Saltillo-tiled courtyard and adobe-like walls.

I knocked on the door of her unit. While I waited for her, I glanced in the window near the door. It looked bare, except for a built-in entertainment center. What happened to her furniture? I saw a light on in the hall and some luggage.

Marny opened the door with a surprised look on her face. "Lana. Hello."

"I was driving by and I wondered whether you still wanted to get that drink. Looks like you're moving."

"I'm sorry we never got to have that drink. I don't have time now. I'd invite you in, but I have to get going. I got a job—in Chicago."

"Well, that was quick."

Marny laughed. "I called Carone earlier and told her. Actually, I got the job last month, but they weren't ready for me. Sorry I didn't tell you. I shipped most of my things today. I'm down to my clothes."

Before she could stop me, I stepped inside. "I wish you luck. I'm good at making last-minute checks. I've moved so many times. There's always something you leave behind."

She didn't have a choice. I began opening the drawers of the entertainment unit. Then I went into the bedroom.

Marny trailed after me. "I don't think I left anything," she called out.

"You might as well be sure." I opened the closet. "Aha! You left a roll of paper." I grabbed it. It was too flimsy to have a painting wrapped inside, but I had to make sure. "It looks like a poster."

"Oh, I forgot. It's *The Red Room* by Matisse."

"That's one of my favorites. Do you mind if I unroll it?"

"Well, if you want. You can have it. I've already packed. I don't have room for it."

"Oh, I couldn't do that."

"I insist."

"All right. Thanks. So what kind of job did you get?"

"It's a great job. At a real museum."

"Which one?"

Marny looked embarrassed. "I'd rather not say yet. I don't want it to get back to Carone until I'm sure they like me."

"I understand. But I won't say anything."

"I know. It's just that I'm on a three-month trial basis. They're not checking references until then. I'm sorry we didn't get to know each other better. Thanks for stopping by. I have to run. My ride should be here any minute."

"But aren't you taking a big chance—in moving to Chicago, when your job isn't secure?"

"I have family there. If it doesn't work out, I'll find something. Anyway—"

"You know, your suitcases are bulging. I can help you pack better. I'm an expert."

"Thanks, but I wouldn't want you to bother."

"You'll never get that carry-on to fit under the seat. It won't take long."

"Well, if you think so."

I opened her carry-on and took everything out. Nothing of importance, just cosmetics and books. I had a hard time putting everything back, and my efforts were little better than hers. I didn't think she'd let me tackle her other two bags, but I reached for one anyway.

A horn honked outside. "Lana, I don't have time for any more repacking. But thanks." She ran to the front door. "That's my ride."

Marny took one of the suitcases and sprinted to a car from one of those airport transport companies. The driver, a young man, put her suitcase in the trunk. Marny ran back and grabbed the other two suitcases. "Thanks for stopping by," she said.

"Just one more thing—"

"I don't want to miss my plane."

"Did you see Eddy Hansen in the gallery the day I was knocked out?"

"Are you still on that? I don't remember. If I were you, I'd quit. I know someone killed Clyde, but I don't think anyone came in broad daylight and knocked you out. Okay? Thanks for coming over. Bye!"

"Sure. Good luck." I waved and walked to my car.

"Lana, wait a minute."

I ran toward Marny, getting to her before she closed the door. "Yes?"

"Hansen was there that day. He's in and out so much I didn't remember to put him on the list. Bye!"

I waited until they got down the block before following them. I needed to make sure Marny told the truth about going to Chicago.

I got to the airport around the same time as she did and saw where she checked her luggage and got ticketed. The ticket was for Chicago.

I had reached a dead end with Marny. I had nothing against Chicago, but if I had stolen a Picasso, I wouldn't be going there in the summer, when temperatures climbed into the triple digits. By now, a thief would have had the money from selling it.

But someone who stole a Picasso might stay in the same spot, to avoid looking suspicious. Finding out Eddy was in the gallery that day made him a plausible suspect. Accusing him of stealing the Picasso was another story. Maybe buttering him up on his importance in the art world would gain his confidence, enough to discover what connections in the art world he had. Few people could resist admirers of their expertise.

He didn't like me because he thought I was after the Merry-weather fortune. Carone thought he had money, but maybe he didn't. So he decided to steal the Picasso. Would the Modigliani be next? Had he put it in the wrong place on purpose? Or did the mix-up delay his scheme?

CHAPTER TWENTY-TWO

The next morning I called Carone at the gallery. I wanted her opinion of Marny, though I had all but written her off as the Picasso thief.

"Carone isn't in."

"Do you know when she's coming back?" I didn't recognize the female voice on the other end.

"Later."

"Who's this?"

"Jane."

"Oh, I met you at Carone's house. I'm Lana Davis. When did you start working at the gallery?"

"Today."

I didn't allow her flat, bored tone to put me off. "Is the alarm company installing the new system today?"

"I don't know."

"It should be on the calendar, on the desk. It's important. Could you look, please?"

She put me on hold several minutes. Then she said, "Four o'clock."

"I wonder if that's going to give them enough time to install everything. Do they work after five?"

"I don't know. I can't. I hope Carone gets here by then, because I have to leave."

"Well, I'll drop by, so someone's there."

As soon as I hung up, I received a call from Lieutenant

Travers of the Los Angeles Police Department Frauds Division. He asked me what I knew about art forgeries at the Boulange Gallery. So Lieutenant Seastrom had put the wheels in motion.

Donald Walker must have finished the Matisse by now. I pictured Amanda and Jason, thinking they had pulled off another con, waltzing into the Boulange Gallery with the police waiting for them. No doubt, Carone had split from Jason already.

I found out soon enough. I got to the gallery at three. Jane sat at the reception desk, in jeans and a T-shirt. She didn't look up when I walked in. Carone greeted me with red eyes and a blotchy face.

"It's about time you got here," she said. "Come into my office."

Once we went inside her office, she slammed the door. "He's gone. He and Amanda. I don't know where they went."

"If they go to L.A., the police will get them. I had a call—"

"Yes. Isn't that great? It wasn't bad enough he left me, now the police are involved. I said I wanted to keep this quiet. Look what you've done."

"What do you mean? You said I could go to the police. People have been murdered."

"All Jason did was take work that belonged to my family. I'm not pressing charges against him."

"Is that what you told him?"

"I didn't tell him anything. He left before I got home yesterday. The maid said he left in a hurry."

Carone's office line buzzed. Jane announced Eddy Hansen. "Send him in," Carone said. "Please go."

I ignored her and took a seat.

Eddy rushed in with a big hug for Carone. "I came as soon as I could. How's my baby," he said. He noticed me. "Would you mind leaving us alone?"

"Sure." But I didn't get up. I wanted to know Eddy's angle in this.

Eddy turned to Carone. "You know how I feel. If you need some time off, I can help run the gallery. Or maybe you should close it—after the auction, of course. It's been too much for you—"

Eddy glared at me. "You must have some work to do, with the salary I imagine Carone is paying you."

"Of course. I'm leaving."

I went to my office. Now why would Eddy want Carone to close the gallery? He knew that's what her father wanted. But he'd never agreed with him on that.

Eddy didn't stay long. I ventured out of my office to get some coffee and saw him leave with a very pale Carone under his arm.

It wasn't that I didn't empathize with Carone. She loved and hated Jason. I knew that emotion well from my divorce. I should have told her how sorry I was, but I hadn't expected her to tell me this was my fault.

Before I returned to my desk, Jane buzzed me in the break room. "You have a call. I rang your office, but you weren't there. I transferred it here."

I would have preferred my office, but I put the phone to my ear. "Lana Davis here."

"Lana, it's me, Darlene. How've you been?"

"Fine. I can't talk right now."

"I wanted to know—did you get me an invitation to the auction?"

"Not yet. But I'm working on it."

At four, the security people came. Although I had asked Bentley to stay, he dashed out the door at five. I called Rodney, but it was his day off and he didn't pick up. Jane had already said she wouldn't stay past five, so that left only me.

I didn't like being alone in the gallery with the two men from the alarm company. But at five after five, they walked out.

I ran after them. "Hey—I don't think you finished. How do I lock up?" They had removed the lock from the back door.

"We have to finish tomorrow."

"You can't leave us like this. We need an alarm system. And a door that locks."

"We don't work overtime unless we have a prior agreement. The boss won't let us."

"But you have to finish the job today."

"Sorry. We'll be back tomorrow."

I didn't know what to do. How long was I supposed to stay here? I called Carone on her cell and at the house. No one answered. Not even Rothwell.

I locked the front door. They had left that deadbolt intact, but not the one for the back door. I barricaded it with a chair. It wasn't much. Anyone could push it out of the way. I was about to call the alarm company when I saw the chair move.

Terrified, I ran to the chair with a telephone directory, ready to throw it at anyone who walked in the door. It was only Jane.

"My books . . . I forgot them."

"I didn't know you were in . . . school."

She looked at me and at the phone book. "Yeah. Art history."

She put her fingers through the hole where the deadbolt used to be. "Can they fix this?"

"They left. I was about to call the alarm company. They have to send someone out now."

"Too bad. Rodney could fix it. If he calls."

"Thanks." That seemed like a long shot.

She picked up her books from the reception desk and left the same way she came in.

I called the alarm company, leaving an urgent message with their answering service. I made another frantic call to Carone.

This time I got Rothwell. No, Carone wasn't in. I told him what happened. He gave me Eddy's number, but Eddy didn't answer. I called Bentley and left him a message. Then I called Lieutenant Seastrom, but he wasn't on duty.

At six, hunger pains set in, so I had dinner delivered from the gourmet pizza place down the street. I stuffed myself with pizza, waiting for someone to call me back.

I tried Bentley again. He had just finished with having dinner with a collector. "All right," he said. "I'll be there in a few minutes." His voice sounded strained.

I left the door open to watch for Bentley's car, sitting on the chair I had used as a barricade. The restaurant across the alley had a band playing, and the music eased my mind. Several customers came out. I heard a car drive up, followed by some laughter. I didn't pay attention to it. Sometimes the restaurant's customers parked in the gallery's lot. They weren't supposed to during the day. After hours, no one cared.

I didn't want people from the restaurant stumbling in, so I shut the door. That didn't do any good because—of all people—Darlene walked in.

"Hello. What's going on?" I asked.

She had a tall blond man with her. He had pale skin and a thin face. They both wore black jeans and black shirts. Her friend stared into space like a zombie.

"You sounded in a hurry when I called," she said. "I thought the gallery was having an opening. Where is everyone? Any free food?"

"There's nothing happening tonight. But now that you're here, maybe you or your friend can help me find a way to lock this door." I told them the problem.

"You work too hard," Darlene said. She giggled. "There's a party on Cerrillos Road. Come with us. Oh, this is Demi."

Demi's expression didn't change. He seemed too drunk or

drugged to acknowledge me.

"Well, if you aren't going to help, then you need to leave."

"Come on. We want to party. If you change your mind, give us a call. Demi, what's their number?"

Demi didn't answer. "Never mind," Darlene said. "I'll text you when I get there. Bye."

The barricade needed another chair to make it secure. I didn't like leaving the door before Bentley came, but it wouldn't take long. I ran to the break room to get a chair.

Maybe I should have gotten Darlene and her friend to stay. What if Bentley was the murderer? Had I walked into a trap?

I heard someone come in the back door. I picked up a chair, so I could throw it if necessary. "Is that you, Bentley?"

A dark-haired man with a pockmarked face stood in the doorway of the break room. He wore a dramatic black cape over his baggy gray trousers. He looked like one of Darlene's crowd.

"Hey. The gallery is closed. You have to leave." I didn't see any weapons on him. If he attacked me, I could always hit him with the chair.

"The gallery is closed," he mimicked. "Yes. That's exactly what I intend to do. I am going to sue your asses off and close this place down."

"Any business you have with the gallery can wait until tomorrow."

The man picked up a coffee mug from the counter and threw it on the floor. It broke. "That's what I do to anyone who throws me out. Nobody throws Sergio Serrano out. Nobody."

So that's what this was about. "Hey, look. I'm dealing with a crisis here. If you insist on hanging around, you have to help me lock the door. We don't have a deadbolt."

"Why should I? I'm going to tear this place apart." He picked up another mug and threw it against the wall.

"Stop it! How will you get any money out of this place if you wreck it?"

He considered this. "I would rather die than do anything to help this place." With a swirl of his cape, he stormed out.

I went after him, dragging the chair so I could use it for the barricade. At this point, I didn't care what marks it made on the carpet.

The lights went out before we got to the door. "Is that you, Bentley?" I said.

No one answered. In the dark, I found Sergio's cape. I pulled on it. "Stay here. I'll turn the lights on. It could be the circuit."

He pushed me away.

"Stay here. You might trip on something." I didn't want to give him another reason to sue the gallery.

He grumbled and rushed forward.

The door from the stacks opened. I heard a loud blast. "Get down," I screamed.

I let go of the chair and dropped to the floor. I thought I saw Sergio lying on the floor. He didn't move. I got a glimpse of a man holding a rectangular object, silhouetted by a street lamp shining through the back window.

I moved and the shooter fired at me. He missed. I slid to the wall, wishing I could disappear into it.

"Don't take this personally, love. It's either you or me."

Rodney?

"Why are you doing this?" I cried.

"Money and greed are great motivators."

"But you're an artist . . . you have a good job."

"I owe the wrong people. If I don't pay up, love, I'm dead. So I have no choice."

"*You* took the Picasso."

"Yes, love. That's why I can't let you live. You know too much."

"But why take another painting?"

"Why not? Now move out. Where I can see you."

I stayed where I was. He fired another shot. It missed again.

I had to take a chance. I swung my leg out and hooked it around the chair, moving it closer to me. He fired at it.

I threw the chair at him, hitting him in the torso. I heard the dull thud the gun made when it hit the carpeted floor. I leaped toward it, colliding with Sergio's body. My fingers closed around the handgun. Rodney yelled and rushed at me.

I fired the gun, not knowing where I aimed it. I missed both of us.

We struggled with the gun. Rodney wrenched it out of my hand. I kicked him in the shins and the gun went off. This time the shot found its mark. Rodney fell and landed on top of me.

That's how Bentley found me.

CHAPTER TWENTY-THREE

"Bentley! Call the police."

"What happened? Where are the lights?"

"Rodney—stole a painting. Don't touch it. Don't touch anything."

"What?"

"Just call the police."

"What are you doing on the floor? Who are the others?"

"Call the cops. I'll explain."

While Bentley called nine-one-one, I had to extricate myself from the bodies of Rodney and Sergio. I scooted from under Rodney, bumping into Sergio in the process. He moaned. "Call an ambulance, Bentley," I yelled. "He's alive."

I got up on one knee and then stood on both feet. Other than a sore leg and a concussion, I wasn't hurt.

Bentley finished the call and I told him what happened. "Sergio is still alive. I don't think Rodney is. Where's the main switch? Rodney must have flipped it off."

"I can't believe this. Rodney? What did he steal?"

"Let's get the lights on."

"The panel is in the stacks. Are you okay?"

"Just get the switch."

Bentley started for the door, but then yelled.

"Don't shoot," a man's voice called out. "I don't want trouble. I didn't do anything."

Oh, my God. "Tyler? What are you doing here?" I said.

I never got an answer. Two seconds later the police came. They caught Tyler before he got away, thanks to Bentley shouting at them not to let him go.

This time, Lieutenant Seastrom didn't chastise me for finding another dead body. And when I told him what happened, I included the theft of the Picasso in my explanation.

Sergio suffered a minor gunshot wound, and, fearing the worst, he had played dead. When the paramedics attended to his wound, he livened up by continuing his tirade against the gallery. Without meaning to, he also backed up my story about Rodney.

By the time Carone showed up with Eddy Hansen, the police had removed Rodney's body and the paramedics had put Sergio in the ambulance. Too bad she missed all the excitement.

Carone gasped when she saw the Modigliani zipped in a plastic bag. "You can't take that painting. It belongs to a collector of mine."

"We'll give it back," Lieutenant Seastrom said. "Right now, it's evidence."

She gave Tyler a puzzled look as the police escorted him out. I shook my head. I didn't have the energy to explain who he was. And Bentley—I didn't know what happened to him. He left before Carone got there.

The next day, the local news media buzzed with the sordid details of a rich gallery owner's life, her cheating spouse, the shootings and the attempted theft of a Modigliani. But nothing about a stolen Picasso. A search of Rodney's house turned up a small amount of cocaine, but no stolen paintings. The police considered my ramblings about the Picasso hearsay since Carone insisted the theft never happened. Even Sergio didn't corroborate that part of my story. In his injured state, he didn't remember anything about a Picasso.

But the deadline loomed. Carone needed to find it. I should have asked Rodney where he hid it. He might have told me, thinking I'd take the knowledge to my grave. But I was too scared to think about it then. It didn't matter. Carone fired me—again—because I told the police about the Picasso.

Charley didn't find out about the Modigliani episode because my name didn't appear in the news. I wasn't an important enough player in this debacle, and I liked it that way.

But Charley clamored for results. "I should know something by Tuesday," I told him. I had no reason for picking that day, because after it passed, I'd have to pick another day and continue stalling.

Monday I went to Clyde's funeral at a small church on Cerrillos Road. Carone came with Eddy Hansen, but they didn't stay long. I think she paid for the funeral. I think they were surprised to see me. Jane didn't come. Not many people did.

Tuesday came with some important developments, just not the one I wanted. The police identified the gun Rodney killed himself with as the same one used to kill Angelica, Patty and Clyde. A gut feeling told me they'd pin Max Beely's murder on Rodney too. Just a matter of time.

I wondered why Rodney needed to steal the Modigliani, when he had the Picasso. Could he have owed that much money that the sale of the last Picasso wouldn't have satisfied his debtor? Unless he couldn't sell it. He must have sold Angelica's diamond pendant. The police didn't find it in his house.

As planned, Frank Ortiz and I went to Calle Fernando. We caught George unlocking the door of the middle apartment, the one rented to the guy named Arby.

"Hey, George," I yelled.

Frank and I got out of the truck.

George looked shocked. He must have thought when we didn't show up Monday, he didn't have to worry about paying me back. "I don't have any money," he said. "The thing is . . ."

Frank gave him a dark look.

"Were you going in that apartment? Isn't it rented?" I said.

"The owner told me the guy stopped paying rent. It smells bad. Something rotting in there. You can smell it from here. Can't you?"

It did smell.

Frank pushed George out of the way.

"Hey, you're not supposed to be in there," George said.

"Looks like I'm already in," Frank said. "It's like something died in here."

I knew that smell, and I didn't like what I knew. "You don't have the hundred dollars, so I'm coming in too."

George followed us in. I covered my nose with a tissue before I gagged. The two men used their sleeves to do the same.

As George had said, the tenant used the apartment for storing . . . paintings that looked familiar.

The smell emanated from a man crumpled on the floor in a corner. I couldn't see his face from the way his head tilted. His shirt had a dark red stain by his chest. I didn't see a gun nearby so it had to be a murder and not a suicide. The man had a finger missing on his left hand.

Antonio Chavez.

Poor Antonio. If I had told him about his inheritance at Angelica's funeral, would that have altered his fate? How sad.

Frank and I turned to George.

"Hey, I don't know—nothing about—this," he stammered. "I heard nothing. Arby used this place to store things. That's all I know. I'm calling the owner." He ran outside. We heard him drive off.

Frank went outside. I stayed behind to search the place. I found a rental receipt on the kitchen counter. George had said the tenant's name was Arby. He didn't realize Arby wasn't a name. It stood for two initials, R.B., short for Rodney Bracken. That's why the paintings looked familiar.

I saw a cigarette lighter next to the receipt. A silver art deco lighter, like the one Marny described. Antonio must have seen Rodney steal the Picasso and told Angelica. Maybe they threatened to talk or Rodney figured he had to kill them in case they did.

Unlike the unit Antonio rented, this place had a real closet. Rodney had hung some clothes and stacked some books in there. I spotted a small roll of canvas, secured by a rubber band, half-hidden behind the books.

I grabbed the canvas. I had to get out of there. The smell of Antonio's body overwhelmed me. But my curiosity couldn't wait.

I unrolled the canvas and held the last painting of Picasso's in my hands. Although no art connoisseur, even I appreciated the significance of its place in the world. How unceremonious of Rodney to leave it wrapped with a rubber band. But now I understood why Rodney needed to steal the Modigliani.

Before or after he took the Picasso out of the gallery, he tried to remove it from the frame and the stretcher bars. In doing so, he sliced the bottom of the painting with a box cutter or a knife. What an idiot. It looked accidental because the gash almost reached the middle of the painting. The photo of the original didn't show a painting with a gash in it. Finding a restorer who didn't ask too many questions probably took more time than Rodney had. Another dumb scheme gone awry.

I rerolled the Picasso and got out of there before I fainted from the smell of death.

Chapter Twenty-Four

Frank sat on the ground by his truck, staring into space. "He was a good friend," he said. "Why would someone kill him? He was good to Angelica. He was good to me."

"I'm so sorry."

Frank shook his head. "The police are coming. I don't know what happened to George. Stupid old man."

"Do you think he shot Lefty?"

"Nah. He talks big. He couldn't hit anything if he tried. He's drunk half the time. I just don't get it. Lefty never hurt anyone."

With Frank still on the ground, I opened the passenger door and hid the Picasso under my purse in the space between the seat and the door.

I left Frank alone with his grief and trekked up the hill near the back of the property. When I reached the top, I looked down at the landscape, seeing miles of sagebrush and sloping hills. Living in such a place changed people. Some drew inspiration from its vastness. Others experienced terror or desperation because of its limited opportunities. Or they got lost in its eerie majesty. New Mexico had done its number on me. I had experienced all it had to offer. I knew I had to leave, but part of me wanted to stay.

Lieutenant Seastrom was right. I had a knack for finding dead bodies. Antonio's body saved my job and let Charley off the hook. I just didn't want it to end this way. Even finding the Picasso didn't console me.

"Hey, Charley, guess what? I found Antonio Chavez, but—"

"Good going. Give him the forms to fill out."

"Charley, he's dead. Murdered."

"Oh . . . can you get a . . . death certificate?"

"Sure. Could take a week or so. I don't know how things go in New Mexico. But I have a feeling they don't move fast."

I knew Charley didn't want to hear the whole story, so I didn't go into it. He wanted the claim paid and the ruckus forgotten. Even in this day of computerized records, insurance administrators measured a good day's work by how many pages they unstapled and re-stapled after processing. Charley could hardly wait to re-staple this claim and file it away.

I half-feared they'd send Lieutenant Seastrom to investigate Antonio's death, but instead a broad-shouldered and personable man named Officer Nestor Hernandez showed up.

Officer Hernandez and his team didn't search Frank's truck. No reason to, though I took a risk removing the Picasso from the apartment. But what good would it do to charge Rodney with stealing it? I mentioned the cigarette lighter to Hernandez and gave him Marny's name. I told him to ask the gallery for her address, in the event the lighter belonged to her.

I asked Officer Hernandez about getting Antonio's death certificate.

"They'll have to do an autopsy. It might take a few weeks. You'll have to fill out some forms, to show cause—why you should have it. It cost five dollars. There's an office in Santa Fe. Here's my card. You can call the station to see when the autopsy is done and when they'll send the information to the county."

We left as the coroner's van drove up. Frank took me back to the Ortiz house. When he parked the truck, I asked whether he knew any of Antonio's friends.

"Just Angelica and a cousin of mine. I mean, he knew people, but I don't know them. I guess he doesn't get the money then."

"No. They'll give it to the next of kin. Did you know any of his family?"

"He said they were in California."

I lingered a moment before I opened my door, to make sure Frank got out first. I said goodbye to him while holding my purse and the Picasso behind my back. "Please relay my sympathies to your family again."

"I'm sorry you didn't get the hundred from George," he said.

"That's the breaks, Frank. Thanks anyway."

He went into the house and I trudged back to my car. I felt tired, but not from the concussion. The sight and the smell of death had shaken the headache out of me. But the thin air still made me lightheaded. I needed a nap. The Picasso had waited this long. It could wait another day.

The only thing that moved fast in Santa Fe was bad news. Carone called me about Antonio before I even got to my hotel room.

"What did you say to the police?" she demanded. "They asked me about him. They found my business card in his pocket."

"I didn't say anything, except to ask how to get his death certificate. As I told you, his death resolves the life insurance claim I was working on."

"Oh. Well, fine."

"I found Antonio's body in a place Rodney rented. They're bound to pin this on him."

"Well, they arrested Jason and Amanda in Los Angeles. Arrested, do you hear? And it's all your fault."

"I'm sorry, but they did try to pass off at least one forged painting. That's—"

"I don't need the police thinking I knew anything about this." She hung up before I had a chance to tell her the *good* news.

Now I felt more angry than sleepy. I skipped the nap and ordered dinner in. I didn't want to run into anyone I knew. Darlene and Lieutenant Seastrom had a sixth sense when it came to finding me.

Before the pizza and side salad I ordered arrived, I unrolled the Picasso and studied it. I took in every detail. I had to admit, this Picasso guy knew how to make the most of his brushstrokes. With a few dabs of color and line, this woman came alive. Her name didn't matter. She represented all women. Maybe I wasn't as dense about art appreciation as I thought. What a shame that Rodney ruined the bottom of the painting.

Because I would never have a real Picasso in my possession again, I took pictures of it—with my camera, not my cell. I wanted good pictures. Something for my memories.

The next day, I called Carone at the gallery. Jane answered. I wondered how she felt about Rodney's death, but I didn't ask. Always with the monotone voice, she didn't sound too different from before.

"Carone is out. Won't be back for . . ."

"For how long?"

"Uh, a day . . ."

"So she'll be back tomorrow?"

"Uh . . . or two . . . or . . . I don't know."

I should have said something about Rodney to Jane, but how could I be sorry about his death when he tried to kill me?

So while Carone disappeared for two days, I played tourist and took pictures of the town and the scenery. I still had some of the money left over from working for Carone, so I bought some clothes and knickknacks for my apartment. I checked out some art galleries, knowing my money didn't stretch far enough to buy anything there.

And at night, in my hotel room, I studied the Picasso, as if mesmerized by its grace and its history. By the time Carone got back, I knew every inch of it, as if I had painted it myself.

I brought the Picasso to the gallery in a cloth shopping bag. Because I had to make an entrance, I wore some of Carone's clothes. I didn't want Jane or Bentley to see me in my drab insurance clothes and realize I was a fraud. They must have known Carone fired me, or maybe they thought my contract had ended, because I didn't come in anymore.

So much for my worries. Jane didn't look up from her art book and Bentley wasn't around. I went past Jane to Carone's office. I knocked. Without waiting for permission, I opened the door and marched in.

"What do you want?" Carone said. "I don't owe you any back salary, if that's what you think."

I shut the door. "I have something to show you." I handed her the shopping bag. "Look in the bag."

Carone glared at me, but dug into the shopping bag. "What is this?"

I had planned to let her discover the contents herself, but in the mood she was in, I was afraid she'd damage the painting even more without realizing it. "If you unroll the canvas, you'll see it's the Picasso."

"Oh." Treating it with proper reverence, she undid the rubber band. She gasped. "What happened to it? Where did you get this?"

"You can thank Rodney for ruining it. I found it in the same place I found Antonio Chavez's body. Rodney took the painting off the stretcher bars. I didn't see the frame or the stretcher bars in the apartment, and I didn't have time to look for it. The police were on their way. I didn't report it to them. There wasn't any reason to. You were gone, and I didn't want to leave you a message."

"I suppose . . . it can be . . . fixed. She looked at me. "I'm happy to give you another week's pay."

I could have taken it, but I didn't. "I have to stick around anyway. My company needs Antonio's death certificate. It won't be available for a week or two. I have to wait for the autopsy. In the meantime, they're paying me for loafing because they want me to pick up the report in person. They don't trust the mail."

"Well, you'll be here for the auction then. Here's an invitation. It's the least I can do. Take a few invitations. You can bring some guests."

I picked up several from her desk. Hey, why not? Now all I needed was a dress to wear. Something that didn't come from Carone's closet.

CHAPTER TWENTY-FIVE

If I lived in Santa Fe, I could never wear sweats to the market or leave the house without makeup. Although I knew so few people here, I always ran into them when I least expected it. While shopping for something to wear to the auction, I spotted Donald Walker coming out of Cardos, an upscale restaurant on Del Palacio. The guidebook in my hotel room described it as having award-wining northern New Mexican cuisine. A little expensive for Donald's wallet, I should think.

At first, I didn't recognize Donald. And he glanced at me as if he thought he knew me, but wasn't sure. We both looked different now. Since the demise of my curating career, I now tootled around town in designer jeans, with my hair down. Donald had given up scruffy clothes and unkempt hair for designer jeans and a new polo shirt.

I remembered him only because I had faked my identity to him. Under normal circumstances, seeing someone out of context wouldn't have jarred my memory. And not wanting to test his memory, I went the opposite way. I wondered about his sudden prosperity, though.

I perused the Plaza area, hoping to find the right dress in one of the boutiques there. I skipped the store where Darlene worked, slinking by in case she saw me. I should have given her one of the invitations, but the idea of hanging out with her made me tired just thinking about it.

I didn't keep up with the news these days. I didn't want to

know anything. I did what I came here to do, and then some. Not everything worked out the way I hoped, but that was the luck of the draw. I wanted only pleasant days ahead.

But I couldn't resist noticing the screaming headlines of *The New Mexican* in a newspaper vending machine I passed. Tyler had confessed in return for a lesser sentence.

I put change in the vending slot and pulled out a paper.

I read the story as I leaned against a wooden post along the walkway. Tyler pled guilty to being an accessory in Rodney's theft of the Modigliani. He was supposed to be the lookout while Rodney got the painting from the stacks. My guess was he chickened out, letting Rodney leave the stacks first and hiding when he heard the gunshot.

The article explained why Rodney felt the need to kill so many people. Tyler and Rodney sold cocaine, supplied to them by a gang of drug dealers, one of whom was David Chasem. Yes, Santa Fe was a small town. Everyone knew everyone else, and not always in a good way. Chasem wasn't in the gallery that day to look at art. He must have gone to see Rodney.

According to Tyler, one of their customers ripped them off big time, leaving them with no money to pay Chasem. Rodney got the idea of stealing art from the gallery to drum up cash because Tyler told him he knew of a guy who had a friend who could sell stolen art. Tyler said Rodney made plans to steal a painting, but they never tried it until the night he died. Tyler denied any involvement in the murders Rodney committed.

When Rodney knocked me out and shoved me into the closet the day I started with Carone, he didn't realize what I knew. I just got in the way. If he had known the reason Carone hired me, or if Carone hadn't shooed him away the first night I approached her about Antonio, he might have tried to kill me sooner.

Chasem must have threatened Rodney when he showed up at

the gallery. At that point, Rodney already had the Picasso but still couldn't pay Chasem. Antonio freaked when I called his name at the funeral because he didn't want anyone but the family to know he was there. He either got involved with Rodney or saw him steal the Picasso. And Angelica must have known as well.

Tyler admitted he didn't have any connections to sell stolen art. He let Rodney believe that because he figured once they had a painting they'd find a source. Both were desperate to come up with some way to pay Chasem, who had no qualms about shooting them. Reduced sentence or not, if I were Tyler, I wouldn't want to be in the same prison as Chasem.

I folded the newspaper and stuffed it in my purse. Maybe on one of the other pages I'd read about Jason and Amanda. I had lost interest in art forgery after I turned over the Picasso, but seeing Donald Walker looking so spiffy had sparked my curiosity. I had taken some damning photos of him, and here he was walking the streets.

I should have known better than to stand on a corner in the middle of town because I saw Bentley coming up the street. I hadn't talked to him since Rodney's death, and I didn't feel like talking to him now. The memory of that night still haunted me. Too late to duck out, though. He saw me. He had on a brown suit, so he must have come from the gallery, or was on his way there.

"Hello, Bentley."

"Lana. How are you? I—"

"I'm okay. I'm not working at the gallery. I'm going back to California. But I'll be at the auction."

"I guess I'll see you then."

"Just one thing I wondered about."

Bentley cringed as if he dreaded what I had to say next. "What is it?" he asked. The murders had changed him. He no longer spoke with arrogance in his voice.

"When Rodney knocked me out and shoved me into the closet, because I know that's what happened, how come you didn't hear anything until I screamed? You didn't hear any footsteps? I saw you in the stacks. Where did you go?"

"I washed my hands. They got dusty from taking paintings out of the stacks."

"Oh." If I had thought to ask Bentley before, I wouldn't have spent that long evening in my car, waiting for him to commit a crime. I should have believed my gut reaction about him. He couldn't have knocked me out because he didn't like getting his hands dirty—literally. And in his present state, he looked scared of his own shadow.

"Lana, when the police . . . came . . . I didn't mean to . . ."

"It's okay, Bentley. It was a difficult night. You called them. I couldn't have done it. And I'm glad you did. Anyway, see you at the auction."

I went to my hotel room and read the rest of the newspaper. Nothing on Jason and Amanda. On the Internet, I found a short blurb on Jason. He made bail. I bet Carone got her father to pay it. Better for the family to get him out of jail, with the auction coming up.

The article didn't say anything about Amanda. I told that police detective in L.A. about the Browns' collection, but the article didn't mention them or the Boulange Gallery. But they dropped charges against Donald Walker. Maybe Carone gave Donald something for his trouble, enough for new clothes and a free lunch. That's something Carone would do. Maybe she gave him an invitation to the auction too. She wanted a full house, regardless of how she got it.

I felt bad about Donald. He had talent. I hoped his new clothes and fancy lunch came from the largesse of Carone, or from sales of his work, rather than from a misguided expectation about receiving a grant. I felt I owed him the courtesy of telling him the truth. Besides, since First Century Life demanded so little of my time now, I could afford to right my prior wrongs.

Donald didn't live far from the hotel. Well, no one did. I could drive from one end of the town to the other in less time than it took to get a pizza delivered in L.A. I would miss that when I got home.

For my visit to Donald, I didn't wear any of the curator clothes Carone gave me, but I tied my hair into a ponytail, the way I had worn it when I went to his house. I wanted Donald to remember me.

When I got there, I saw a *For Rent* sign in front. The old cars Donald tinkered with were gone. The elderly lady of the house next door stood on her front porch, staring at my car. I undid my ponytail and shook my head until my hair fluttered around my face. I didn't want her to recognize me.

I got out of the car. "Hello," I said.

"May I help you?" the lady asked.

"What happened to the artist who lived next door?"

"Him? He moved. You look familiar."

"Really? I don't think we've met. Where did he move to?"

"Hah. Said he got a grant. He could afford to move. Imagine, anybody giving him a grant. Always working on the cars, with the loud music. Who would give him a grant? Don't I know you from somewhere?"

CHAPTER TWENTY-SIX

I arrived at the auction gala about a half hour after it started. I wore a black dress and heels. I picked the dress up at a department store the day before. I heard the new fall fashions had come in, and a new black dress would look better than the faded one I had. I used to wonder why stores showed fall fashions in July and August, since summer still had a ways to go. But after having searched Santa Fe for a summer cocktail dress that didn't cost a fortune and didn't look like it came from the local bridal shop, I realized how their strategy paid off.

The gallery was packed. A string quartet played, and a buffet table laden with northern New Mexican cuisine looked inviting. I hadn't realized the auction was a silent affair. Along the wall beside each painting was a sign-up sheet where people wrote their bids. Each bid had to be ten percent more than the preceding one. When the auction closed at the end of the night, the last bid was the winner.

Carone, surrounded by a group of elegantly dressed people, looked ethereal in a white floor-length gown. She noticed me and smiled. Then she frowned and came toward me.

I soon realized why. I turned to my left and my eyes met those of Lieutenant Seastrom. He stood next to another man. They must have followed me in. They both wore suits. Seastrom had called me the week before to see if I had anything to add to my statement on Tyler and Rodney. When I told him about the auction, he got dibs on my invitations. I didn't mind because if

Darlene called I could tell her, without lying, that I didn't have one to give her. But Darlene never called.

"Why Lieutenant Seastrom, how nice to see you," Carone said. "Can I assume this is a social visit and not an official one?"

"We're here to enjoy ourselves like the rest of Santa Fe."

I edged away from him. I didn't care what Carone thought, but I was a little surprised Seastrom made it sound as if I had come in with him and his friend. When he introduced his friend as Lieutenant Scott Travers, I almost gasped. He was the one who'd called me about Jason and Amanda.

Carone responded to the introduction with characteristic grace. "Lieutenant Travers. We finally meet. So nice of you to come. Well, I need to circulate. This is a big night for a good cause. Have a nice evening." She dashed off without acknowledging me.

I slipped away from Seastrom and Travers. With a copy of Antonio's death certificate now in my possession, this was my last night in Santa Fe. I wanted a good time, and hanging out with two cops didn't fit the picture.

I sampled some salsa and chili from the buffet. Delicious. It came from a well-known restaurant in town, as a donation. Every dish on the table had discreet signage next to it, noting which restaurant had donated it.

I got a glass of mineral water at the bar, feeling like Cinderella. Would I ever mingle with such high society again?

I felt a tap on my wrist. Eddy Hansen was smiling at me. That was a first.

"I never got around to thanking you for saving the gallery," he said.

What a surprise. I guess he forgave me for my treatment of Herbie. "Well, thanks. I didn't really do anything."

"Now, don't be modest. It was amazing the way you caught

Rodney Bracken. I'm happy he didn't take any more paintings. See the Picasso over there? That is his last painting. It's a good thing nothing happened to it."

I smiled. Words failed me.

"That business with the other one they caught, Tyler . . . Veller. He and Rodney were in it up to their necks, forging paintings and selling them in California. If I have anything to say about it, they're going to revisit Mr. Veller's plea bargain. That's the real story."

Life in the bubble. It went on and on with Carone's crowd. Did Hansen actually believe Tyler and Rodney consigned forged paintings to the Boulange Gallery? As Clyde might have said, the merry Merryweathers. They couldn't admit one of their own had betrayed them, however much they didn't like Jason.

"Please, before you wander away," Eddy said, "I want you to know I never wanted Carone to give up the gallery. I only wanted what was best for her. I didn't mean to be so hard on you."

"It's okay. But thanks."

"And seeing this night happen, I'm glad she kept the gallery open."

"So am I," Herbie cut in. He had his arm around Darlene.

Will wonders never cease?

"Lana, you've met Herbie, haven't you?" Darlene gushed.

Herbie didn't wince when she called him Herbie. He even smiled at me.

"Hey, I'll call you, Lana," Darlene said. "We'll talk." She and Herbie drifted into the crowd, their arms entwined.

A match made in heaven. With any luck, neither of them would get their show at the Merryweather Galleries, but not for lack of trying.

I excused myself from Eddy. Of course, I gravitated to the Picasso. Since giving it to Carone, I missed looking at it.

A uniformed guard stood near it. There were several of them stationed in the gallery. With a crowd this size, I could see why. If Carone had hired security guards before, nobody would have died.

The Picasso, as impressive as ever, looked different framed and restored. I stared at it, trying to figure out why it had changed so much. A restorer must have dropped everything to work on it, getting it finished and framed in less than two weeks. I couldn't tell where the gash used to be. Sure, the frame made a difference, but I didn't think that was it.

"Enjoying the exhibit, Ms. Davis?" Seastrom asked.

I hadn't realized Seastrom and Travers had sidled up to me. Was one of them attracted to me, or did they have something else in mind?

"Yes," I responded. "This painting is the last Picasso. Painted just before he died."

Travers nodded. "Is it for sale?"

"I think so. But it's not part of the auction."

I saw Bentley coming toward me. "Lana, someone wants to meet you," he said.

Bentley led an older, white-haired woman forward. Like me, she wore black. But while I had a string of turquoise beads around my neck, her fragile neck held diamonds—lots of them, as Herbie might have said.

"I'm Eleanor Peabody," the woman said. "This is my Picasso. Do you like it? I just had to meet you. Bentley told me how you stopped that thief from stealing a Modigliani. Very brave of you."

"Well, thank you. And yes, I do like your Picasso." I introduced her and Bentley to the two officers. "You remember Lieutenant Seastrom, Bentley."

"Nice to see you again, Lieutenant, under better circumstances," Bentley said.

"And are you selling your Picasso, Mrs. Peabody?" Travers asked.

"Oh, no. I decided to keep it. But I wanted Carone to show it off tonight. Isn't it nice how she framed it? The frame fell apart and she couldn't salvage it. It doesn't matter. It was just a frame."

Donald Walker strolled by, looking almost dapper in a black suit. He was too busy looking at the Picasso to notice us. I got the impression he found something funny about the painting, especially when he walked away laughing.

It didn't take me long to figure it out. I guess I'd laugh too if I painted a Picasso and everyone thought Picasso had painted it instead. When Mrs. Peabody decided not to sell the Picasso, Carone had to go to plan B. She got the real Picasso repaired and sold it to someone who didn't care about its provenance. She had those connections, if anyone did. Then she paid Donald to paint a copy for the elderly Mrs. Peabody, who would never suspect anything. Or maybe, Carone had already hired Donald to paint the copy, thinking she'd never find the original. With the money from the sale, Carone paid her debts and Donald for his silence. To Carone's credit, at least she bought his silence with money, and not with murder. Carone, with her elegant face and helpless demeanor, had succeeded where Rodney had failed.

"I'm so grateful to you, Lana," Mrs. Peabody said. "That terrible man might have run off with my Picasso."

"That would have been . . . awful," I said.

Carone surfaced from the crowd, taking Mrs. Peabody's arm. "Oh, Eleanor, there you are. I've been looking for you. You shouldn't tire yourself out. I have a chair for you."

"Oh, I'm not tired. I love the way you framed it, Carone. It complements the painting. Isn't it a nice frame? I know you wanted to sell it. But I love it. How could I sell the Picasso?"

Yes, how could she? But I was thinking of Carone, and not Mrs. Peabody.

With two cops standing next to me, I felt empowered. "Mrs. Peabody, it is a nice frame. But the painting is a forgery."

I saw Carone's jaw drop, her calm demeanor shattered.

"Oh . . ." Mrs. Peabody moaned.

"Maybe you want that chair, Mrs. Peabody," Lieutenant Travers said.

Bentley looked confused for a second. Then he grabbed a chair for the distressed Mrs. Peabody.

I didn't instigate this out of meanness, but out of fairness. Mrs. Peabody deserved to get a real Picasso back. And the people murdered because of it deserved to get some retribution.

As Carone once asked, is anyone above corruption? Yes, and those who aren't sometimes rise to the occasion. This was my occasion, and judging from the encouraging looks I got from Seastrom and Travers, I had a captive audience. So I told them the whole story, starting from the beginning.

ABOUT THE AUTHOR

Vanessa A. Ryan is an actress in Southern California. She was born in California and graduated from UCLA. When not writing or acting, she enjoys painting and nature walks. Her paintings and sculptures are collected worldwide. At one point, she performed stand-up comedy, so her writing often reflects her love of humor, even for serious subjects. She lives with her cats Dezi, Teger, and Riley, and among feral cats she has rescued. She is the author of *A Blue Moon*, an urban fantasy, and *Horror at the Lake*, a vampire trilogy. Follow Vanessa A. Ryan at http:// vanessaaryan.com, https://www.facebook.com/VanessaRyan33, and https://twitter.com/vryan333.